P9-DCV-290

ST. MARTIN'S

MINOTAUR

MYSTERIES

ZEN

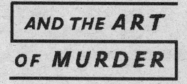

AND THE ART OF MURDER

ELIZABETH M. COSIN

St. Martin's Paperbacks

Author's note: Although many of the places in the book are real, the author took liberties with the details. That means she made it up.

ZEN AND THE ART OF MURDER

Copyright © 1998 by Elizabeth M. Cosin.
Excerpt from *Zen and the City of Angels* © 1999 by Elizabeth M. Cosin.

Cover photograph by Ed Holub.

Library of Congress Catalog Card Number: 98-19402

ISBN: 0-312-96948-1

Printed in the United States of America

St. Martin's Press hardcover edition / October 1998
St. Martin's Paperbacks edition / October 1999

10 9 8 7 6 5 4 3 2 1

ACKNOWLEDGMENTS

Special thanks to everyone who stuck by me these last few years, too many to name without leaving someone out. But to Mike Ventre, Amy Dawes, Linda Shayne, Jennifer Frey and Sean Piccoli, and Bruce Britt: thanks for being there when I needed you. (And to Gery Sommer for keeping my phone working.) I'd especially like to thank my family: my sisters Anne and Susan, and my brother Jonathan, for humoring me all these years. Thanks also to my new colleagues in crime: Bob Crais, Jim Hall, April Smith, Suzanne Wickham-Beaird, and Keith Perez, who were kind enough to read the early drafts and encourage me onward; and to my wonderful editor Joe Veltre: you have a magician's touch. A toast to all the regulars at Father's Office, who shared the process and many brews (you know who you are). And finally, a humble, heartfelt thank you to my agent, Dino Carlaftes, who from the beginning believed in me more than I did.

To my parents,
Toby and Allen,
for the past,
and
to Inaki,
for the future.

ONE

It rained the day I said good-bye to my best friend; the kind of storm that was packaged in a San Francisco–like cold front. December in Santa Monica could blow in from the Pacific like the draft from a meat locker.

Perfect funeral weather.

Even posh Montana Avenue was dulled. The shops had lost their hard-fought elegance, and darkened and drowned by the weather, they melded into the worn sky like so many strip shopping malls.

I kept my gaze downward as I stepped out of my Alfa. I was clutching a dark-red-and-brown vase—K-Mart Dynasty circa 1994—and trying to stay dry. I was looking for something to kick. A small dog, perhaps. A lawyer. I was feeling sorry for myself.

The rain plunked down, rapping a disco beat on the brim of my baseball cap. Last night's hangover was still trying to push my eyes out of their sockets from places inside my head I never knew existed.

A dark sedan buzzed by suddenly, cutting a tight corner out of the alley in front of me as if I wasn't there. Startled, I rocked backward, lost my footing for only a moment, and watched, as if in a dream, the pieces of the vase bounce off the pavement in every direction like popcorn in hot oil.

I stood over the shattered urn, the rain sheeting over the rim of my cap, and stared at the jagged-edged clay pieces now congealing with a fine, grayish-brown dust.

It was all that was left of my dead cat.

I watched until the last of his ashes rolled off the pavement with the rest of the rain water.

So much for respect for the dead, I thought as I stood in the rain long enough not to notice it anymore. I was mesmerized by the streaks of reddish-brown dye that ran off the cheap pottery, like blood from a new wound. I was thinking of bad omens and wondering if I was looking straight down at one.

The rain was seeping into my skin now and I let it run over me for a while, catching a glance or two from the early-morning-omelet-and-cappuccino set that had come out of hiding for the day.

It was still early, the day after Christmas, and the few people who did look up didn't seemed to be in any better mood than I was. Maybe Santa had forgotten the Tiffany tea set. I didn't care.

I felt stupid standing there in the rain, my reflection staring back at me from the window of the corner barber shop. I tried to straighten out my kinky hair—gypsy hair, my mom called it—and ended up shoving it under my Giants cap; sweeping dust under a rug.

I yanked the hat downward, tugging the brim at a well-bent spot so it cast a half-moon shadow over my face, partially hiding my eyes by design. I didn't like the way they could say more about me than I wanted most people to know. My nose stood out, too small and delicate, making my good family cheekbones give the impression I hadn't eaten since the Giants left a pile of broken hearts and rubble that was once called the Polo Grounds.

The rest of me fit more or less into a gray UCLA sweatshirt—part of a collection of items left by former lovers—and a pair of blue jeans which, like everything else, was hanging on to my skin like a new marine layer.

I cursed myself for drinking too much, pressing my temples to stop the throbbing. As if it was going to make a damn bit of difference. I thought of that bottled-water commercial; something about having 365 days a year to change your life.

Tomorrow, I could head up to the psychic bakery for some multigrain bread, a glass of carrot-pineapple juice with tofu for eggs, and a palm reading, then go home and jog a few miles. I could stop feeling sorry for myself and I could go out to the pound and get a new cat.

I looked at my watch, squinted at it, really. Tomorrow was still a good day away.

I peeked first before stepping back into the alley and circled behind to the back of Father's Office, my neighborhood pub.

TWO

Nat was waiting for me in the empty bar when I sloshed inside.

"Where's the deceased?" Nat was looking at me like he didn't like what he saw. "Did you swim over here?"

I could only shrug on my way to a barstool, the water running blue off my Levi's.

I held a piece of the broken vase a few inches above the shellacked bar top, waiting a moment before letting it drop.

Victor, one of the day bartenders, was leaning against the wall behind the counter, leafing through a tattoo magazine. He was a big, muscular man, though his girth rounded soft around the edges like his personality. He could look pretty dangerous sometimes, the gruff goatee at his chin one reason, the book-long display of tattoos up each arm, like matte pink skin had been added, certainly another.

He was the kind of guy who would wait to be asked for his opinion on the weather. But what Victor lacked in natural meanness he made up for in what I liked to call artificial outrage. It was unwise to make him mad, though at times it had helped me to do just that.

At the moment, he was studying the piece of tile until it rattled still.

"Is that . . . ?" he started. I shrugged. Nat put it into words.

"You *dropped* Ira?" He was incredulous.

So was I, but I didn't voice this. I closed my eyes, wishing myself out of my clothes, out of my skin, really. Nat had poured three beers and was standing behind me, smelling like laundry detergent. He was a big man, too, and while he could hide it better, he always looked as if he'd never outgrown his baby fat. He had the kind of even-handed temperament commandeered by bartenders, preachers, and social workers. The quiet authority born from years of calming down sinners, eighty-sixing drunks, or talking jumpers off the ledge. The performance of everyday miracles.

It was a minute before I realized he was waiting for me to say something.

"It was an accident," I said finally, swiveling my stool around so I was facing Nat, holding the beer but not drinking. "The alley. A car and . . . wham! That was the end." I slapped the top of the bar for effect, then shrugged my arms out, swishing the off-white foam of my beer until its head spilled over the glass. My own volcanic eruption.

I could see Nat wondering whether I'd be able to keep track of my head if it didn't happen to be permanently attached, but he kept this to himself.

"To Ira." It was Nat who broke our silence, raising his glass. "The only cat to get run over twice"—he looked at his watch—"in twenty-four hours." The clink of the toast to my late pet echoed through the bar, muffled a bit in the dense air. The only other sound was the plop-ploppety plop of the rain above our heads.

We sat there listening to it.

Nat's belch broke our reverie, or whatever it was. Victor followed with one of his own and in its wake finished the last two-thirds of his beer in one swallow.

I caught Nat's eye briefly and an awkward silence followed. Victor, feeling like the third wheel, coughed nervously and looked around for something to do. He finally decided he was needed in the back room.

Next to Ira, my cat, and my sometime partner and soul mate Bobo, Nat was the best friend I had. That was saying a lot because I wasn't exactly what you would call social. More like social retard. We had managed to exist pretty much as we were now—sharing silences—and Anchor Steams.

I really didn't know much about him, except that, behind his barroom cheer, he kept a knot of pain bigger than a beer keg. It was more complicated, of course, but I'd always figured a woman or two had put him through the relationship garbage compactor, and very likely vice versa. I never asked about his history and he never asked about mine. It was an unspoken understanding between two people on the hard side of life who had let the wrong person get away with their hearts and money and the right one simply get away.

"You look like you've been up since last week," he broke the silence, his deep voice a strange echo in the empty room. "Working on a case?"

He said this hopefully and I managed an appreciative smile, knowing my traitorous eyes were saying much more. I was a small-time private detective, a job I'd fallen into after making a name for myself as a sportswriter just in time to experience a flame-out that was now the stuff of legend in a business full of legend-telling. I never thought of it as anything more than a really bad day, but then in some places slugging the World Series MVP in the locker room is front-page news. My mistake.

Now I spend my time either finding people, which I like a lot and am good at, or following errant spouses, which I'm even better at, but hate. Unfortunately, more people cheat on their spouses than turn up missing, at least here in LA, and that means I spend most of my working day doing something that makes me feel like a heel.

It tends to make me miserable, but lately I'm not doing well enough to turn anyone down. If only they'd ask.

"Just a hangover," I said. "Nothing's come my way lately. Guess love _can_ exist in LA."

"Fair point," he said, the sudden ringing of the phone seeming to emphasize his words. "Don't let the lull fool you. Give it some time and those angry wives will be beating down your door. You can count on it."

"Yeah, whatever." I was skeptical and still very wet, pressing my hand against my thigh to wring some of the water out of my jeans. "Right now I could use a change of clothes."

"It's for you," Victor said to me. He was in mid-yell as he walked to where we were sitting with the business end of a cordless phone in one hand and a fresh beer in the other.

Nat's look was of the "see, I told you so" variety.

I have a unique answering service, a 1930s B-movie star for whom I'd helped recover money a few years back. She'd been conned out of her substantial savings by the kind of lowlifes who make their money preying on weak people's weaknesses.

Now she felt she owed me a debt—apparently my generous fees hadn't been enough. So she handled my calls from her home. It had turned out to be a wonderful setup—most of the time. It gave her something constructive to do and it gave my clients a soothing voice that didn't come from a little black box. The only problem was that Vivian had this maternal instinct for me that included knowing where I was twenty-four hours a day and giving my phone number to single Jewish doctors.

"Zen here," I said.

"Mr. Zenaria Moses?" It was my given name, an unfortunate combination my parents thought might grant me some kind of mystical powers. It only mystified everyone who had to use it. Few people ever did, and most of them were dead or had a G-rating before their job description.

"It's Ms. Moses to you," I said to the voice that wasn't Vivian. It was a 180 from the singsong Brooklynese that made her put R's on the ends of words ending in vowels. "Who wants to know?"

"Your government." The voice, a woman's, was trying to be amusing. It was generic-sounding with an official tone to it, but there was something else beneath it

"Very funny," I said pleasantly. "What part of me does my government want to rip out through my throat today?"

"I wouldn't look at it that way, Ms. Moses." She was back to the land of officialdom. "We're only doing our job."

This was getting good. "Who would 'we' be, ma'am?"

"Uh, I'm sorry. Marcia Atwood, IRS. Didn't I say?"

"No, you didn't say." My heart was in China.

"This is probably nothing." Uh-oh. "But there were some, ah, discrepancies on your 1989 federal tax filing. It's a routine thing, but you've been scheduled for an audit."

Well, at least I'd filed.

"And I was just having a wonderful morning."

"Excuse me?"

"Nothing."

"Ms. Moses, it's very likely nothing to be concerned about." That was the second time she'd said that.

"Then why call? It's practically still Christmas," I said. "Couldn't you just skip over my case? Surely someone else is more deserving of government intervention." Like Bosnia.

She barely broke stride. "Why don't you schedule a time when we can sit down and talk? Chances are we can get this all settled. Is this your office number?"

"So to speak," I said, then arranged to meet her at my home office Friday afternoon—she had a few more poor souls scheduled for IRS critical organ transplants between now and then.

"Bad news?" Nat asked.

"It's the IRS," I told him. "They're after me for crimes allegedly committed in 1989."

"What specific crimes?"

"Beats me. I barely remember what I did last night, much less in a previous decade. Seems like I'm getting audited, though."

"It can't be too bad," he said. "I get audited once a month." He laughed, though the way he ran his business, I was sure he was telling me the gospel.

"I just don't know why the idea of that doesn't just lift my spirits." I smirked. "Now, where was I?"

"Going somewhere to dry off, I think."

I was thinking about a dry pair of jeans, pushing myself away from the bar and trying to remember 1989. The whole thought process was a strain. Maybe I needed a nap.

Victor came in from the back with an empty glass, walked

around the back of the bar and yanked one of the handles. A pile of foam slopped into his glass.

He poured the foam out and tried another handle. The same. "Must be the CO_2," he said to Nat. "Want me to take a look?"

Nat nodded and we watched Victor lumber to the back. When a tap spits out foam, it usually means the keg is empty and a new one has to be hooked up.

Out of our view, to the right, was the walk-in refrigerator where Nat kept the kegs for the thirty-odd microbrews he served. Victor peeked around the corner. "You change the temp of the walk-in?" he asked. "It's set below freezing."

Nat was frowning. He was very particular about his beers and how they were served. Anything warmer or colder than 37 degrees meant serving an imperfect product.

Nat gave me a "that's strange" look and got up to inspect the situation for himself. I was tagging along behind when we heard a muted yelp from the back room. It was Victor. We found him leaning against the keg cooler, holding his hand to his mouth as if he were keeping something big inside.

Nat had gently pushed by Victor and had his head in the cooler. "Oh my god," he said and I peered in over his shoulder.

The walk-in was named so for obvious reasons. It was eight feet deep, four wide; one wall was lined with metal racks and the other with round metal kegs, most attached to plastic tubing. One was attached to something else. Or rather, *someone* else.

It was sitting on the cement floor, arms and legs wrapped around one of the kegs. I went inside, the frozen air turning my wet clothes to ice. It was a man, tanned, well-fed, and dark-haired, his mouth grotesquely hooked up to a makeshift tap. I felt for a pulse. No beats. No surprise.

"Christ, Nat," I said, "he's dead."

"I guess I should call the police." It was Victor. He said it from outside the cooler. He'd seen enough.

Nat sent him to do so, stepping back to the door, leaving

me with the body. I took a quick look around.

I was supposedly trained for stuff like this, but I'd managed to avoid corpses whenever possible. I had no stomach for them, which seemed normal to me.

I took a deep breath and squatted down to check for a wallet, but his pockets were empty. I noticed a watch on his wrist, a shiny gold Rolex turned so it faced downward. It was his only identifying mark, that and a small caliber hole in the back of his head near his neck.

I pulled at the sleeve of his leather jacket, its shiny black finish had the just-off-the-rack look, though from the soft nap I was certain it hadn't been bought at discount. I was trying to turn his arm so I could get a closer look when the body moved slightly. I flinched, grabbing the air for something to keep from falling on my ass. I got a handful of chilly skin instead. I'd grabbed the guy's cold, wet, limp wrist.

The sensation shot up my arm and I yanked it back quickly, grabbing at the keg instead, where I steadied myself. Only once I got my balance, I realized I'd gotten my sweaty hand stuck to the metal of the freezing barrel.

I could feel the gentle pinch on my flesh which made me pull even harder, the action dragging the keg and the corpse toward me. Both teetered for a moment, held in place by the hold, then toppled when the connection broke.

In the midst of this, I got a good look at the guy's face and my heart stopped.

I was rubbing the back of my hand, afraid to look and see if all the skin was still attached. The body lay, half-stiff, on its side in a grotesque fetal position, now separated from the metal barrel, which was rolling back and forth on the floor, metal on metal. Clank, swish, clank.

I heard someone call my name, but I couldn't move, frozen in the freezer.

I finally looked up to see Nat hovering in the doorway, making some joke about my making a mess of things. Little did he know. I noticed he didn't come inside. I didn't blame him.

He pointed to the keg. It had nearly come to a stop, but was still rocking slightly.

"Keg's empty," he said. Another time, he would have been smiling.

I nodded, slowly bringing my mind's focus back to the present.

"Well, at least we know one thing," he said.

"What's that?" The words seemed to come from somewhere else. I was edging closer to the door—and fresh air.

"He died happy."

I managed the thinnest of smiles. He put his hand on my shoulder.

"Are you all right?" he asked me.

"Yeah, sure." I was far from all right. I was going mad.

Nat didn't know what I knew: that the man in his walk-in had died twelve years earlier.

I knew. I had killed him.

THREE

Victor had phoned the police and then vomited. Helping someone consider the existence of an afterlife—something he'd done for me on occasion—was apparently a little more palatable than dealing with the mess afterward. It was that way for most people.

Two uniforms had arrived promptly and told us not to leave the country; or the bar, for that matter. They were "securing" the scene as it were, which left me a moment to gulp some air.

My clothes were weighing me down, but they were feathers right now compared to my conscience.

Life brings regrets. This is not earth-shattering. Live a little and they pile up, those moments when you realize you have given the wrong answer to one of life's little quizzes. Live a little longer and you end up dragging one or two things around you wouldn't brag about. You can bury them, but there just isn't a place deep enough that somebody's dog won't dig up.

If I'd always thought this, I never really knew it until now, standing at the pub's open back door, hyperventilating into the alley and drowning in regrets and raindrops.

My life was a child's flip book, speeding before my eyes in jerky, clouded moments, stopping at a point a dozen years ago I thought I'd finally made peace with, but knew somehow I never could.

It was a matter of time before my past finally caught up with me and I'd just stared it in the face. Its name was Daniel. Daniel Moses.

It was from a time and place I'd kept hidden somewhere I'd thought was gone forever, a moment that—in its own quietly persistent way—had haunted me, settling somewhere in my gut where dread goes to die. Reminders of a blip in my moral radar. The shame was palpable.

Nat called me from inside the bar, where several cops were busy at work, most hovering around the walk-in. Nobody looked too happy. Murders weren't exactly commonplace in Santa Monica. Having one the day after Christmas certainly didn't add to holiday cheer.

Detective Jonathan Brooks took charge of the scene for Santa Monica's finest. He was a tall, attractive man with a striking skin tone on the gold side of brown. He was in jeans, work boots, denim shirt and colorful tie, all wrapped up nicely in a black leather jacket.

Even though he was tall, his broad shoulders made him appear squat, like a fullback. His hair was cut short, leaving a fine layer clinging to his head that looked so soft, I wanted to run my hands through it.

He was clean-shaven, though the genesis of a beard was starting on his squared jaw and he had dark eyes set a little too far apart, but not so you could really notice. It was just enough that, with his softly angled cheekbones and perfect nose, it gave him the air of a man who was comfortable around kings or the descendants of them.

Brooks had a boyish face, but I'd heard about him and the word was he knew what he was doing. I couldn't help but wonder if he was one of the beautiful people who flocked to LA with a dream and the word "thespian" in their vocabulary. For them, the jobs they take—waiters, salesmen, bartenders, even cops—are temporary until one day they realize it was always the other way around.

He had replaced my best buddy on the force, a half-Mexican, half-Jewish detective named Joshua Lopez, who had left to run the police force in a small, growing city in New Mexico.

It was a big move for Josh, whose only real character flaw was his ambition. He was a great friend, always would be,

who never let his personal goals get in the way of being a
good cop, but they were always there nonetheless. It was
only a matter of time before he followed them out of town.
Unfortunately for me, his leaving coincided with my temporary retreat from society, so I'd have a lot of catching up
to do. Even though I knew there were some guys in the brass
that would stand up for me, it was no secret that the higher
you went, the harder it was to put your neck out for anyone
outside the circle of blue. Certainly not some meddling girl
PI. Josh had always been there to step between me and those
authority figures, saving my ass more than once.

Now I was going to have to cultivate someone else. I was
hoping Brooks would turn out to be the next-best thing.

A captain I knew by sight but not by name was hovering
around Brooks, occasionally barking out orders. He was a
stocky man who kind of reminded me of a beardless Santa
Claus. He wore an out-of-the-box flannel shirt, no doubt
found under his tree yesterday morning. Its fireman's-red hue
matched his face and hair.

I watched from the sidelines, sipping another Anchor
Steam and privately thanking Nat for keeping the taps flow-
ing. The dead man's keg wasn't hooked up to a line, so the
cops didn't suspect the beer had been poisoned, though they
made Nat check his supply anyway.

Brooks saw me and nodded a greeting. I was one of those
PIs who had actually made a few friends among the rank
and file, but a lot of the cops were new to me now. That
Brooks knew me by sight, or appeared to, anyway, meant
he'd been around a while.

A uniform who'd just had a word with the red-faced captain came over to where Nat and Victor and I were sitting.
He was Hitler-blond, his short-cropped hair holding up a pair
of sunglasses. Perfect for a sunless day.

"Who are you?" His name tag said "V. Lennon."

I patiently emptied my beer glass. "An innocent by-
stander, comrade," I said, poking a finger toward his breast
pocket. It also said "Sergeant." Promotions came fast in
Santa Monica.

He stepped back. "What's that, a joke or something?"

"You choose."

"What?"

"You decide if it was a joke, or something."

"We got ourselves a smart-ass here." Lennon gave me one of those looks that made me think his next move would be toward his gun.

Nat must have thought the same thing.

"We made the, ah, discovery," he said, moving between me and Boy Wonder and pleading with his eyes for my best behavior.

"Yeah?" Lennon said. He was young, mid-twenties, and kind of chunky, as if he'd once played football but let the muscle ease in a casual direction. There was no intelligent life in his expression.

I thumbed at Victor. Despite the weather, he was sweating, his jowls latex-yellow, his eyes large, barely holding his pupils in. The corpse had looked healthier.

"Actually, he found the dead guy," I said. "I mean, he was there first. I just happened to be in the neighborhood."

We all looked at Victor. I wasn't sure if he was going to vomit again, or faint, or cry. Maybe all three. Everyone seemed to want to put distance between them and him. Another time or place, it would have been funny.

"It's his first one." I tried out a nod, wanting to let Victor know I understood without embarrassing him. He seemed to be fighting to give the appearance of control.

Lennon wasn't so kind. I caught a tinge of arrogance in his eyes. Guys like him—snot-nosed kids who thought bungee-jumping was some kind of death test—believed they had no fears. This was a tragic combination of youth, disrespect and outright stupidity. It wouldn't last—he'd grow up or get buried before he had the chance.

"And what are you? An expert?" Lennon on the attack.

"In a way . . ." Nat started. I stopped him with a quick wave, a gesture I noticed made Lennon lean forward on the balls of his feet. An infielder waiting for the next pitch.

"What are you?" Lennon asked again. "The F-B-fucking-I or something?"

"Or something," I said after a moment, seeing immediately that it wasn't going to satisfy him. I tried another tack. "I'm just a patron. And you want the truth, dead bodies give me the willies."

"Shit, that stiff's nothing." Lennon was talking to me but everyone knew he was directing it at Victor. I felt sorry for him. "Far as bodies go, man, I've seen a lot worse. We once found a bum with half his brains splattered over a quarter mile of Santa Monica Boulevard . . ."

"It's too bad you don't have any practice with live ones," I cut him off, winking at Victor, who managed a brief smile. "Then maybe you wouldn't be such an asshole."

He glared at me, but the radio on his belt wheezed so loud we all jumped. He reached down to squelch it, moving across the room toward his captain. I saw Brooks smiling; he had been listening in. I noticed Victor's color coming back, showing his embarrassment. In a minute, he'd be well enough to be angry and we might have to pry him off the little creep.

As far as I was concerned, his was the only humane reaction. The rest of us had forgotten how to feel.

Movies don't do justice to dead bodies. The real thing has a presence, as if its spirit is trapped somewhere nearby. It's an eerie feeling, a sense that you're treading on someone else's private karma in the clumsy way puppies trample gardens. I didn't like it.

But at least I knew enough to fear it. There were significant advantages to some kinds of cowardice—like living longer.

Lennon returned with the captain, while Brooks edged his way toward us, probably waiting for the show to start. I wasn't in the mood.

"I'm Captain Watkins," the big man said, reaching out a stubby pink hand the color of steak tartare. He could be Santa on Christmas and not have to rent the suit. I let Nat take it, introducing himself. He was good at that.

"We'd like to go over what happened," Watkins said officially. He and the IRS woman should get together; their children would all sound like high school principals. "I was hoping we could talk to you each separately."

A kid I didn't know was assigned to talk to Victor; the big man was finding his equilibrium again. Nat got Watkins and I was left sitting on a barstool wondering if underwire bras could rust.

FOUR

"Could I stand you to a beer?" I asked Brooks when he finally came over. Up close, he was even more impressive.

He didn't answer, but his gaze told me he'd noticed my appraisal.

"On duty, right?" I said, taking an exaggerated sip. "Life's tough, I guess."

"From what I hear, you would know." The remark struck me at first as biting, but his glare softened so quickly it erased the thought from my mind. He stretched out his hand. "How does a woman get a name like Zen?"

"Long story." We shook. "I've heard good things about you, Detective."

"Then we have something in common." His eyes blazed with humor and intelligence, and my respect for him deepened. He gestured with his chin toward Lennon, who was unraveling a roll of yellow "police-line" tape. "I see you and the sergeant have become fast friends."

I gave him a helpless shrug. I was good at it.

"That innocent act is a bit much for someone with your rep," he said. "I mean, I heard you were tough, but man, you really gave it to the kid—not that the prick didn't deserve it."

"Yeah, well, sometimes I just let my mouth get loose in heavy traffic. It's a bad habit. You'd think I'd have learned by now. I keep getting run over."

"Not always."

"What do you mean?"

"You're kind of a star in these parts, what with the Leontine Kidnapping case and—"

I cut him off. "Years ago," I said, and it was. I hadn't worked much the past two years, not since I'd accidentally helped solve the kidnapping of a child of the rich and famous. I even got my picture in the paper. "I was just in the right place at the right time."

"They didn't say you were modest. So what have you been doing these past two years—besides, ah . . . well I heard you . . ."

"The Big C?" I said. "It's okay, you can say it."

"I didn't want to . . . pry. It's none of my business."

"Don't worry about it," I said with more pain than I meant. I had always tried to forgive and forget; most of the time, that's exactly what I did. But having cancer shows you not only who your friends are but who they aren't, too. "They consider me one of the lucky ones. I'm still here."

"Sorry."

"Forget it," I said. "I lost a lung, not my sense of humor. Now that would have been tragic." I said this last thing in a way I hoped would let him know he was treading on ground I didn't feel much like going over. It said a lot for him that he didn't press the issue, giving me a long look instead.

"You're an unusual woman."

"Been called worse," I said; trying again to sponge some water out of my jeans.

"Got caught in the rain?"

"As a matter of fact, yes. Do you think I could be released so I can go home and change—or am I your prime suspect?"

"It depends," he said. "So it was you who found the stiff?"

"Not exactly." I retold the story, and he remained silent throughout, nodding or crinkling his brows every so often.

"Nasty business," he said when I'd finished.

I agreed. "Know who the guy is?"

"Not even a clue. There was no identification on him. No

wallet, not even a library card. The only pictures he had on him were of dead presidents.''

''Yeah? Are they the kind that sponsor white sales, or do they fall into the military-hero category?''

''Everybody's a comedian,'' he said. ''The stiff isn't laughing.''

Ouch. I nodded. The surprise of finding Danny had worn off, but I was still having trouble separating Danny the dead guy and Danny my first cousin, my best friend, the closest thing I had to a big brother, one I thought his father and I had buried twelve years ago. I cried a lot back then, but much of that was for myself, and what I'd lost. There was a dull pain, a hole where my stomach was. It was all I could do to keep from turning it into tears.

''Are you all right?'' It was the second time I'd been asked that this morning. He was looking at me sort of through the corner of his eye. I just shrugged.

''Anything you'd like to add to this discussion?''

I shook my head. But the pure effort necessary to keep from thinking about Danny had set off my headache again. I couldn't keep my hands from sweating. I needed air again. I needed to get the hell out of there.

''Penny for your thoughts.'' It was Brooks, this time eyeing me a little suspiciously.

''What? Oh, sorry. Just thinking.''

''Anything you want to share with the police?''

I left the question unanswered. I had every intention of telling Brooks who his corpse was, had felt the words teeter on the edge of my tongue, but a bevy of emotions kept me quiet.

Brooks was smart enough to catch on.

''I wouldn't want to think you'd been keeping something from us,'' he said, pointing toward the back room, where Nat was attached to his cordless phone. ''You two seem to have a special rapport.''

I looked up at him a little too quickly.

''Don't let your imagination run wild, Detective. The proprietor and I are just friends. Sorry to disappoint you.''

"I'm not disappointed."

"I bet all the girls love that line," I said, draining the rest of my beer. "Not about to work on me."

He smiled, clearly amused he'd fazed me.

I was through playing for today.

"Just a joke," he said.

I looked up a him. "It's just been a long morning," I said. "I'm wet and I'm a bit hung over and I got a dead cat for Christmas." And here I was hoping for a peaceful holiday.

"Look, Detective, you know where to find me, can't I at least go home and dry off?"

He nodded. "Now, don't be going too far."

"No farther than my living room," I said.

"Let's hear what's on your mind first. Just between you and me." He was smiling as if we both knew he was making a promise he couldn't keep, even if he wanted to.

Nat came over holding the cordless.

"You have a call, Detective." He held the phone out, but I held up my hand.

"Wait," I said, thinking for the first time that morning that Danny deserved a lot more than being left in a cold cabinet in the morgue with a "John Doe" tag tied around his big toe. Brooks took the phone, but held it down by his belly, covering the mouthpiece with one of his large palms.

"Go ahead," he said.

"His name is Daniel. Daniel Moses." I said it as evenly as I could.

"Who?" he asked.

"Your corpse," I said, watching their eyes widen. Nat looked as if I'd told him I won the lottery. Brooks put the phone to his ear, spoke a word or two and then hung up.

He eyed Nat. "Over here," he told me, grasping my elbow to pull us both out of Nat's hearing. I knew later I would pay for this. Nat always wanted to know everything. What's a bartender if he can't dish the dirt, anyway?

"You were saying?"

"It's a long story," I said. "Besides, you wouldn't believe it if I told you."

"Try me."

"He was my cousin," I said, filling him in on the particulars. Danny was the son of my father's half-brother Sam. We had been raised practically as brother and sister.

"When was the last time you saw him?"

"That's a bit complicated."

"Please, Zen," he said. "I could make this official, you know. I'm giving you a break here."

"I know," I said.

"So when did you last see him?"

"Twelve years ago," I said.

"No contact at all?"

"There were what you would call mitigating circumstances."

"And those were?" Brooks had raised his eyebrows. With his arms folded against his chest, he was tapping one set of fingers against the sleeve of his leather jacket.

I really *was* going to say, "I was under the impression he was dead," but managed somehow to suppress this. The shock wouldn't do either of us any good and I wasn't about to spend the rest of the day talking to the cops, no matter how noble their reasons. "Family problems," I finally said, giving my voice an underlying angst that was sincere if not totally honest. "We had a falling-out. Frankly, I couldn't have even told you if he was dead or alive." I couldn't help myself.

Brooks formed one of those expressions people have when they are working out a response to a situation they've never faced before. I kept my mouth shut. This was a good thing, considering what was careening around in my head.

I was reaching back into a twelve-year-old ditch that I thought was inaccessible to anyone without a pulse or a shovel.

"Are you sure it's him?" he said after a moment.

"It's him," I said, holding back my grief. I wasn't about

to shed tears in front of Brooks, no matter what I thought of him.

"What more can you tell me about him? Any family?" If he'd sensed my condition, he never let on. All business.

"Not much," I said. "It was a very painful time for my Uncle Sam and me. We haven't spoken since."

An idiot could see I was hiding something, but I was hoping Brooks would just see it as a clumsy effort to keep family affairs where they belonged.

"Here's one for you," he said suddenly. His impatience was so obvious it was as if it were a third person in our conversation. He was reading me about as well as anyone could, and while I found it a bit disconcerting, I also knew it was what made him good at his job. "What would he be doing on the floor of the beer freezer?"

"I have no idea." Even knowing what I knew, I was still vexed. I couldn't give more information if I wanted to; I just didn't have any. "I assume he must have been here to see me, but for what and why, I have no idea."

"I see." Brooks's look was a bit askance. He knew I was holding something back. I just wasn't ready to air Danny's dirty laundry, not until I knew more about what was going on. Danny had been a lot of things to me, most of them good, and I owed this to him. I was being selfish, too, but that was okay. The longer I kept the cops out of it, the easier it would be on me.

"I'm glad one of us does," I said. "I hope you can appreciate my interest in the case. I mean, if anything comes up, could you keep me informed?"

"I suppose," he said. "I hope I can expect the same cooperation from you."

I nodded. "Am I free to go now?"

"I guess so," he said. "We'll talk again soon."

"One more thing," I said. "The body . . ."

He nodded.

Nat caught me as I was sneaking out the door.

"What's that all about?" he asked.

"My past," I said. "Before you knew me."

"So let's hear it."

I shook my head. "This one's buried too deep," I said, edging closer to the door. "I'd rather not talk about it. Nothing personal."

"I understand," he said, though I could see a trace of hurt behind his eyes.

I touched his shoulder, giving it a slight squeeze. "Everybody's got secrets," I said. "Even in the town that tried O. J."

I winked at him and stepped back out into the storm.

FIVE

The rain had eased to a drizzle by the time I pulled into the alley behind my house, a small stucco building surrounded by rent-controlled apartments on Euclid Street. Mine was the last house on a street that dead-ended into the back of a private pet cemetery. I used to rent the place, but bought it cheap from my landlord after the Northridge earthquake had remodeled it from three stories to two and a half. "Cheap" was a relative term, and if it weren't for a nice donation from FEMA, I'd probably still be in a studio in Venice. Sometimes the government is your friend.

It wasn't particularly big, but it had everything I needed, including a garage out back and enough land for a tiny urban garden where I grew tomatoes and chilis and, last year, corn. It was newly renovated, thanks again to Uncle Sam, right down to the nifty front porch. Earthquakes were hell, but if you managed to survive in one piece and knew your way around government aid forms, you could get back what you'd lost, maybe even a little more.

It was the right time to be out of the rental market. Santa Monica has had artificial controls since the late seventies, ostensibly to keep landlords from artificially hiking up the rents. Tenants and liberals loved it. Landlords liked to refer to the city as the People's Republic of Santa Monica, which used to be funny. But tougher laws and whining landlords were gutting the rent laws, and it was getting harder and harder to find a reasonably priced place.

I liked mine because it reminded me of home up north: hardwood floors, a nice-sized fireplace, two bedrooms—one

I used as an office—and lots of closet space. The block, like many in Santa Monica, was home to various 1950s Spanish-style stucco apartments ranging in size from one story to three, with as many as fifteen apartments or as few as six.

Most had been belted, too, by the big quake and at the very least repainted since, giving a purely LA postcard tinge to the entire block. Most had been painted in varying shades of white and off-white, except the triplex next door, which was aquamarine and orange. Howard Johnson's was alive and well and living next door to me.

The bills had already been delivered, along with a sheaf of junk mail, which I systematically tore in half without bothering to open the envelopes. It was simply amazing what mailing lists I had managed to get onto in my lifetime. From socially responsible MasterCards to *Guns and Ammo* magazine. I'd obviously skewed somebody's market survey.

My answering machine was blinking notice of two messages, both from Vivian: the first warning me that the IRS was looking for me and the second that she'd ratted me out. Timing was everything. The phone rang again while I was in the bedroom changing.

To the irritation of my friends, clients, creditors, and loved ones, I do not as a rule answer my phone, preferring instead to screen my calls. I do it for a number of reasons, not the least of which is so I don't have to talk to people I owe money to.

I let it ring and listened in from my kitchen—coffee seemed a good idea at the moment. It was a woman's voice, smooth and sensual, with a slight hiss on the *s*-words.

"Mr. Moses, this is Evelyn Mulwray," the voice said, pronouncing each word deliberately, drawing out the syllables like a dinner-theater actress trying to sound aroused. It sounded more like a cat in heat. "I am in need of your services. I understand you can be discreet." She gave the number.

My name would have been confusing if I were a man, but owing that I was, as far as I could tell, anyway, a woman, it was even more complicated. The nineties and Sara Paretsky notwithstanding, letting people think they were hiring a man had its advantages. By the time we sat down to talk business, most clients were too far into their stories to change PIs. Either that, or they were so mesmerized by my innate charm, they wouldn't have cared if I were a trained seal.

Evelyn Mulwray, I thought, got us a movie buff. I checked my watch. Had to give the appearance at least that I was out when the call came in.

The number was a 310 exchange, which meant it could be almost anywhere on the west side of Los Angeles, from Santa Monica to the west, Beverly Hills to the east, on down south all the way to Manhattan Beach and Torrance. I matched it in the crisscross directory and came up with a name: L. V. Maxwell. Had to be only one person: Latisha Viola Maxwell.

Maxwell was a talk-show host, a breed of television folk that had multiplied over the past few years at twice the rate of rabbits. And while many had fallen into the abyss of bad ratings, some of them had not only survived, they were one-person media conglomerates. The nineties have been a windfall for amateur shrinks with microphones.

If talk is cheap, it's nowhere cheaper than on these shows that exploit the growing American phenomenon of publicizing the most intimate and distasteful details of people's private lives.

I vaguely remember reading that Maxwell was closing in on Oprah as the queen of the genre. The only thing I knew about her was from an article in the LA *Times* about her rise to stardom. She had a typical rags-to-riches story, from modest means to small-screen mania.

I knew she'd been arrested recently at some kind of antitelevision-violence rally, a move catapulting her to celebrity status. I guess I'd been wondering why her show and others like it weren't what was really wrong with television.

Her Beverly Hills address got my attention. Beverly Hills meant money, which in turn meant there was a good chance I could get some. Lord knows, I needed it. Besides, at least it wasn't a spousal thing; she was single. *People* magazine said so and that was enough for me.

Still, I wasn't in a hurry to make the call.

Plopping into my cushioned black futon with my coffee mug in one hand and the remote in the other, I leaned back and juiced up the CD player.

I watch a little TV now and then, but what really inspires me is music. My tastes ran all over the map, but lately I'd been stuck on a collection of Billie Holiday's last recordings.

Made shortly before her death, they were originally panned by the critics. By then, drugs and fame and a million other things had reduced her to a fragment of her former self and her once-angelic voice was gone. It creaks and sputters through the material like a sports car with a bad choke. And the overly sentimental string arrangements would be almost laughable in another setting. But through it, Billie was able to convey meanings to me that I felt deeply. I'd always found her frailness and honesty and the starkness of her pain very real, very touching, and very, very sad.

I'd needed her a lot these days and not simply because I'd been in a slump.

Life had been pretty good over the years, and I counted myself among the lucky few who had found something they were good at that also happened to pay the bills.

But it had taken me a while to get there. I'd grown up a lot since my first job out of college as a sportswriter, a career path that had brought me money, a little fame and glory but not much happiness. Success in professional sports is the kind of thing that's woven into the American dream like red thread in the American flag. From a distance, it's exciting, glorious, gallant. But up close, it's scary as hell.

Men who think they're gods and act like kids. Money and corruption in your face with television cameras and an often pathetic cadre of groupies who want money, sex, or both. Somewhere buried in all that is the game, but while I still had a soft spot for the idyllic battle of the athlete in games no mortal could conquer, I knew in my heart that part of me had long been left for dead.

I had an awakening of sorts, and in a few short years I'd extracted myself from a contentious but brief marriage, squandered a good amount of money, lost a dear friend or two, and survived a bout with cancer, but I was free and I had people around me who cared about me and whom I cared about. Somebody once said that was all you needed. Most times, I even believed it.

Daniel Moses had once been in that circle. But I'd turned my back on him because of a million things wrapped up in youth, arrogance, and some morality I would laugh at now if it hadn't cost me so dearly.

I didn't actually kill him. But I might as well have. To me, at least, it was one and the same. That's the way I'd always see it, even if I didn't think about it much. Time and survival instincts and therapy had helped me to tuck it away. I suppose I was waiting for the day when I was strong enough to face up to it. Truth be told, I was hoping I'd never have to.

But now I would. All these years later he had come back into my life and it looked like I'd failed him. Again.

I closed my eyes for a moment. I could feel the dampness outside, hanging in the stale air of my house like a rotting woodpile. The problem with rain in southern California is mostly that there's never enough. But every so often, it comes down with a vengeance. One of God's ways, along with earthquakes, tornadoes, and such, of reminding us how powerless we all really are.

Billie was dragging herself nobly through "The End of a Love Affair," the bland grayness of the day faintly illuminating the room. I followed the pattern of intricate lines reflected on the floor by the streaking droplets of rain, finding their own roundabout way down my windowpanes.

I stared at the phone.

Sometimes I was too good at feeling sorry for myself, and hating that feeling was probably what kept me getting up each morning. Sooner or later, I was going to have to get something accomplished after I did.

When Billie finally sang her heart out, it left an empty

silence in my living room. I almost nodded off when Ira, my cat, dashed across my eye's path, or what I thought was Ira. It was an omen. My second of the day.

Either that, or I was going crazy. I stuck with the first—my mother once told me that signs were all around us. It was just that some people can see them and others can't. In her mind, that's what separated the living from the dead.

I rang up Beverly Hills and the mysterious Mrs. Mulwray. She picked up before the second ring. "Mrs., ah . . . Mulwray?"

"Um, yes. Who is this, please?" She sounded out of breath.

"Zen Moses," I said. "You rang."

"You're a woman." It was more a statement than a question.

"Why, yes. Is that a problem?"

"Ah, no."

The voice wobbled slightly. This was the future queen of talk shows? A silence followed. I decided to wait her out.

"Well," she said finally. "I need a private detective."

"That much I figured out."

She sniffed at this.

"Perhaps you could come to my office so we could discuss your case," I said. "Or I could come to your home or office."

"No, no," she said, too quickly. "We can't meet. I mean, I'd like to take care of this over the phone."

"You'd better find someone else then." I was firm.

"Excuse me?" I'd caught her off guard.

"I have a rule about meeting my clients in person. I'm sure you understand." I never take on a case without eye-balling a client first. I've been burned too many times.

"I can assure you that you can trust me," she said, her voice gaining what seemed a familiar tone of authority. She was almost dressing me down. The TV star finding her on-air persona. "I have powerful friends and I am in a tenuous position. This is why I need to be discreet. And from what

I hear about your current financial situation, you really don't have a choice.''

"Perhaps not, Mrs. Mulwray." I spit the name out. "But let's get a few things straight. First—I repeat—I never, ever take a case without meeting with the client first; second, my 'financial situation,' as you put it, doesn't have anything to do with whether I take a case or not; and third, I have no reason to trust you because you have already lied to me. At least once." I paused for effect and could hear her breathing.

"Ms. Maxwell, I presume?"

It worked—for about a microsecond. That's how long it took her to get her feet back. "It's not what you think."

"I don't care why you called," I said. "It was you who called me. If I can be of help to you, I will try. If not, I'll be on my way."

"Okay, all right," she said. "I need your help. I'm just not good at these things."

"You have at least that much in common with practically all of my other clients."

"How did you know who I was?"

"Suffice it to say I'm good at my job, ma'am." I didn't have to tell her that it took me less than thirty seconds to look her up in a directory that lists people by their phone numbers. "Besides, *Chinatown* is my favorite movie."

"Nothing gets by you, does it?" She sounded sad all of a sudden and very young, nothing like what I expected from someone who made her living talking to millions of people.

"You sound like you could use a drink." I softened, the point having been made.

"I suppose you know where I live." She was resigned. An interesting woman, this one. She had a wide range of emotions and I'd heard all of them in the span of a five-minute phone conversation. "Can you be here in an hour?"

I told her I could.

"And . . . Ms. . . . Moses?" She tripped over the "Ms."

"I know, I know," I said. "Be discreet."

I was a mind reader as well. She rang off without even saying good-bye.

SIX

Latisha Maxwell lived among LA's beautiful people in an obscenely affluent neighborhood in Beverly Hills, within Gold Card distance of Rodeo Drive.

I considered taking the freeway, but the thought of making this woman sit and wait a moment was something I couldn't resist. I fired up the Alfa and headed east up Wilshire to the coiffed green lawns and security fences of Beverly Hills. It was still raining.

No matter what anybody says about southern California, it isn't a natural paradise. Not by Adam's and Eve's standards, anyway. Woody Guthrie was right about that ''Do Re Mi'' stuff. LA is modern man's feeble attempt at paradise, a mirage of four million people rising out of the desert. Some paradise. More like paradise lost.

What else could be said about a place whose inhabitants live with constant fears of water shortages, brush fires, race riots, earthquakes, and God knows what else. Talk about shaky ground.

Sure, it was sunny and eighty degrees every day, but all this did was melt the pavement, trap the fumes of civilization under a layer of yellow smog, and parch anything that had a pulse or a cell structure.

And I loved everything about it.

The thing that was so contagious about LA was that nearly everyone who lived here, certainly everyone who moved here, was after something they could never catch. It was a city of tail chasers.

You could get a tan, a face-lift, a million-dollar makeover, and your own personal trainer, and you'd never get any younger. You could buy a house with fifty rooms, have a table at Spago's, two front-row seats next to Jack at the Forum, drive around in a Hummer, and even make a movie, but you're never gonna live forever. A whole city looking for the fountain of youth. Tailor-made for detectives.

"Let 'em wear black" was my motto.

The center of this phenomenon, of course, was Beverly Hills. To the rest of us in these 34,000 square miles of former desert, the natural color of grass was brown. But on the hottest days of the year—weeks, even months into dry spells—the lawns in Beverly Hills are as green as golf courses and big-league ballparks; a thicket of jungle and exotic plants, colorful flowers and perfectly trained shrubs, all often surrounded by a well-monitored fence. And, depending on the time of day, protected by immigrant gardeners and a small cadre of armed (and dangerous in ways barely imaginable) rent-a-cops.

It only proved that success buys lots of green.

It was still Christmastime, and the rich and famous displayed their particular brand of excess in ways that usually stayed behind closed doors. As in the rest of the country, Christian homeowners had brought out their holiday decorations. Here, whole mansions had been outlined in white lights, others had decorated fences or large living Christmas trees, and still others had propped up mangers and sleighs and reindeer on their front lawn, alongside six-figure sculptures. Nothing too tacky, now. But more than a enough to add a few more zeros to the electric bill.

Latisha's entranceway was no exception, although the smatterings of white lights around a front-yard tree and along the roofline of her house were among the more subtle in her neighborhood. There was a fence, all right—wrought-iron; the kind that said "Stay out! Please"—but the house itself didn't seem as foreboding. It was set back, like other houses in the neighborhood, though smaller, more in scale with what regular folk like me were more accustomed to. I kind of liked it.

I pulled up to the gate and pressed the button—everything these days was like entering a mall parking garage—and Latisha's voice came through, the intercom static adding to her sultry s's.

"Ms. Moses?"

"It is I," I said.

She let the gate do her talking and it clicked and choked slightly before dragging itself slowly across the mouth of her driveway. I drove the Alfa up the modest drive and nosed it in next to a forest-green Ford Explorer and a shiny Chevy pickup, the kind with the exaggerated fenders. Both were shielded from the elements by a carport that appeared to have been added after the house had been built. I could see the marks where it was attached to the main building, faded a lighter shade of yellow than the makeshift garage.

I hopped out and hurried through the rain and up to the main door. She let me wait several minutes before cracking open the door.

I didn't expect Faye Dunaway and was well aware what the wonders of the small screen could do for the big stars who made millions off the medium, but it looked to me like Latisha Viola Maxwell didn't need much upkeep.

Small and delicately angled, she gave the impression of being much taller. She was a blonde, her hair clipped short and styled with mousse to give it an orderly messy look. She had a model's figure—slender and well-proportioned in those places most men—I was told—thought counted for something.

She would have been a perfect photograph, except for the barely noticeable bruise that accented her right cheekbone. She had covered it up expertly, but I'd seen my share of battered women, and although I was sure it was not a recent mark, I could see the outline of fingers stretching from the dark center.

It occurred to me this was why I was here, but I decided to keep quiet for now. There was something about her that was all control, the TV person, but there was something else visible that made me wonder whether the trip up the mountain had been a hard one. It was a fast first impression, one I'd probably update later, but in the mild way she rocked in the doorway and the constant movement of her eyes I saw something vulnerable. I would have to give her some room.

Her makeup was her only attempt at appearances, however. She wore torn-at-the-knee jeans, the kind that come with the rips in them—costing extra for each tear. She had loosely tucked a black T-shirt into the jeans, and on her feet was a pair of white Keds. She wore no jewelry.

I had dressed appropriately, it seemed, opting for jeans as well, plus my waterproof Timberland hiking boots, a heavy black cotton blouse and my favorite leather jacket, a grizzled veteran of my wardrobe whose lining had been in shreds for years.

"Please come in." She was curt. I couldn't tell what was real and what wasn't. I had a sneaking suspicion she didn't know either.

While the outward appearance of the house seemed pedestrian for the neighborhood, the inside was even less typical. It was too clean, lacked much in the way of furniture, but did have character, the kind found in places people actually spent time living in. Snapshots were everywhere. Some were of children, and nearly all of them looked happy, or seemed happy, anyway. The most prominent was of a woman who easily could be Latisha's sister. Very similar in build and appearance, but much younger and thinner. Another photograph stood out of a much younger Latisha, the sister, and a thin, fragile woman who was probably their mother. They were standing close together, not really touching. It was a bright summer day somewhere, and you got the impression water was nearby.

It was clearly a blow-up of a snapshot, maybe a Polaroid. The colors were blurry like a Monet painting.

Latisha and the older woman and the sister, who must've been no older than five or six at the time, were staring straight ahead at the camera. Their faces held similar thin smiles, but their eyes, even the child's, had an emotion in them I couldn't name. It was as if they were all mad at the world—or something else.

Their chilly gazes seemed to follow me as we passed through a tiny foyer. A short shelf lined one side of the hallway, stacked high with magazines, mostly copies of *Elle* or *Cosmo*, with a few *Daily Variety's* and one or two dog-eared copies of the *Hollywood Reporter*.

A carved wooden bowl sat on top, filled with mail—mostly bills.

I was led into a large living room that ended at the back of the house in a wall of glass. Beyond the floor-to-ceiling panes was a nice-sized green lawn, ringed with flower beds and knee-high shrubs, and beyond it a fenced-in swimming pool complete with a 1940s Art Deco cabana. By itself each element would have been just fine. Taken as a whole, it was modern disaster design—another specialty peculiar to LA.

"Make yourself comfortable," she said, as I gazed out at her jumble of a backyard. I sensed she was looking a lot farther than that. But her moment of reflection passed quickly and she snapped into what no doubt was her efficiency mode.

"There's coffee if you like." She gestured toward a silver Art Deco carafe that highlighted a tray on the center table, which stood in front of the house's most extravagant feature—a white leather couch. "If you could bear with me, I was in the middle of something when you came. I'll just be a moment."

I nodded acquiescence, but it was toward her back; she was already flying out of the room.

Latisha's big, cushion couch and two matching chairs were surrounding a cut-glass table in the shape of a kidney. On one end it had an artistically placed hole whose purpose eluded me, other than making a game of placing one's coffee mug.

A wall unit ran along one wall holding a stereo system I'd kill for. It was a melting pot of components from England and Germany that must have cost more than I'd made in the last five years. She even had a turntable, a snazzy Swedish thing that was thinner than a coffee-table book, though from what I could see she didn't have any records.

The shelves were filled with knickknacks, more pictures, and a collection of gadgets and toys of all shapes and sizes and materials. She also had, I noticed with a surprise that made me feel like a snob, a collection of books that actually looked as if someone had turned their pages.

I had a first-edition Chandler in my hand when I heard someone behind me.

"Looking for pointers?" It was a male voice, authoritative, brisk, perfectly in control. I turned around to see Latisha standing next to a man who I imagined was quite used to the art of persuasion.

He had on a Hugo Boss suit, knit shirt, no tie and a pasted-on grin as if he'd swallowed a lot more than just one canary. The uniform of the young and affluent.

"Excuse me?" I said to him, probably sounding as puzzled as I felt.

"The books." He was grinning so hard I was waiting for his lips to crack. "A PI reading detective books. It's classic. I asked if you were looking for pointers, tips of the trade, so to speak. Get it?"

I could have answered and part of me was disappointed that I didn't. The retorts flew into my head at a speed that would make Jay Leno envious, but something checked me. I don't know if it was decorum, the veiled look of discomfort on Latisha's face or just my unfamiliarity with the situation, but whatever it was, it shut me up.

"And you are?" I replaced the book on its shelf and walked toward them.

"This is Lawrence Kay," Latisha answered for him. "He's my manager . . ."

". . . and publicist and agent and water boy. Just your all-round gofer." Still grinning, he shot his hand out like a snake's tongue. "Hiya, Zen. Mind if I call you that?" He giggled at the name in a way that made me want to slap him.

"Go right ahead. Everybody calls me that."

"Well, great. You can just call me Lawrence," He

thought this was funny, too, and his grin impossibly seemed to widen.

The weird thing was the guy didn't come off like a stand-up wannabe. It was a different kind of humor. Something he had perfected to remind people he didn't think much of that he was better than them, or maybe, in my case, to register approval, as if I was being welcomed into his club.

Either way, he was still condescending and it was all I could do to keep from looking for something to hit him with. He was brash, caught in that age that's too old to think they can learn anything and too young to realize they don't know shit.

I didn't like him and I didn't think much of a woman who would entrust her career to such a pip-squeak, but then again, they probably all did. No self-respecting person would take the job of baby-sitting the scions of Hollywood fame and fortune. I hoped for Latisha's sake that he was better at managing her life than he was at telling jokes.

I looked toward Latisha for some assistance and noted with a degree of relief that she was nearly rolling her eyes. She had her thin arms folded and her right foot a little ahead of her left. I could almost imagine her tapping it on the floor, completing the picture of an impatient woman.

"Please, sit," she said, taking one of her leather chairs herself and leaving me the couch. It gave a funny crunch when I sat down.

Kay remained standing, finding a spot where he would lean against the wall, casual-like.

A collection of what I thought were toys sat on the coffee table, but when I picked one up, I could see it was a kind of sophisticated puzzle game. Too sophisticated for me.

I reached for an easier puzzle, two horseshoes fed through a metal ring.

"Ever seen one before?" It was Kay.

"I think they're called Tavern puzzles," I said. "And the object is to remove the ring without a blowtorch."

"Elementary, my dear Watson," he said in a lousy British accent. "I'm impressed, Detective."

I rolled my eyes at him but turned toward my prospective client instead. "Pardon me for saying so—and I mean no offense to Sherlock here, but I like to meet with clients on a one-to-one basis. It's, well, less complicated."

She flashed a look at her manager that I could not see, but it must have been fierce because his face changed suddenly. All business. It was then I knew for certain where that little bruise on Latisha's face hadn't come from.

"I think we can proceed," she said. "Lawrence is my most trusted friend and adviser and is privy to everything I do. I'd feel much more comfortable with him here."

"Whatever you like," I said, starting to work on the Tavern puzzle, the metal clinking in my hands. It was a moment before I realized they were both staring at me. I looked up sheepishly.

"Knock yourself out," she said, as if we were best friends sitting for tea and scones. "Everybody plays with them. My sister loves figuring things out."

"Ahh," I said, noting my impression of a family resemblance was right on the mark. "The woman in the pictures."

"My kid sister." She smiled the warm smile of someone who knows the real value of family. Maybe she wasn't so bad after all.

"Listen, I'm sorry about the other thing. I didn't really know what to do."

"It can be difficult." I held out my mug. "I'm willing to forget it happened, okay? Let's just start all over. Besides, I love *Chinatown*."

"Actually, I've never seen it," she said. "It was Lawrence's idea."

I looked up at Kay and he had one of those self-satisfying smiles, clearly impressed with his feat of cultural intelligence.

"Jack's the man," he said.

"Whatever you say, Lar." He winced at my pronunciation of his name.

He started to say something but Latisha cut him off.

She took a practiced, dainty sip of the coffee—lots of

cream and sugar. No wonder she had rapid mood changes. I took advantage of the lull in the titillating conversation to get things started.

"Ms. Maxwell," I began.

"Latisha," she said.

"Latisha," I repeated, the puzzle still keeping some of my attention. "How can I help you?"

"It's rather complicated," she said. She was still slurring her *s*'s, but in person it didn't sound sexy at all. And I was considering giving it a try.

"I don't know where to begin, Ms. Mos—"

"Please, everyone calls me Zen."

"Zen. Such a strange name." She laughed and seemed to think about it for a moment. Her thought process was very visible. "Okay: Zen."

"You were saying?"

"I was saying I didn't know where to begin."

"I understand."

"How could you possibly? I haven't said a word." She was in her indignant phase now.

I was at a loss and told her so. "I just assumed," I said, trying to be delicate and gesturing toward her face. "Your bruise."

"Oh, this? It's nothing," she almost snapped, showing a glimpse of temper which she quickly covered with a laugh that, though not unkind, was clearly dismissive. "No, this is . . . it's not why I called you here."

"Did you walk into a door?"

It was a cruel thing to say and I wanted to take it back just as soon as it came out. But I was also not up to getting a runaround and was wondering if she really needed my services. Her mood changes were starting to annoy me. It was irritating that I couldn't pin her down to one personality.

"I'm sorry," I said quickly, seeing that Kay, whose attention had begun to wander a bit, was turning it back toward us. "That was uncalled for."

"Forget it," she said. "But please, can't we get down to

business? This is hard enough as it is, and I don't know when Sara is expected back.''

"Your sister?"

"As I said, this is very complicated. Sara has no idea I am meeting with you. I don't want her to know.''

"Is your sister in trouble, then?"

I sat back in the leather sofa, draining the last of the coffee. I was very confused, but I said nothing. Instead, I went back to the puzzle.

Latisha remained silent as well and I half-watched her, practically seeing the gears churning in her head. I suppose she was having second thoughts. So was I.

Kay kept looking over at me, then back at Latisha as if he was trying to signal her. Finally, he just came over and parked himself in the other leather chair. He leaned toward Latisha and they fell into a private exchange of whispers.

I waited them out, turning my energies back to the puzzle and trying not to think of my own problems. Finally, Latisha broke our silence.

"No one's in trouble," she began. "I just need you to find someone.''

Now we were getting somewhere. "That can be done.''

"We heard you were pretty good at these things." It was Kay again, making it clear he was in on the whole thing. I nodded, but underneath I was wondering from whom the recommendation had come. I didn't know I had that many fans.

"The problem is," Latisha said, "that I don't want anyone to know I'm looking for this person. The press is very persistent, as you can imagine.''

Talk about calling the kettle black. "You don't have to worry about it coming from me," I said. "I don't do press releases.''

She nodded.

"So," I said slowly. "Who's missing?"

SEVEN

Kay had his ears up again. This was his moment.

"You understand that this is strictly confidential," he said. "Our conversation can't leave this room."

"Of course," I said to Latisha, trying to be professional. My you-can-trust-me look. I felt like a used-car salesman. "Conversations between private detectives and their clients are essentially treated in much the way as those between confessor and priest and lawyer and client. I believe strongly in the ethics of confidentiality."

Kay huffed, but Latisha just nodded. She seemed to be measuring her words, sizing me up, and God knew what else was in her head. Maybe the room needed recarpeting.

"I need to find my father," she said flatly, trying on words she didn't seem familiar with. No wonder. If there was one thing even I knew about Latisha Viola Maxwell, it was that her father was dead. There had been a big stink in the tabloids a year or so ago about it after she had done a show on single parents. She broke down in tears on the air when she related her troubled childhood and how her father had died. Even the tabs thought she went over the top.

"Well." She was looking at me and I smiled. I had let myself drift off for a second. Guess I wasn't always the consummate professional.

"Forgive me," I said, once again attacking the puzzle. "But didn't you say on TV that your father was dead? So are we looking for a grave site, or are you going to destroy all my illusions by telling me the camera isn't the only thing that lies?"

"There were . . . reasons," she started. "What I do on TV is mostly performance. Don't believe everything you see on television. My private life is my business."

I really didn't want to get into a discussion about whether that fact gave her a license to lie, partly because I didn't want to know what she would say. It wasn't always necessary actually to like your clients, but it sure helps if you can trust them. I didn't want to take a case that forced me to keep looking over my shoulder. Besides, in a way wasn't I lying myself? I'm sure Brooks would see it that way.

"It'd be nice if you could stick to reality with me," I said.

She glared back. I guess this wasn't going to turn out to be a mutual-admiration club.

"Of course." The color that had risen in her face seemed to drain a little. Her emotional changes were making me dizzy.

"My father moved us around a lot, but we basically grew up in the South, wherever he could find work," she said. "It was just me, my sister, Sara, and my parents. My father, well, he wasn't exactly Mr. Cleaver, if you know what I mean. I don't know if he ever really loved my mother, but they stuck it out, probably because she *was* Mrs. Cleaver. I last saw him fifteen years ago, when I was a teenager. We had been living in North Carolina. Anyway, we had an ongoing argument and I finally ran away from home. We haven't spoken since."

"What did you fight about?"

She waved her hand. "You know that's the funny part. I don't even remember. There's just been so many things that have happened to me since, that it almost doesn't seem important anymore."

"It was then," I said, seeing Kay fidget. He wasn't liking where I was going and this made my alarm go off. "At least to a certain teenager."

"You know how seventeen-year-old girls can be." She was almost laughing, turning the tables on me—now I was uncomfortable. It was an obvious lie—people don't forget the reasons why they run away from home. She wasn't winning me over.

"You're certain he's alive?"

"I've been trying to find him on my own for some time and have reason to believe he is," she said.

"And that is?"

"He's been in contact . . ." Kay put his hand on her leg, a slight movement that I almost didn't notice. She looked at him before continuing. "He's been in contact with family friends."

"Why do you want to find him now?"

She looked up quickly at this, then at Kay, who registered a look that I couldn't read at all, though it seemed to say something to the effect of "You're on your own now."

"I suppose you'd want to know that," she said, as if talking to someone else.

"Actually, no," I said. "It doesn't matter to me, but it might help."

"I understand. I just didn't expect the question." She seemed to have a great need to control things, staging her words as if she were sitting before a camera. I had a compelling urge to turn around and look for cue cards. Instead, I just listened, still fiddling with that puzzle in my hands, glad to have the distraction.

"My mother died recently," she said.

"I'm sorry."

"Thank you, she'd been very sick." She went back to her faraway place again. "She asked me to find him, if he was still alive, and, you know, try to reconcile things with him. My father was very old-fashioned. The truth is that all I have now is Sara, who lives with me. She hasn't had an easy time of it, especially lately. She was very close to my mother.

"And to be honest, I guess I want to try and close some old wounds. I mean, no matter how awful your parents are to you, they are family. Maybe I'm mature enough to deal with it. Maybe he's changed. I suppose I want to find out before it's too late."

It was a story I'd heard a thousand times from a thousand different people, all victims, for lack of a better word, of the dysfunctional family. For a lot of them it didn't matter what horrors—real or imagined—had been committed behind closed doors. In the end, it was family and forgiveness and burying the past. It was a human kind of justice in an often inhuman world.

Maybe it was pure need, maybe it was just wanting to be part of something that was really yours, or maybe it was just our race's own brand of insanity. Whatever it was, it had a pull that only things like religion and maybe politics have, and most times there wasn't anything you could do about it. Ask questions now, pick up the pieces later.

I hoped there wouldn't be too many left lying on the floor when we were done.

"So," Kay said. "Will you be taking this case?"

I looked at him then back at his client.

"Is there anything else I should know before I say yes?"

She thought about this for a minute and shook her head.

"Of course, you do understand this must be kept in strict confidence," Kay said. "If anything, and I mean anything, leaks to the press, all bets are off. Latisha's company is in a major network negotiation right now, and the last thing we need is to have this blow up in the tabs."

This was the third time I'd been cautioned, but I nodded. Typical modus operandi for the Hollywood elite. It was a wonder they didn't all walk around with paper bags over their heads. And, of course, she wouldn't want *this* to get in the papers, not after what she'd copped to on the air. I wondered how she would explain it all. Everything comes out eventually. It's the nature of things that nothing stays underground too long. I was just finding this to be painfully true. I wanted to warn her, but I decided some lessons are best learned firsthand.

"I will do my best," I said. "But when you start opening doors, people take notice. You can't control that, especially in a world where folks get paid to talk about people like you."

"It won't come out," Kay answered again, this time with a certain ferocity that reminded me of my first impression of him, that he could be trouble if he wanted to be. "If it does, I'll make sure you never work in this town again."

I wanted to laugh at this butthead's gall, thinking he could command the attention of the city's entire pool of prospective private detective clients, but I turned back to Latisha.

"Look, I'm good and I'm discreet. It's nice to be prepared for the unexpected. That's all."

"Thanks for your concern." Kay again. "We'll take care of our end. You just take care of yours."

"Fine," I grumbled. "Will there be anything else?"

"Yes," she said. "You are simply to find my father. Verify it's the right man, go and talk to him, but do not tell him that I am looking for him. Then report back to me. I said I wanted to find him, but as you can imagine, I'm not really sure if I want to *see* him. I hope you understand."

"That's not unusual," I told her, and it wasn't. "What should I tell him?"

"Use your imagination." It was Kay. "I'm sure you have a vivid one."

"I'm glad you can see this from my point of view," said Latisha, ignoring, as I had, the dig from Kay. "You don't know how much this means to me. I've been losing a lot of sleep over this."

I solved the metal puzzle, finally, the ring slipping off to freedom and bouncing off the white shag carpet. I picked it up and slipped it back on for the gadget's next victim. As I laid it back on the glass coffee table, Latisha's bigger puzzle was whirling around inside my head.

Nothing Latisha had told me made taking the case seem risky. Missing persons was run-of-the-mill stuff, and you didn't have to produce to get paid. But I was tempted to invoke my first two rules of self-defense: Run, and run like hell.

While there was something about this woman I liked, there was something about her story that I didn't. I had no basis for thinking so, but my gut was churning.

Plus, I had Daniel on my mind. Somewhere in the last few hours, I had vowed not to let him down again. I was in this business because I loved it. I was prepared and well-trained, but I'd survived this long because I didn't take stupid chances.

Yet, even as I counted off the reasons to walk away from Latisha and her weasel of a manager, I was feeling myself fall in, plotting a course of action.

There was something about her that made me feel for her and I couldn't place it. Maybe it was the homey quality of her house, the books and pictures, or perhaps it was her desire to make a broken family whole again.

I certainly had reason to find this compelling, even a little admirable. She was willing to walk through territory I had been content to avoid. If Danny hadn't turned up, I wondered if I ever would have talked to Sam again. I had put it all away where I wouldn't have to deal with it, and here was a woman who wanted to drag it out, shake it up, and try to make sense of it.

Besides, even if I didn't like her, it didn't mean I couldn't take her money.

"I'll tell you what," I said. "Give me a couple of days and I'll see what I can find out."

Her face brightened as much as I thought possible, which wasn't saying much at all.

"Great, that's great. Hang on a moment." She got up and went back toward the hallway and I took the opportunity to lean in toward Kay. I beckoned him with my finger and he moved closer.

"Never work in this town again?" I told him with as much menace as I thought I'd ever display. I swear I almost scared myself. "That's original."

"Don't think I don't mean it," he hissed back at me, though I cut him off with a pointed finger.

"I'm not sure, but that sounds like a threat to me." I said this slow, calming my voice to the point of disinterest, the way madmen do in movies. My way of making sure he understood the weight of what I was saying. "I don't like being threatened and I certainly don't like being threatened by an arrogant weasel like you. I don't think much of people who spend their time measuring their dick size to everyone else's. Get with the program. Not everyone has one, you know.''

"You don't scare me," he said.

"I should," I told him. "The fact that I don't means you're a lot dumber than you look."

He just smirked at this, while I leaned back in the couch and glared back at him. Zen as tough guy.

Latisha returned with a black leather knapsack, the kind that was in vogue, the latest urban pocketbook. She sat back down across from me and fished out a wad of bills thick enough to make my mouth water.

"What's your fee?" She was counting out the money, laying hundred-dollar bills on the glass table between us like playing cards.

I wanted to say four hundred dollars a day but I was nothing if not honest and I didn't have the heart. Another sign I was growing soft in my old age.

"Two-fifty a day, plus expenses," I said. "A week's advance is normal procedure. And I'll need you to sign some papers."

"Fine." She nodded, then made an obsessively neat stack of Ben Franklins on the table. I counted twenty-five of them, all the while watching Kay, who was leaning back with his arms crossed and his bottom lip sticking out slightly. I couldn't tell if he was stewing or moping. "Here's twenty-five hundred dollars to start with. Twice your normal fee, which I am hoping will convince you to keep the paperwork out of this."

A vague sense of decorum was the only thing keeping me from snatching the money off the table. "That's not really normal procedure. I like to keep records."

"If someone breaks into your office, I wouldn't want them to find my name on a contract."

"What if it were Evelyn Mulwray's?"

"What? Yes, yes." She actually smiled a second time. "That would work. I like it."

I didn't, but I was counting the beer and bills the cash would cover, and besides, I wasn't Jim Rockford. I couldn't remember the last time someone had tried to steal anything from my office.

"Thank you," she said, rising from the couch, with Kay a second behind. Her way of telling me the interview was over. "Thank you very much. This means a lot to me."

I managed to keep from drooling as I scooped up the cash. It felt good. We walked back to the front door, pausing for a moment in the foyer, leaving Kay and his glares behind in the living room. I saw him fiddling with the Tavern puzzle that I had left on the table. He was trying to pull it apart with his bare hands.

"I'll send you a receipt for the money," I said. "Here's my card. I can be reached twenty-four hours a day if there's anything you need."

She nodded, thanked me again and held out her hand. I shook it gently, getting a cold, wet palm in the process. She pulled back, but I held her hand a moment. When our eyes met, it occurred to me she was either very nervous, very frightened, or hiding something. Perhaps all three.

"Is there something else?" she asked.

"How *did* you get that bruise?"

She paused for a beat, then smiled. "You were right," she lied. "I walked into a door."

She managed not to cause any more marks on her face as she opened her front door, letting in a burst of cold, wet air.

"Now if that'll be all . . ."

I wasn't going to push it, not now anyway. I had to admit she didn't fit the battered-woman profile, and I was no shrink. Yet I knew her reaction to be typical. I had trouble with a society that not only allows this kind of thing to happen, but produces the kind of victims who permit it to continue.

I stepped out into the rain, gathering my coat around my neck and turning to look back at Latisha Maxwell. Her small-screen presence was obvious just then, a kind of surefooted demeanor marked the way she stood in that doorway, just a step of two from the outside world, confidently standing on the brink. I had one of those feelings, the kind that you never know the source of, that she could be a very dangerous woman.

"You tell that door something for me," I said evenly. "If it gets in the way of your face again, I'll kick it in."

Her answer came swift, sure and pointed—in the form of her allegedly abusive door slamming in my face.

Guess I was going to have to work on that Good Samaritan thing.

EIGHT

The bad weather eased a bit, turning the day into a sloppy, partly sunny afternoon in the land of the affluent. But as I got closer to Santa Monica, the fog added itself to the sky like a low, smoky ceiling. Nothing new here; Los Angeles always looked in need of kidney dialysis.

It was a scientific fact that Santa Monica was not as smoggy as the rest of Greater Los Angeles, and those same ocean breezes that kept the pollution out could also play games with the weather, especially at the bookends of the day.

That meant sometimes the sun wouldn't show itself until late morning, when a light, white fog would finally extinguish itself, and then seem to lose its brilliance just before setting in the cool shadow of evening.

Folks who had fled to the inland valleys (for more space and less expensive housing) also liked to say the weather tended to be much warmer and more stable than at the beach. But LA could get as hot as the desert it was, and they'd all end up driving their Toyotas and Hondas back to the edge of the Pacific for relief.

I stopped first at the bank. They had changed the decor since the last time I'd been in. They had had plenty of time. The blurp-blurp of my car phone interrupted Joe Henry on my tape deck. He was a kind of Southern rock and roller who wrote like Dylan and sang like Merle Haggard. Nobody ever played him on the radio, but that was usually a good sign for me, considering the state of radio these days.

He was getting through a song called "She Always

Coco," in a way that made me feel sorry for the old boy. This was okay; change the pronoun and I could do a reasonably honest job making someone feel the same for me.

I had picked up one of those tabloids with Latisha's picture on it, plus a copy of *People*, which had been gracious enough to have a feature on her this week. Not exactly prime bedtime reading, but it was a necessity. An important tenet of detective work is "Know thine client." A day or two of talk shows and I might be as well-informed as the average American. Now that's a scary thought.

The call was from Nat, pleading with me to meet him at his favorite steak place. I went by the pub, arranging to meet him outside. His climb into my tiny car was almost comical.

"Hey, baby," he said, smiling at me as if we shared a secret. In a way we did; we'd been an item once, though it was essentially a secret to even our closest friends. I liked to keep it that way. Our relationship, if you could call it that, had been brief and never really serious. We had comforted each other during some hard times and become lovers by accident, but I'd discovered that Nat was faithful to only one person—himself.

I'd been angry with him initially, but his friendship always seemed too important to hold a grudge, and although I felt at times that I barely knew him, I was sure he'd been hurt pretty badly. I didn't know the details, but I'd heard he'd been burned a couple of years ago and decided the only way he would live life was on his terms. So he surrounded himself with people who would give him that luxury.

I realized somewhere along the way that I didn't really want or even need what he was willing to give. I missed him sometimes, particularly on those nights when his kind of company was the only thing I wanted, but I knew that, like playing center field in Candlestick Park, there were things in life I was never going to have—and perhaps didn't really want anyway.

Besides, I found that one of two things happen to single women on the fall from thirty. Either they widen their net in hopes of catching the first-best thing to come around, or they begin to see men as a want, but not necessarily a need. The latter tends to make them choosier, and smarter. Having Nat as a friend seemed a lot more comfortable than either of the alternatives, and I considered our current relationship a sign of my own maturity.

I smiled back in the only way I could let him know how I still felt about him.

"Dinner's on me," I said.

"A case?"

I nodded.

"That's great," he said. "It'll be good for you to get back to work, get back into the flow. Just what you need."

I parked behind Knight's Inn on Wilshire and pulled my radio out of its slot in my dashboard. I was tired and figured on draining more than one glass of Scotch with dinner, which meant I'd have to leave the Alfa here. I cared too much about my radio to leave it for some junior car thief to heist.

The place was practically empty when we walked in and found Nat's usual table in the back. The whole room had a kind of deep cherry-colored glow to it, as if you were standing inside a submarine. Red leather banquettes horseshoed around mahogany-stained wood veneer tables that faded into a dark carpet you could barely see because the lights were kept so dim it was hard to say if they were really on.

No doubt a stray tourist might catch a glimpse of the wrought-iron knight-on-horse that graced the faux brick facade and find this place hard to pass up, but this was home mostly to old-timers and their regular routines. Like its heart-attack menu of rare steaks, greasy sides and iceberg lettuce with underripe tomatoes slathered in bottled blue-cheese dressing, Knight's was one of those places that watched the world go by without paying much attention.

The guys who came in last Monday had probably not missed a Monday here since the Great War. Inside, the names and faces never changed, they just got older and drunker and, maybe, heavier too.

There were two ancients at the leather-trimmed bar when we walked in, both facing half-empty Budweisers and half-eaten plates of steak and onion rings. One sat on each end of the bar and every once in a while they seemed to say something to each other, the acoustics apparently good enough for them to converse in a mumble across the room-length bar. Either that, or they were talking to themselves. It was hard to tell.

Our waitress smiled at us as if we were old acquaintances, which surely was true, though I couldn't pull her name out of the cobwebs if I'd been given a road map. Nat was good at this kind of thing and greeted her like the regular he was.

I wasn't much of a meat eater, but there was little else on the menu to choose from except for what I knew would be an undercooked baked potato. I ordered it anyway with the Black Label that I'd been thinking about since I walked in.

Still, I was a bit hesitant. Scotch and steaks were how Nat and I had gotten into trouble in the first place, and we'd kind of kept that activity to a minimum.

We spent most of the meal talking about things other than what we both really wanted to talk about. Nat, I knew, wanted to be let into whatever it was Brooks and I had kept from him earlier. I didn't really want to talk about anything at all. I had too much stuff in my head at the moment. Trying to voice any of it would be too difficult right now. I hoped Nat would understand.

"You're quiet tonight," he said, leaning back in the red leather seats. I had to squint to see him, the low light and the liquor leaving a film over my eyes. "After an evening with you, I usually need to get away for a while."

"What can I say, I'm a lot younger than you," I said. "I guess I can change my bad habits easier."

"You never miss a chance," he laughed.

I emptied my last Scotch.

"Let's get out of here," I said. "It's been a hell of a day and I have a client to attend to tomorrow."

"Hold on a minute," he said. "I kept my tongue all evening. A guy was murdered in my bar. I figure I deserve to be told something."

"I wish I could, Nat. Really, but I can't," I said. "Besides, I thought we had a deal to keep our pasts to ourselves.''

''That was before yours turned up dead in my freezer.''

A part of me wanted to tell him, but another, bigger part wanted not to tell anyone at all, even my best friend.

''You're going to have to give me some room here.'' I was trying to sound firm and solid, but I felt anything but. ''This is something I've got to do myself. I'll explain everything to you when I'm ready. Promise.''

He seemed to accept this, though from the way he bit his lip, I could tell he wasn't quite ready to let it go.

We had made our way outside the deserted restaurant. Tuesday night on Wilshire Boulevard was pretty quiet, except for a few passing cars and a mild breeze that was making preparations to drag the next morning's fog across town. In the distance we could hear the rapping of thunder. God was fixing a fine ending for my day.

''I'll forgive your bar debt,'' he said, suddenly wrapping his big arms around me, and I was reminded again of why they called it a bear hug. He pressed his lips against my ear. ''What do you say?''

I was melting. ''I'll think about it,'' I said, trying half-heartedly to pull away. ''Don't start what you can't finish.''

We remained there, in that embrace, for several moments, feeding off each other's warmth. Sex, as it had always been with us, was in the air. But this time the feeling for me faded so quickly, I shivered.

I rested my head on his chest, though, and considered how nice it would be to have him with me later, but along with desire came foreboding. I broke the embrace and reached up to give him a friendly peck, but it turned into a too-friendly kiss. I pushed back, knowing I'd feel better in the morning.

''We've been through this before,'' I said.

He smirked the way he did sometimes in serious moments. I knew he meant no offense—it was just a habit—but it was still irritating.

Our condition merited a cab ride and he had the hostess call one. It was already at the curb when we got outside.

Nat opened the door and held it for me, a lost child's look on his face. I shook my head.

"I think I'll walk," I said, watching him climb into the cab and then leaning over to shut the door. "Just give me a couple of days to work things out, okay?"

His nod came with a smile that lasted even after I'd closed the taxi door.

For not the first time since I'd known him, I watched him go and wondered why two people who had grown so close could be so far apart and what kind of pain or fear or humility kept us there. I couldn't tell my future—hell, I could barely work out what I was doing tomorrow—and I wasn't much of a believer in fate, but I knew somehow Nat and I had crossed paths for a reason. And somehow, somewhere down the line, we would find out why.

I just wondered if we'd recognize it when it happened.

NINE

The walk home cleared my head enough to let my hangover begin to settle in. I was restless and feeling sorry for myself for a long, troubling day. Another night alone wasn't making me feel any better.

I wasn't hurting for male companionship, but I had what my friends called the bachelor complex. Although I could be gregarious and charming when called upon, I preferred my own company to almost everyone else and jealously guarded my own space. Add that to a general fear of commitment, a sometimes trying personality and an active dislike of social situations, and suddenly the pool of available prospects dwindled considerably.

By the time I got to my block, the night's chill had found its way under my jacket and the thunder began to creep closer. An orphaned raindrop plunked down on my face.

My place was at the end of a dead-end street, facing the high back fence of one of Santa Monica's three graveyards and the only one in the Southland especially for man's best friend. The wrought-iron fence had long been covered by climbing plants and ivy and was as dense as a high-security barrier probably, to keep the ghost of Fido from haunting the neighborhood cats.

Except for the dull light I'd left on outside my front door, the street was darker than usual, the moon's glow covered by the rain clouds. I was adjusting to the low light and trying not to trip over myself when an odor wafted up through the dark.

The smell hit me slowly, drifting out of the night so casually that it was hard to place it for a moment.

But when it did, it was familiar enough to bring with it a rash of memories I'd been wrestling with a lot longer than since I'd seen Danny in the walk-in. Dense. Earthy. Exotic.

Cigar smoke.

Another ghost from my past.

This one spoke. "It's been a long time, Zen."

As I approached, I could make out a figure seated on the wooden rocking chair I keep outside my house just for this smoking ritual. He had his legs stretched out and crossed, the ember from the cigar aglow and unsteady in what now must be sixty-year-old hands. His face came into some focus, his hair, I could tell, even in the near dark, faded white along with a well-coiffed mustache, the old-fashioned kind that loops upward at the ends, Hercule Poirot style.

"Sam," was about all I could say as I plopped down on my stoop so we were almost side by side, both looking out toward the cemetery as if we could see it clearly through the foliated fence. I was trying to imagine the demons that raged beyond that fence when Sam finally spoke, his voice clear, unforced, in the strong tones of a news anchor, only not quite as perfect.

"Doctors still let you have these?"

I looked up at the short, fat cigar he was waving at me. I took it from him, automatically holding the business end toward my nose. Its smell was complicated, nutty, a bit spicy. I gently pried off the tip with my fingernail and took the lighter Sam handed to me to stoke it up.

Cigar smoking was one of my passions. My friends knew about it, but I rarely smoked in their presence, preferring to save mine for moments when the only company I was keeping was my own.

It had lately become the newest fad among young professionals and, recently, young women, which was okay with me, but I was a different sort of smoker. I was the daughter and niece of tobacconists and had been raised behind the counter of one of San Francisco's oldest cigar shops.

Cigars were a requirement in the Moses household. Cigarettes were another story.

There's no middle ground with cigar smoking. Most people find them stuffy, stale, smelly, and distasteful, but true connoisseurs smell something entirely different. Cigars are pure tobacco, unfettered by the tars and nicotines and other chemicals that go into cigarettes.

I was sure it wasn't wise to continue to smoke, not in my condition anyway, but giving it up felt like giving up part of my history, and these days it was the one tangible thing I had left. Besides, being perfect might hurt my tough-guy-detective image, and anyway, decadence was okay in my book as long as you sinned in moderation.

As we sat there, the smell of smoke and memories settling into the damp air, these thoughts didn't seem very important. I was trying to think of something to say, but for maybe the second or third time in my life, no words of consequence came to mind. Nothing that could give justice to what I was thinking and feeling. Nothing at all.

TEN

So much came flooding back through my mind that I was afraid to tilt my head, sure that it would all tumble out my ear and onto the porch.

Sam was my dad's half-brother, the true black sheep of a family of Russian immigrants, dropped in San Francisco on the wrong side of the Great Depression.

They had been close in age and shared everything from a cigar shop to a multifamily brownstone in the city's Noe Valley. Their wives had also been childhood friends, and each bore only one child, though only Sam's stayed around long enough to see her kid grow up.

We all lived a couple of houses down the block from the shop, a remodeled turn-of-the-century confectioner's shop, complete with ice-cream-parlor chairs, a long metal-plated counter and those ornate sterling soda fountains that hadn't been used in years.

Danny had taken over the shop, not because he was the only boy in the family, but because I'd never wanted anything to do with the place. It was really a second chance for Danny, who had left home for Wall Street with an MBA degree and a kid-on-the-rise cockiness.

It was a crazy time, the early eighties, when every American boy, at least every prep-school boy anyway, thought the world was his own personal oyster, as long as he wore the right suit and tie, drove the right car, found the latest crack in Wall Street's potholed facade, and learned how to outrun the SEC. It was there for the taking, and Danny saw no reason why he shouldn't be the one to grab it.

Like all the other MBAs out there, Danny was in it only half for the money. The real lure was the game and the buzz of making something out of nothing. He had been a good trader at first, made more money than I'd ever seen, but he was always hustling the next big loophole. He got nailed in an insider-trading scandal and avoided prison by finking on some of his colleagues.

Danny didn't come back with any guilt about what he'd done, which was the thing that irked Sam and my dad more than the fact that he'd actually broken the law. To Danny, the guys he turned in deserved what they got. Either they weren't smart enough to play the game or they'd committed one sin too many.

Danny always liked to say he hadn't hurt anyone who hadn't deserved it and, for the most part, he hadn't, but the pain he'd caused his family had always weighed heavy on his conscience.

Robert Frost says, "Home is the place where, when you have to go there, they have to take you in." That's pretty much what happened for Danny. When he came back with nothing, my dad was too sick to run the store and Sam was just too tired to do it by himself.

It seemed a good setup, mostly because underneath it all Danny had had his father's heart; it just didn't always seem to be beating. And he made a good go at it, taking to the family business like the only son he was.

But then Danny found religion. And not the kind you get at the Jewish Community Center. He had hooked up with one of those post-hippie gurus who preach inner peace and self-discovery, but end up going for the soul of guys like Danny who are still trying to find out if they have one or not.

Danny was a perfect mark for their insidious mix of friendship and persuasion. He'd begun to feel as if he'd let his own down, that his crime against his family was the one thing that was truly unforgivable. I thought then, we all did, that his guilt was just part of a self-indulgent phase, but now I wonder how much we added to his feelings. Our disappointment was obvious, our forgiveness, perhaps, was not.

Maybe he would have gotten over this too, but our family had already had enough history with used-car salesmen masquerading as messiahs. My mother, a wonderfully strange, slightly mad and very uncertain woman descended in part from real gypsies, discovered her guru after reading an article in *Rolling Stone* (what this woman of the Benny Goodman generation was doing with the bible of the air-guitar kids, I'll never know). She left home in our old Ford station wagon, the one with the fake wooden panels on the sides. It was a quiet, sunny Sunday morning around the same time a Watergate security guard was stumbling into a burglary in our nation's capital. She was off, she explained in a letter she left on the kitchen counter, to join her savior. She still lives on that same commune, somewhere in Idaho where nothing much grows, not even potatoes.

There wasn't a one of us, not even my father, who thought perhaps my mom wasn't better off among people as crazy as she was, but that didn't mean we were willing to let her go. She had her moments, my mom did, and she had her unexplained visions too, but her mental imbalance was no reason to leave her family for a money-sucking, robe-wearing fat guy in Idaho just because he said he had been visited by God on a barren plateau in the middle of mid-western nowhere.

I still don't forgive her for not waiting long enough for Prozac to come along.

My dad was bit more charitable and I think he thought she would come back sooner or later, but when Danny got the call, I guess he started to see the whole thing as being more permanent.

And perhaps Danny would be living in some commune somewhere now too, if we had dealt with it a little better. But we didn't trust Danny's emotional stability at the time, and the more involved with the commune he became, the more we pushed to get him out. The more we pushed, of course, the more he turned away from us and toward his new "family."

It was heartbreaking to Sam and to my dad, and when Danny started giving his guru money, the whole thing went downhill fast.

The problem was that Danny had no cash to speak of, not since he'd used it to help buy his freedom from the Feds, so he was dipping into the shop's till for donation money. It was a while before any of us realized what had happened, but when the books came up short, it wasn't long before we suspected Danny.

Actually, it had been up to me to confront my older cousin. He denied it, but there was no one else who had been close enough to the accounts to pilfer. He finally confessed on the same night he took off for good to live with his new people. The guru had a wooded private estate about ninety miles south along a sparsely populated section of California's famous Pacific Coast Highway.

My dad had always treated his nephew like his own, just as Sam had done with me, and the whole thing hurt him deeply. It was a great disappointment to him, the kind you don't get over, that makes you believe you can actually die of a broken heart. My dad did.

He died angry and hurt and I never forgave Danny for letting my dad down. I drove down the coast to see him and our last conversation is not one I will ever be proud of. I wanted him to know what it felt like to be betrayed. I pushed him, hard.

The circle of disappointment went through my dad and me right to Sam, completed horribly when Danny, along with a dozen other cult members, linked arms and threw themselves off one of those picturesque cliffs that bring millions of visitors to Route 1 every year. Most of the bodies were never recovered, mixing with the sharks and rocks and sea life that churns forever in the cold Pacific.

It was quite the news item at the time and many questions remain, as why did only a few cult members jump? All I know is that Danny had plunged into the Pacific mere hours after I'd left him, no doubt with feelings of guilt and torture and confusion. I didn't need to know anything more than that.

Neither, it turned out, did Sam. I knew he had been angry at Danny for what had happened, but he was even more disappointed in me. I'd never forget the last time we spoke, after we'd buried the remains of his only son—only a couple of months after we'd put my dad to rest.

It had been raining on and off for days and the city was sealed inside a cold February fog. We were standing beside the black Lincoln the funeral home had used to taxi us to the cemetery. The elongated, dark car dwarfed Sam, who seemed vulnerable in a way I'd never seen before.

His breath came fast, his words shooting out between his teeth like bullets, given finality with the way he waved at the air for emphasis with one hand and tightly gripped the side-view mirror of the Lincoln with the other.

"I'd always asked a lot of both of you," he told me, his whole body shaking, more from anger than the chill. I had been holding an umbrella over both of us, but had moved it absently so only part of me was sheltered. The rain hid my tears.

"But you?" he said. "Danny was never able to control himself, he was weak that way. You never were, but you let yourself be controlled by your anger and your disappointment. Wasn't one death in the family enough?"

He started crying then, the way I've seen men do many times since, a tear or two rolling down the check or nose, followed by another and another, a controlled march. I dropped my head, wanting to say I was sorry, but still too blinded, too proud. Too stupid.

"You've done a terrible thing, Zenaria. A terrible, terrible thing." He opened the door of the car just then and looked up at me. My tears raced the rainwater down my face. "You should've tried to help him," he said. "You should never play with a man's demons. They don't belong to you."

It was the last thing he said to me—until tonight—and I wondered, staring into the darkness, feeling the coolness raise a shiver under my skin, whether he was replaying the same scene over in his head, whether, like me, he'd been doing it ever since Danny had jumped into the Pacific.

And as far as we'd both run from it, and there was no doubting we had done just that, we'd come back to each other as if we'd been running in place the whole time. Go figure.

ELEVEN

"How'd you know?" I asked after we'd been silent long enough to hear the thunder creep toward us, its grumbling gaining in decibel with each new crash.

"Been keeping track," he said. "I wanted to come see you when you were sick, but I was afraid you wouldn't want to see me. I'm sorry; that's when I should have come."

"That's okay, Sam. Some things you gotta do yourself, you know." I said this like I meant it because I did. To me there was no better time for solitude than when facing one's own mortality. For a while that's exactly what I had been doing.

"Sounds like the girl I knew," he said. "Good to see she's still intact."

"For the most part," I said. Another sound of thunder, this time close enough to make us both jump a little. "Maybe we should go inside."

He nodded and got himself up out of the chair as if he were pulling invisible handles. Old age had settled into Sam, but I was glad to see not too unkindly.

I set up Sam in a big fluffy chair once reserved for the resident feline. But since Ira had been flattened, the chair was no use to him anymore. I figured he wouldn't mind if I let Sam use it.

I sat on the floor in front of my futon where I could see the shadows from what little light was outside. There was a subdued bright glow, the kind that comes before big storms and that makes it seem as if daylight were only a moment away. Another one of nature's deceptions.

"So, here we are, again" was all I could think to say and I felt stupid as soon as I'd said it. It made me think of something Bobo likes to say: people sometimes have too much to talk about to say anything useful. And that silence often says a helluva lot more than talking all night.

The ember of Sam's cigar went from a dull orange to a bright red glow as he breathed in. Even in the low light I could see the smoke swirl around his face. I could also make out the small smile he flashed at me.

"Here we are," he repeated back to me. "I suppose it's hard to know where to begin."

I nodded, though I doubted he could see my gesture. I let it stand as my reply anyway, hoping he would help us get through a moment that was growing more awkward with each passing second. I was sorry for how I'd acted toward him and Danny all those years ago, but I was also angry at Sam. He was supposed to have been wiser and smarter than me, but he let his pride rule his actions as sure as I did with my own. He should have known better. We both should've.

Perhaps it was disappointment or the old childish hurt that wouldn't let me tell him I was sorry. Whatever it was, it had burned a hole inside me for a dozen years. A long time to stew about anything. Not something you can deal with just like that.

Right or wrong, I was going to let him do the talking.

"We got a lot of ground to cover, Zen," he said. "We did and said some hard things back then and I know it hasn't been easy on you. We may never be like we were before, and if we do, well, we don't have to do it all in one night."

He stopped, took another drag on the cigar and waited while another blast of thunder slapped the air. The storm felt as if it was directly overhead. The light drained out of the sky and the air suddenly bulged with the smell of rain.

"The truth is," he went on, "we're pretty much all either of us has left. That ought to count for something. It's a start, anyway. I'm willing to make a go at this if you are."

I could have easily shed a tear—I was one of those people who can cry during a McDonald's commercial—but I didn't.

It was as if there were two people inside my head going at each other like prize-fighters. One was sticking to her guns, keeping her distance, wearing her pride like a bumper sticker. The other couldn't believe she wasn't doing anything about it.

I felt guilty sitting there in silence.

Maybe to bail me out or maybe because deep inside he knew me better than anyone else, Sam took my silence as the olive branch he was asking for.

"Well, at least I'm not hearing a no," he said.

It was during Sam's next long silence that I started to wonder what I should have been wondering as soon as I saw Sam on my doorstep.

"How did you know about Danny so quickly?" I blurted. I spoke too fast, too anxious to realize fully how I'd be so disrespectful. But I realized the answer before he could even say anything.

"Jesus, Sam, you *knew* . . ."

I angrily stubbed my half-smoked cigar out on my parquet floor, the one I'd spent last summer refinishing. Tomorrow there would be a fresh scar on it. I pushed myself up and felt my way across the room to my desk, where I keep a humidor. I took out one of those short, fat Dominicans I favored, then crossed back to my seat on the floor.

"Yes, I knew," he said, finally. His words hung in the air with the cigar smoke, just as fresh. I could feel the skin crawl on the back of my hand where it had stuck to the keg. I rubbed it and felt strangely like Lady Macbeth.

What was that line? "And all our yesterdays have lighted fools the way to dusty death." I knew my part well.

I was glad the room was dark. Come light of day, I knew I'd have to deal with reality. But in the dark, it didn't seem real. I could keep it under cover.

Then the rain started. First a couple of heavy drops, plop-splat on the roof, then a couple more and a few more and more after that, until it was pounding down in steady waves.

"Don't be angry, Zenaria," he said. I'm certain he used my given name to invoke gentle parental authority, the kind that's supposed to make you believe there aren't any monsters in your bedroom closet. "Danny only came to me a few weeks ago. Up till then I thought he was dead, just like you did."

"I still can't believe it." I was rolling my cigar between my thumb and forefinger—a nervous habit. "I checked out that story. Bobo checked it out, too. We were there. Why didn't he contact us? He must have known how much pain he had caused you. I mean, he could be a selfish bastard, but he was never unkind. Not to us."

The words came out of me like pounding rain. It was as if everything I thought was coming right out of my mouth and I couldn't stop it.

"I wish I knew." He took a long puff on the cigar, turning the tip red-hot, the glow illuminating his face. "I wish I knew."

The more I ran the possibilities through my head, the more questions came to mind and the more devastatingly complex the scenarios became. One in particular stuck there, one I didn't even want to consider. I pushed it to the back of my mind. "What did he want from you?"

"He came to see me. I have a place in the Marina. I moved there a couple of years after Danny . . ." He left the last part unspoken. All these years and he had been living right here, a few miles away.

"He was not the same," Sam continued. "Oh, he looked the same, a little heavier, maybe, but still full of energy, always moving. He apologized, in his own way, for everything. He asked me to keep some things for him, told me he'd be back."

"Did he say where he'd been all this time?"

"He just wanted me to hold some things for him. He was frightened, running from something or someone, he wouldn't say anything, though. I didn't want anything to do with it, but how could I turn him away? After all those years."

Sam had a father's anguish in his voice. An anguish I'd heard before but without ever realizing how close to my own life those emotions really were.

"What was he like?" I asked him.

"Different in a strange way," he said. "Sadder, not as cocky. I can't explain it, but it wasn't like the old Danny. He was more mature, solid. I believed he was in real trouble."

"He was always in trouble, Sam."

"True. Yes, this is true. But this time, I could tell he hadn't gone looking for it. Something else, too. He was blabbering on about God and the Jews and going to temple. I don't know where he got it. He said he was close to something big, that he was going to make it all up for both of us."

I smiled at this, realizing again he couldn't see it. I turned the dimmer switch up a notch on my floor lamp, just enough to see shadows. Our Jewish heritage aside, Sam and my father weren't very religious. Danny hadn't even had a bar mitzvah.

"That's better," Sam said about the light. He was looking around for a place to lay the stub of his cigar. I took the glass ashtray on my coffee table, the one with a Willie Mays baseball card encased in it (payment from a former client), and slid it across the floor to his feet.

"You know, he asked about you," he said after putting the last of his cigar to bed.

"Me?"

"He said only that he knew a lot about you, that you were working as a detective and that he needed your kind of help, that's exactly how he put it." Sam stopped. "He said if anything were to happen to him that I was to see you, that you would know what to do. As soon as I heard about Danny, I came over here."

"How did the cops know to call you?"

"They didn't," Sam said. "I called them."

Sam had his hand up to keep me from asking the obvious. "We were supposed to meet Sunday," he continued. "He told me to call the police if I didn't hear from him for a few days. I thought he was kidding."

"He knew something would happen to him?"

"I don't know, but he was pretty scared," Sam said. "The police sure were surprised to hear from me. But I didn't say very much. They want to talk to me tomorrow. I was hoping you could be there."

"Of course," I said.

"And Zen," he said evenly, but with some force, adding emphasis by the way he leaned forward in his seat.

"Yes, Sam?"

"You'll help me, won't you? I'm too old for this, to go through it again, alone. I need to know what happened to Danny and who was responsible. I don't know what to do."

He had to know it was a moot question. Pride or not, I still would do anything for this tough old man.

Maybe twelve years ago, Danny did what he did on his own, but I didn't need a shrink to know for sure that I might as well have pushed him into doing it.

The pain and humility of it had followed me down every road I had traveled since. I was always thinking about it, even when it was the farthest thing from my mind. It was the only thing I was thinking about now. It would be that way until I put it to rest.

I knew I wouldn't be able to make peace with Danny or Sam or with the things we'd done, until I did.

"I know things have been hard for you," he said. "I can pay your fee."

"Forget it, Sam," I said. "We're family."

And for the first time in years, I felt a part of one again, even if the feeling left as soon as it hit me.

TWELVE

I've never been much of a sound sleeper, and with everything that was rolling around in my head, the night passed by like a documentary on manufacturing shoelaces.

I meant to get an early start on the day, but when I finally fell asleep, around 5 A.M., it was deep enough to keep me under until midmorning.

I stumbled into the shower around 11 A.M., then brewed a mugfull of espresso, very black and very strong. I brought in the LA *Times*, sat on the floor and tried to read the paper. For a former journalist, I was a lousy newspaper reader, preferring to skim everything but the arts and sports pages. It was all so damned depressing.

But with hockey and baseball on strike, even the sports pages had lost their luster for me and, except for the New York *Times* Sunday paper, which I essentially read in full, I was down to reading book reviews and doing the crossword.

This morning my heart wasn't into either.

I had turned the phone off sometime during the night and had missed a couple of calls, according to the blinking red light on my answering machine. One was from Vivian, the other from Nat.

I called Nat first. He was supposed to meet with Brooks later and wanted me around for moral support. I wanted to help out, but there was nothing I could do, and truth was I didn't much feel like going back to the pub. Besides, I would be seeing Brooks later, when Sam went by to talk with the cops.

I knew I was letting Nat down, but I also knew he mostly

wanted in on the details of my latest crisis. Normally it wouldn't be a big deal, but this was something I didn't feel like talking about, even with Nat. I hoped he would understand, but from the sound of his voice, I knew our friendship was being tested.

Vivian didn't wait for me to call her. She buzzed in while I was on the phone with Nat.

"Hello, bubala," she said. "How are you?"

"Tired, Vivian, but holding up. What's up?"

"A Detective Brooks called for you but said he'd reach you himself later." I looked at the mantel clock on the bookshelf, one of the few things I had that had belonged to my mother. It was always running about ten minutes slow. At the moment it was showing a few ticks before noon.

"He has the most soothing voice," she said.

"Vivian!" I scolded.

"Sorry," she said in a way that made me feel bad. "I'm just trying to help. Having a man around can be a good thing, you know."

"I know, Vivian," I said. "I'm not against having a man around. I just would like to choose one for myself."

"Of course, dear," she said, making me smile. I knew we would have this same conversation tomorrow. "Any other messages?"

She said there weren't and I was about to hang up when something else occurred to me. "Hey, do you watch Latisha Maxwell?"

"Why, yes," she said, seeming pleased I had asked. As much as we spoke and as close as I thought we were, I realized we didn't talk about much besides my work, the weather and single men she wanted me to date. "She's very good with her guests, very kind, but it's still trash in my book. I don't much go for those shows, but I like watching her. She seems so nice, very genuine. Why do you ask? Are you going on her show?"

I had to laugh this time. "No, no, just curious, that's all. Thanks."

I rang off and phoned Sam. I let it ring several times, got

his machine and hung up. Then I called Brooks. He wasn't in, but one of his assistants told me that Brooks wanted me to know that Danny's autopsy would take an extra day, maybe two. He would call when they were through with it. As if I were in a hurry.

I wanted to get to work, but it was time to clear my head. All that had happened the last couple of days was whirring around my brain too fast for me to keep up with and, like it or not, exercise was key to my survival. I liked beer and good food but wouldn't be able to enjoy either if I didn't get on that bike on a regular basis.

The weather had changed back to its normal southern California pattern—sunny and a warm, but a brisk sixty-five degrees—so I pulled out my only form of exercise and one of my prized possessions—a silver Richey mountain bike with front and rear suspensions. Just the thing for riding down mountain trails or hopping over city sidewalks.

I headed over to my office, a cramped space on the top floor of a small building on Arizona Boulevard, perfectly situated halfway between my humble abode and my favorite drinking hole. I tried to make my life as simple as possible and, most of the time, this made me a very happy woman.

It was an easy ride but I wanted a workout. I took the long way, riding down Pico to Ocean Boulevard, then south into Venice. I rode along Main Street, then east up Pearl Street, which runs right through Santa Monica College to Twenty-sixth Street and across to Olympic before cutting north by way of Eleventh to Arizona. For years, I'd followed a pretty rigorous exercise schedule, but my time at UCLA Medical Center had changed that and I was reminded of my deficiencies almost every time I worked out.

Today was a good day and the whole ride took about ninety minutes, almost all of which I spent cranking the pedals. But when I had carried the twenty-five-pound bike up the stairs to my office, I was ready for a nap. Passing out on the floor seemed a good option.

I decided instead to start up the coffee machine.

My office was a simple one-window room on the top floor

of a four-story building that had once been a kind of YMCA for wayward men back in the fifties. A variety of businesses filled up the top three floors, including a credit adviser, a chiropractor and an acupuncturist. All services I probably could use, but either couldn't afford or couldn't stomach.

A well-respected mid-size architectural firm had the entire first floor. They had been responsible for renovating the building, and as far as I was concerned had done a wonderful job, right down to keeping the basement showers.

I still had to ride back home, so I passed on the shower for now, but, more times than I can count, having a place to freshen up in the middle of the day without leaving the office had been a lifesaver.

With the two floor-to-ceiling file cabinets hidden under only a small part of my phone-book collection (invaluable reference guides in my line of work), there was barely enough room for me, two chairs, a desk, and a coffee machine.

I had the latest electronic office necessities: a copy machine, computer, and fax, all fighting for space on a metal desk I'd bought when the old *Herald Examiner* had had a fire sale. It had always reminded me of how I'd once wanted to save the world.

I grew up with a reverence for journalists that I was betting few kids these days would share—not for the right reasons anyway. There aren't many role models anymore. Mine was Dan Rather, a tough-nosed, old-fashioned Texan who had stood up to Richard Nixon back when reporters were still supposed to treat presidential news conferences like coronations.

But as the business faltered, so had the people in it. Even Rather had shown his blemishes.

I had wanted to be just like him and had shown promise as a young reporter and later as a sportswriter, rising far enough to pen a column for LA's second newspaper. But I had this problem with authority figures at a time when the new brand of editor began taking over newsrooms: the kind that spent more time watching their bottom lines and their than ball games. It made me start to second-guess my profession's integrity and my part in it.

Television news had long ago sold out to the ratings gods, but now newspapers had joined the fray, making everything from a football star's murder trial to floods, fires, and other disasters just another fight for footage. Somehow, in the long, long line of brilliant American reporting, journalism had turned into a distasteful feeding frenzy. Cronkite had gotten out in time, and Murrow, well, there was no question what he was doing in his grave. Plenty of people were out there doing it right every day, but they were laboring fiercely in obscurity, overshadowed by tabloid news shows and factoid-filled newspapers—people like my client.

It was nauseating and it scared the shit out of me.

I had stayed around long enough to develop a kind of expertise in investigative reporting and it was Bobo, an ex-Army cop, who first suggested detective work. He had wanted me to try the LAPD, but there was my question-authority complex to think about, so I trained under his tutelage and got my private detective's license instead.

That was nearly three years ago, and I was left wondering, as I squeezed into my tiny work space, what it had all gotten me.

I had the phone rigged to ring at Vivian's house so she didn't have to go anywhere, but she did like to come in a couple of times a week to tidy things up. I tried not to keep too much stuff on my desk just for that reason. I knew she'd been here when I couldn't find anything.

I kept two lines—one was switched over to Vivian's and the other went directly to my office. So I called Vivian to let her know the doctor was in and answering the phone.

Then I called Nat, who kept a spare set of my keys, and asked him to get my Alfa, which still sat parked behind the Knight's Inn. He didn't have a car of his own, which meant he'd probably run a few errands with mine first. It was worth the favor of having it returned to its garage.

Sam and I had pieced together as much about Danny as we could before he'd left for home last night. He had no idea where Danny had been staying in Los Angeles; his last known address was still somewhere up on the four hundred acres of land owned by the Guru Tama Tai.

I knew, sooner or later, I was going to have to go up there, back to where this whole thing had started. But first things first. I had to find out if Danny had left any tracks here. He had come to LA, to see me, for a reason.

I needed to go back to the scene. I'd been too shaken up the first time and I easily could have missed something. Brooks might help in that regard, too. But I was going to have to be careful. I knew I was being stupid and selfish, but I felt strongly about taking care of this myself. I didn't want anyone in my way. Not this time.

I would be seeing Brooks later and afterward would pass by the pub for another look around. Until then, I had a paying client to tend to. Frankly, I needed the money as much as a reason not to think about my own problems.

THIRTEEN

Latisha had kept tabs on her estranged father for years, but he never stayed in one place long enough for his daughter to track him to a real address. His name was Harry Ford Winchester. Latisha had long ago discarded her given surname for reasons we didn't get into, but I can only imagine. Pain runs deep in the hearts and minds of seventeen-year-old runaways, especially the kind like Latisha, who don't stop running until they create a life so unlike their old one that they might as well be totally different people.

From the little I was learning about Harry, I didn't blame her. He wasn't one of those militia boys who lived in log cabins in the hinterlands of the Midwest, strapped a gun named Shirley over his bed, and kept his worldly possessions, along with a supermarket aisle full of Spaghetti-O's, in boxes under the floorboards, but he might as well have been.

He had dragged his family through most of six states on the trail of the better blue-collar job. These didn't exist, at least not in the way most Americans dreamed about, and Harry's vision of the perfect job had started going out long before he even got here. His particular trade was in newspapers, as a pressroom typesetter.

Newspapers began downsizing when web sites still were places spiders called home. So, as modernism began to take hold a half century ago, the first jobs to go were in the pressroom, where the Linotypes and their brethren were replaced by film-setting machines, computers, and pagination.

Harry showed his love for the old-fashioned trade of

hand-setting type by naming his eldest daughter Latisha-Viola, after a classic typeface.

His adjustment to the pressroom was tougher, taking him from Detroit to Ohio and West Virginia, back west to Illinois and then south to North Carolina before he gave up, settling into a factory job in a canning plant just south of Fresno. Harry wasn't too hard to track. Every place he went, he left a paper trail of letters to the editors of a dozen different small-town newspapers, many of which he had actually worked for.

Latisha had saved sheets of this mostly typed correspondence that covered issues as far-ranging as garbage collection and the Ku Klux Klan. He was against the former (waste collection was a waste of taxpayers' money, he wrote) and for the latter (freedom of speech, he argued).

He railed against a host of other evils, too, from same-sex marriages (though he used much more vivid language) to the horrors of abortion and the shortcomings of Jimmy Carter ("that no-good Georgia moron" was his exact description).

It was curious his daughter had taken the time to collect and save these letters. She didn't strike me as the sentimental type, so her reasons for saving the stuff puzzled me.

Latisha left her ranting father and his family behind in North Carolina, in a small town off Tobacco Road near I-40, where a two-lane highway runs through thinly populated evergreen forests, hiding a hundred tiny towns that remain mostly separated from the rest of the world in the way small towns in America once were but aren't anymore.

I knew the area well from my days covering college basketball. Back when I started, North Carolina, which played in Chapel Hill, and Duke, practically next door in Durham, were among the best in the nation each year, but an enormous local kid was about to put Wake Forest, a smaller college a few miles down the road not known for its athletics, on the college basketball map. I remember there was a road sign near Chapel Hill that read "Wake Forest, 85." Someone had scrawled "North Carolina, 100" across the top.

What had happened to Latisha's family was a mystery to me, and a few calls to some old newspaper buddies proved I wasn't the only clueless one. Latisha wasn't spilling any details either, which made me wonder again if I was right in taking this case with so little real information. I called Leland Heath, an old colleague of mine who had left high-powered political reporting to run a small but well respected farm paper near where Latisha grew up, and promised to see if he could dig anything up.

"I wouldn't hold your breath," Heath said, his drawl long ago having lost the urbane tones he'd picked up covering politics in Washington for the LA *Times*. "Latisha is a local hero down here."

"You mean they don't want her to look bad?"

He laughed. "Where you been, girl? Tibet? Contemplating your navel?"

"You're making fun of me," I said. "Don't forget, us city folk carry concealed weapons."

"You forget," he said. "We mount 'em in plain view on the back of our pickups."

"You got me there," I said.

"Seriously," he said. "Latisha isn't only our star, she's a national celebrity. You should know that means she ain't got no secrets. Every six months or so, some guy from *Hard Copy* or the *National Enquirer* or the fucking London *Sun* comes down here and starts waving around U.S. Grants."

"And in the South, no less," I said.

"Now you're starting to see the picture," he said. "Factories are closing, cotton's no longer king, hell, even tobacco companies are cutting back. This is the nineties. Information is gold and there isn't a soul down here who wouldn't think twice about giving up the family skeletons."

He promised to check his sources and peruse his paper's archives and get back to me. Once a reporter, always a reporter.

I still have friends at my old newspaper, a 200,000-circulation paper that competed, mostly in vain, for the Los Angeles media market, an area owned and jealously guarded by the LA *Times*, one of America's media behemoths, and dented by a half dozen papers that circulated from the San Gabriel Valley to Ventura. The Los Angeles *Sun* had followed the blueprint set by papers like New York *Newsday* and the Chicago *Sun-Times*, which were basically tabloids on the outside but real newspapers in their guts where it counted.

The pay was terrible, the hours long, but the staff melded well and took on the *Times* with the vengeance of the old-time newspaper wars that had mostly been relegated to barroom conversations between aging copy guys who kept bottles of Jack Daniels in their right-hand drawers and still banged out stories on vintage Underwoods. In a cramped San Fernando Valley newsroom, the battle still raged.

On the front line was Leah Steinbeck, who worked the trenches as the *Sun's* metro columnist and chief investigative reporter. She was the toughest person I knew outside of ex-marines and Bobo. While I admired her work, it was mostly her ability to get buried deep in the muck and manage not to come back up bitter and cynical that truly impressed me.

I found her on her lunch break—typically well past noon—and she promised to send Latisha through the newspaper's library research system and see what fell out. As usual, she wanted desperately to know why I was interested in the biggest name in daytime TV, but I managed to douse her journalistic instincts with a promise that if something juicy came out of my work, she'd be the first to know.

It worked. There's one good way to get a reporter to do something for you and that's to promise a good exclusive in return. All you have to do is deliver once or twice and you've got a friend for life. Politicians and bureaucrats, take heed.

Leah promised to fax me the articles she found on Latisha by late afternoon, so I took a moment to ring up Sam. The phone rang several times before he finally picked up.

His voice sounded older and more tired in the daylight and I felt a little sorry for him. His meeting with Brooks was at 3 P.M., a little more than an hour away. Sam agreed to meet me at my house and we'd drive over to see Brooks together. On the way there, we could get our story straight.

I hung up not knowing yet what that story was going to be.

There wasn't much I could do except hang around waiting for the fax machine to start hissing, so I decided to get back on the Richey. I might just be able to catch a quick nap before Sam arrived.

FOURTEEN

I was a little stiff on the ride home, but the exercise felt the way it should, just enough pain to remind me I was still breathing. Besides, the way back was mostly downhill, though along the ride east up Olympic, I had to compete with fast-moving cars and their choking exhaust.

I was used to getting grazed by drivers who were either on their car phones or had been looking to get back at the last cyclist who had prevented them from making that right on red. That's why I barely noticed the midnight-blue coupe that cruised by me, too close.

It was the kind of thing that happens in a way that doesn't seem notable until later, when you have a moment to consider the details. It wasn't as if the guy was trying to run me off the road, which was probably why I didn't think much of it. Sure, I could see the minuscule scratches in his fine, just-short-of-sparkle finish, but it was around a bend on Olympic that can be hard to negotiate when you're trying to beat it to the next light before it turns red again.

Midnight-blue Mercedes are a dime a dozen in this town, but when I saw the same car come back down Olympic from the other direction, I was sure that it was the same guy. Or maybe I was just being paranoid.

I hadn't worked a case in two years, at least not one that was significant enough to draw attention to me, and the IRS didn't have the money to put luxury car tails on their marks. I certainly could have been losing my grip on reality; it wasn't as if the thought hadn't crossed my mind recently. I was sure I would know soon enough if I was.

*   *   *

I had just enough time to shower and change before Sam showed up. I chose a new pair of jeans, a linen jacket, and a white blouse for our trip to see Brooks. California casual.

Sam showed up in a dark suit I could've sworn was the same one he had worn to Danny's funeral. The first one.

We took my car down to the station, a trip I could tell Sam enjoyed. I got my appreciation for all kinds of strange foreign sports cars from Sam, who, with my dad, had always been tinkering under the hood of a car I could barely pronounce. They had a slew of really neat ones and would go through phases, often keeping three of the same make at one time. Two were for parts.

It wasn't far to Brooks's office at the Santa Monica police station, but it was that special time of day in Santa Monica when cars seem to outnumber even pairs of Oakleys. So, as we crawled through the steel maze, Sam filled me in on the missing years.

He had sold the cigar shop, something I'd already heard from an old friend a while back, and bought a small house in the exclusive, canal-front section of Marina del Ray. That much seemed normal for a sixtyish bachelor looking for a nice, safe neighborhood where he could walk around at night, eat at a decent restaurant, and even chat up the working fishermen that lined the harbor every morning just before dawn, waiting to take a bunch of white guys with green out on the blue. A bunch of Bogie wannabes mostly, guys living out Key Largo three thousand miles away and a million miles off course.

What I hadn't expected, but should have, was that Sam had traded one job in for another and had turned the shitload of money he got from the sale of the cigar shop into a woodworking business in a vacant old building in Venice. It wasn't much more than a one-man operation, though Sam said he brought in a few guys each month to do his upholstering. He just built one or two things at time—a chair here, a table there, even cabinets. One by one, piece by piece. I guessed once a workingman, always a workingman. Why fight it?

When I turned right off Pico onto Main Street, I caught the briefest of glimpses of midnight blue in my rearview. I glanced backward and caught the tail of what could've been a Mercedes, a distinct car if there ever was one, but this was a world where imitation was the sincerest form of corporate R&D, so it also could've been any number of models from the world's cookie-cutter car industry. More paranoia.

The Santa Monica station is tucked on the bottom floor of the City Hall Building, which was kind of a Spanish Colonial affair complete with a color-tiled entrance. I decided to scope out Brooks. Sam agreed it might be a good idea for me to go in alone at first. I deposited him on one of the wooden benches that lined the wide walkway outside and headed in.

I found Brooks behind a cluttered desk in a back office. Government was formed to deal with problems, and the cops, of course, had more than their share. Theirs were stacked up in paper piles like so many old phone books crammed into tiny, fluorescent-lit offices that always gave me the feeling I was being exposed to some kind of mutant-forming diseases.

For a relatively small city, Santa Monica's black-and-blues weren't short of paperwork. Maybe it was the cramped quarters, but from the way these offices looked, Brooks and his boys had me beaten in the problem department. Next to them, I could've been on vacation.

"I hope you got something for me—or someone." It was Brooks. He was leaning back in his chair, his size twelves resting on the only clear spot on his coffee-stained blue blotter. He hadn't looked up, which meant the gruff rent-a-cop at the front desk had done his job. That, or Brooks had eyes in the top of his head.

"It depends," I said, sitting in an empty chair opposite his desk. It was one of those orange plastic jobs with metal legs that never seemed to hit the floor all at the same time.

I rocked it back and forth, partly because I was feeling a buzz from the coffee I'd drunk earlier and partly to see if I could annoy him.

"Why else would you want to see me, unless . . ." He finally looked up.

"Unless . . . you're here to ask me on a date."

"Don't flatter yourself."

"Yeah." He threw the papers he was examining on his desk, dropped his feet and leaned forward. "Yeah, I heard the bartender had first dibs."

I smirked, wrinkling my nose a little. "Old news," I said.

"Since when? You two seemed to know each other pretty well, from what I hear."

"Are you following me?"

He raised his eyebrows, smiled a half-grin and shrugged. It left a crease across his forehead and I thought again how attractive he was.

"Don't you have better things to do?" I said finally, "like writing some speeding tickets?"

"Yes, we have plenty of better things to do, and no, you weren't being followed. Not exactly, anyway. I have my sources."

"I'll remember that," I said, and would. "But you'd better not rely too heavily on them. They neglected to tell you that we went our separate ways after dinner."

"Well, well, well," he said, folding his hands on the desktop like a shrink. "A free woman, huh?"

"Always am," I said. "Look, Detective . . ."

"Jonathan is fine."

"Okay, Jonathan. Let's cut the social banter. I'm really not in the mood right now and I've got a lot of boring work ahead of me."

"A case?" he asked. I nodded. "Wouldn't have anything to do with that certain bar owner?"

"Actually, I can't disclose my client's name, but I'll tell you this much: I'm getting paid well for my considerable services, so that counts Nat out." I rocked the chair so it clicked in sympathetic rhythm with the ticking of an old schoolhouse clock that hung on the wall behind his desk. He gave me the kind of look my mother used to give me when I shook my leg under the dining room table.

"You should know that he might be a suspect."

"On whose planet?"

"I know, I know, but a man was killed in his bar." He shrugged. "It's routine."

"Routine my ass. You have anything on him?" He shrugged at this. "I didn't think so. All you got is that Danny was killed in the pub. I'm a better suspect. I mean, we were related."

"Speaking of which"—he looked over my head as if he were searching for something—"weren't you supposed to be bringing someone along?"

"Yeah, he's waiting outside."

"So you're testing the waters?"

"In a manner of speaking."

"Don't you trust me?"

"Do I have to answer that?"

He almost laughed at this, which was good because the air had been getting a bit tense. Unfortunately, the smile faded quickly.

"Can we be serious for a minute?" He was leaning toward me, his two big hands flat on the top of the desk, as if he was about to spring up. He was whispering. "I don't have to tell you that I had to pass on some of the information you gave me and, well, that kind of does make you look good for it. It didn't help that the kid you messed with yesterday has got connections. Only thing holding them back upstairs is your track record. You must be the only PI in history that hasn't pissed off the local police."

I nearly smiled at him, but I didn't want him to think this was a game to me. Anytime you're in the middle of stuff like this, it isn't hard to get on the wrong list. "Prime Suspects" wasn't one I wanted to be on.

I checked my watch, thinking about Sam sitting outside on the bench. He was probably feeding the birds or chatting up some homeless guy.

"So what do you want from me?"

"How about where you were night before last."

I must've grimaced. That, or those damn eyes again, telling their own story, because he looked up at me in that funny way people do sometimes when they think they've been wronged.

"Bad?" he asked.

"In a way," I said. "I was out of the picture, so to speak."

"Don't even say it." He was holding his hand out in front of him. Stopping the train.

I just nodded.

"Oh, boy." He was shaking his head back and forth. "You were . . ."

"Schnockered, hammered, wasted . . . flat-out drunk. I told you, my cat got run over. We were very close. What can I say?"

"Hey, I'm not making any judgments here. So was this a public mourning or a private affair?"

"The latter. Unfortunately. Just me, a bottle of cheap Merlot, and Billie Holiday. Though I doubt she will confirm my alibi."

"You're not helping."

"What can I say?" I suppose I should have said something here about my impeccable character, but I didn't feel I needed to prove anything. "If I didn't like you, Detective, we wouldn't be having this conversation at all."

"I see." He scratched the back of his hand, leaning back again in his office-issue swivel chair. "But you aren't making it any easier to look elsewhere."

"Wanna talk to Sam?" Me changing the subject.

"It's gonna be like that, huh?"

I spread my hands out to each side, tilting the chair back. The helpless look.

"I know I don't know you all that well, but Josh did and he told me you had this independent streak to you." Brooks was leaning forward, commanding my attention. "I know you know more than you are telling, and I know why you're not giving it up. It's some kind of personal vendetta thing or something, right? Avenging your cousin's death."

He looked at me, the firm gaze of a father disciplining a promising child who had refused to show that promise. He had formed a small space between his lips and was letting out the air, a little bit at a time, as if the store in his lungs was all he had left.

"This isn't some kind of movie," he said. "This is reality, a place where people get hurt for real, you know? You can go off on your own now if you want; I mean, I don't know if I wouldn't do the same for my own blood. But I'll tell you this: It's only a matter of time before I fill in the holes to Danny Moses's story, and God help us both if it leads back to you."

I had no answer for this. What he said made sense, the kind I would probably do well in following. But too many other things had spun out of my control in my brief time on earth, and I wasn't about to let something I could do something about get away too.

I knew there would be a price to pay later. Already, I had this awful feeling that my life history was about to be a gossip item all over Santa Monica. Every minute I was losing royalties. And time.

"I can't help you, Jonathan. I'm sorry."

"That's bullshit."

I shrugged again. I really did like Brooks and felt bad about keeping the details from him, but in my own obstinate, perhaps ultimately stupid, way, I didn't have a choice. Sam had understood when I told him in the car. Though even he didn't like it.

He threw his hands up. "Is stubbornness your only talent, or do you have any more hidden that I should know about?"

"None that I care to divulge at this point in our relationship."

He leveled his gaze at me, his dark eyes direct and determined, but the look was soft in its own way. Perhaps telling me he understood where I was coming from, but just didn't agree, was all.

"I'm gonna be right on your ass, Zen. I mean it."

I didn't say a word. There was nothing to say.

"As long as we understand each other then," he said, leaning back again in his chair and putting his arms behind his head. "So how about that date?" His way of offering me some slack, though I could tell his flirting had another purpose.

I got up, gave him another one of my looks and turned to go. He would want to talk to Sam alone, which didn't bother me too much. Sam and I, we both had the same objectives. I knew he would stick to our story, give Brooks the basics and leave it at that. Besides, as far as I could tell, he didn't know much more than that anyway.

"Don't be mad," he called after me.

I waved my hand. "I'm not mad, just busy. Don't call me . . ."

"I know, I know," he started, but I was out the door and didn't hear him finish.

I waited for Sam in the parking lot outside the station, sitting in my car. I turned up Billie really loud. I needed to think. Some people turned everything off to do this. Me, I found music to be the most calming influence on a brain that was cursed with having no shut-off switch.

I hated that Brooks was on to me. I hated even more that he was a cop. Growing up the way I did, I'd learned to treat everyone basically the same and I'd carried that over to everything I did, including dating. Brooks would certainly not be the first black man I had dated, but I had a rule against dating cops and doctors. Men who regularly saw the underside of life were to be commended, but not necessarily dated. I'd broken the rule before, but only in desperate times. This wasn't one of them.

I liked Brooks and he intrigued me, but the last thing I needed right now was a romance with the man in charge of investigating a murder so close to me. Besides, I was lying to him, which was not exactly a good basis on which to form a lasting relationship.

FIFTEEN

Sam was with Brooks no more than fifteen minutes, the conversation having stuck to the basics: when was the last time he'd seen the deceased; what was his relationship to said deceased, et cetera.

We didn't talk much on the trip back to my house. Sam was off in his own head and I was trying to keep from getting lost in mine. I dropped off Sam by his car in front of my place. There was a briskness in the air unusual even for winter in Santa Monica. The sun had threatened to show itself all afternoon, but the gray-blue clouds had managed to muscle it out. Not a drop was in sight, but the smell of imminent rainfall hung in the air nevertheless.

"I know these are lousy circumstances"—Sam was leaning into my driver's-side window—"but I'm glad something happened to bring us back together. Maybe we can even be friends again."

I smiled up at him, this old man who had once meant the world to me, now almost a stranger.

So much stays the same, but the things that do change, sometimes they are the most important. Those singular, personal memories, the way you build up people who are part of your life because you share the same gene pool.

Parents, uncles, aunts, brothers, and sisters. We make them invincible, stand them tall, never quite holding them to the high principles we give them because we think we have to, because if they don't have them, what does that make us? Thicker than water. That, and then some.

But with time and distance and, I guess, maturity, those

feelings weaken, are altered, sometimes dissolve completely, leaving just another human being in their wake. It was a hard thing to live up to. It was even harder to live down.

I nodded at my uncle, these thoughts running in the background of my head, wondering how much was showing in my eyes and happy to have my shades on. I didn't know really how I felt about Sam, all those years and hurt between us standing here and the way we used to be, but I knew how I had once felt about him. That was enough for now.

"Thanks for helping," he said to my silence.

"Like I said, Sam, we're family. No need for thanks." He bobbed his head; we understood this much at least. "Listen, I'm probably going to be tied up for a day or two. There's something I have to take care of. It shouldn't take long, and besides, Brooks won't let me get a good look at the murder scene until his boys are done."

"I guess Danny's not going anywhere." Sam was flashing his old sense of humor. Only the subconscious memory of things past made me take it as he meant it. Funny the way the mind works. Maybe what I was doing really was thinking too goddamned much. "Let's talk in a day or two, then."

He touched his hand to mine, which I'd absently set on the door. I'd been fingering the edge of the window; it always stuck just short of flush with the door, leaving a ridge that left a mark on my forearm whenever I rested it there.

"Be careful" was all he said, patting my hand and turning to walk across the street where his everyman Chevy truck was parked. I watched long enough to see him climb in and drive off, a little hunch to his back as he sat at the wheel, guiding the truck in a patient U-turn and then back down my street. Someone's father tooling over to see the grandkids, happy and sad all at the same time. I couldn't help thinking about the past and how it always seemed easier, more innocent, even if it wasn't. Here I was putting up for my own flesh and blood just because, and knowing all along that it was a selfish, needy reason instead of some long-held belief in the sanctity of family or some other bullshit. Truth was I wanted to believe, but I didn't anymore.

I'd lost it twelve years ago in a San Francisco rain that hadn't ever stopped. Now this old man was making his case for my redemption and I was nodding my head like I was on the same set of train tracks, wondering if it was possible to recapture what the journey from youth robs you of, wondering if it was worth it.

Maybe I'd never know what it all meant. Maybe nobody ever did.

SIXTEEN

Leah's faxes were waiting in curled-up piles on the floor of my office when I returned from the meeting with Brooks. She was thorough, and I would have to remember to send her a case of Jordan Cabernet Sauvignon when I finished the job for Latisha. Leah was a refined woman, something she liked to remind us beer drinkers, and Jordan was one of the better among the Napa Valley's grape products in recent years. She would appreciate it.

Most of the pages dealt with Latisha's recent rise to talkshow stardom. Her show, which originated out of Burbank, had begun several years ago as a local fill-in, but had been grabbed up by the syndicators. She'd been tabbed as the next Oprah, a moniker that had brought down many a promising talent, but the networks apparently liked her style—and her ratings—and picked her out of the crowd of daytime talkies, revamped the show and featured her in the fall daytime programming advances.

So far, "Latisha Live!" had delivered for her bosses, and rumor was her next contract would add one more digit to her six-figure salary. By all accounts, Latisha Viola Maxwell had arrived.

The only hint of controversy, besides the obvious sleaze factor her show shared with every other one on the air these days, was the thing with her father.

All the stories related the death of her father shortly after she had left the family to make it on her own. No one had dug deep enough to find out the real facts surrounding the demise of one Harry Ford Winchester, except to interview his "widow," Bunny, who didn't hesitate to confirm her husband's early exit from earth, adding some shadowy details about her daughters' horrible childhood. Just another American nightmare turned fantasy.

There were mentions of the widow and the home her daughter had bought her in Santa Barbara. Some of the sister, Sara, and of a mysterious illness reported to be everything from HIV to schizophrenia. No other relatives were mentioned. Funny thing, too, since everyone knows the number of people related to a wealthy celebrity increased exponentially with said person's earning power. You could look it up.

Leah's research was good background, but it wasn't going to help me find Harry. That was going to take some old-fashioned leg work. I had some fairly thin leads, the best came from Latisha, who told me she had tracked her long-lost father to Fresno. But that had been a year ago and there was no telling how cold the trail had become. The proverbial needle was what it was.

All I knew was come morning, I'd be heading north. Some of the most prosaic landscape in California—seven hundred miles or so—lies on the inland routes between Los Angeles and the Oregon border, northward through Sacramento and Redding. Somewhere a third of the way up are the hot, dry plains of the San Joaquin Valley. Miles and miles of flatlands and farmlands and netherlands.

In the middle and even farther east from the state's dramatic coastline lies Fresno, a small town of starter families, yuppies-in-training, college kids, and trailer-park denizens who feed their superiority complexes each morning as they drive to work past migrant farmworkers that cram into piecemeal pickup trucks ten at a time.

Settled 130 years ago, when irrigation came to central California, Fresno had at least one advantage of locale, being relatively close to the grand Sequoia National Forest, which rises in its evergreen glory less than a hundred miles to the east. When the wind blows in the right direction, you can stand in the middle of Fresno's downtown and almost smell the pinesap. Almost.

This is where Harry Winchester supposedly had been living out his golden years until a half dozen months ago, when the old man had moved on. To where was anybody's guess. I was hoping I could find someone up there who could posit one or two. But for a guy who seemed to disappear off the face of the earth, I wasn't expecting much.

As the late-afternoon gray had turned the dusk darker than usual, there was barely enough light for me to make out the intertwined multicolored strings that ran in organized chaos all over the map unfolded on my desk. I was squinting to make out some details when I felt the presence of someone in the room. I didn't look up; instead, I rather casually concentrated on the electronic lock on one of my right-hand drawers.

Inside was one of the two Walther PPKs I owned, which I was one or two numbers away from putting my hands on.

"Not a chance." The voice, a very familiar one, startled me.

I looked up at a large, dark, menacing man who seemed to be grinning, which I knew was just an illusion. He had a weird glow to the whites of his eyes, making them look as if they were hanging in the room all by themselves.

"Doesn't anyone call anymore?" I said.

I brought my empty hand back up to my desk, clicking on my green-shaded desk lamp and returning my attention to my map. He had scared the shit out of me, but I was playing cool.

"Been a long time, Bobo," I said. "What brings you out during a weekday?"

The big man grunted, shuffled over to my only extra chair and gracefully folded his considerable length into the seat. Bobo La Douceur was a good six feet four, an even and very solid 220 pounds, with hands big enough to make two adult-sized paws disappear in their grip. He was wearing a pair of black jeans, a black leather jacket and a loose white T-shirt that said "Centenary Oyster House, Shreveport, La.," in red letters across it. He had an impressive collection of T-shirts with all sorts of sayings on them.

I couldn't see it, but I knew he was carrying. It was always within his reach, sitting in a worn leather holster he kept under his jacket.

Bobo was perhaps my oldest adult acquaintance. "Friend" would be only about half right. I like to think of us as soul mates. We'd met when Bobo was working security at Candlestick and I was that kid who thought she could break the sex line in major-league baseball. They still called it Candlestick then. Now it was named after some Silicon Valley computer company who had paid for the privilege. The highest fucking bidder.

He was the personal bodyguard for a couple of Giants, but most of his work was for the soon-to-be megastars who got beaten up every week in the late seventies for the 49ers, just before they started collecting football championships. He got sick of the greed and the hangers-on and he never did like flying, so he got out a few weeks before the first Montana miracle. All those guys were making good money back then. Now they were raking in fortunes. It would have seemed like bad luck to anyone but Bobo. He didn't give a shit.

He hooked up with a few security companies, then went abroad for a while. Places you read about in the international pages of the New York *Times* but can't quite pronounce, much less locate on a Rand McNally. When he came back he drifted around for a time, changed in a way he never talked about and I would never ask. He finally settled in LA, where he'd been freelancing, or whatever you would call it.

He coaxed me into the security biz when I realized sportswriting wasn't going to cut it for me. I worked for him long enough to earn my PI's license and a ton of other stuff they never asked me on the test. He'd saved my ass on those occasions when I needed it, even saved my life once, but in the decade we'd known each other I can't remember one conversation we'd had that lasted more than five minutes. Shoot, five minutes was a day's worth to Bobo.

He was your classic man of action. Like the Bayou fishermen who were his ancestors, he measured life in increments too small for the rest of us to comprehend. He spoke as if words carried a price tag he could barely afford. It wasn't necessary for a man who didn't need to open his mouth much. His was a manner that could be downright frightening. He just had to look at a man to make him feel like a bug caught in the spray from a Raid can.

I hadn't seen or heard from him in months, which wasn't unusual for us. We had that kind of relationship, catching each other coming or going. Two ships. Most of the time, Bobo showed up when I needed him the most. He was a difficult man, deep down fending off some pretty nasty demons. And while he never talked about it, a stranger could look in those eyes of his once and see here was a man you steered clear of. But I liked his company, his silence, the big, gaping holes he put in the often unbearable loudness of things. And I missed him something awful when he wasn't around.

"Having trouble?" he said, leaving me at a loss as to whether he was speaking in general terms about recent events or specifically about the map on my desk.

"I think I found what I was looking for. Unfortunately." I was fumbling in my top drawer for a magnifying glass.

"Shouldn't leave the door open and the hardware locked up. Bad combo."

"Guess I'm getting lax." I looked at him. He was a living example of America's melting pot, having been infused somewhere down his family line with enough races to start his own United Nations.

He had the polished, exotic skin tone found in the West Indies, but it had been lightened by doses of French Canadian, Italian and Cajun blood. His left eye was hazel and fit fine with his features, but the right one stood out; it was colored a deep-sea kind of blue. When he was tired or tense, it would take on a mind of its own and wobble, moving separately from his other one.

His jaw was prizefighter-solid, running in a straight, no-

nonsense line up to his nose, which, like mine, had been broken once or twice. On those rare times when he smiled, Bobo was beautiful.

"Is this a pop quiz, or have you some other reason for coming back into my miserable life?"

"Paying my sympathies." He had a habit of wiping his hand on the front of his shirt when things made him uncomfortable, like showing emotion. He was a guy who probably would never be able to say, "I love you," even if it was exactly how he felt.

"How'd you . . . ?" I should've known better. Bobo was so well tied in to LA's information banks, he could probably tell you the truth about O. J. "My mistake, Bobo."

"Seems like Danny is the one who was making the mistakes."

"Yeah, I guess." Thinking about it brought back all the melancholia I'd been feeling the last twenty-four hours. Self-pity run amok.

"Know what he was doing here?"

I shook my head. "Sam says he was looking for me. For what, I have no idea."

He nodded at this, sharing my somber moment with me. It was one of his great character traits. Unlike 99.9 percent of the people I knew, Bobo always knew when to shut up.

He looked at my map, leaning over to get a closer view. "What's in Fresno?"

"A case."

"Mmm. Heard you were back in business."

"Nothing gets by you," I said and we lapsed back into quietude, both of us gazing at the map as if, if we stared long enough, we'd suddenly be there, standing in the middle of Fresno.

It was clear to me, without knowing exactly why, that Bobo had more to say. I knew if I didn't say something soon, we might be here all night.

"Something else on your mind?"

"Just some information."

"About what?"

"You." Most times, this was the way we communicated. I asked the questions, he gave the one-word answers. Sometimes, if I was lucky and he was in a hurry, he'd actually speak in whole sentences. Bobo was rarely in a hurry.

"Me?"

"Uh-huh."

Bobo's voice had long lost its Cajun tint, but the New Orleans brogue remained underneath, coming out in the way he poured his speech, slow and easy, a little muddy, just like the Mississippi. You had to listen closely; Bobo was always saying one thing aloud, another, more complicated, thing in the silence in between.

"Seen a blue sedan on your ass?"

"So I haven't been hallucinating."

"Miracle you even noticed."

"An idiot coulda . . ." I started before realizing he was yanking my chain. "Fuck you, Bobo."

"Yeah, all the girls say that." He grinned a bit at this. An emotional outburst.

"Now I know where you've been all this time." I waited a beat. "Comedy-club circuit. I feel sorry for the guys who miss the punch lines."

He didn't even flinch. Another guy who didn't appreciate my arresting wit. At the rate I was going, I'd never get a date.

"So," I said. "The midnight-blue Mercedes. One of my admirers?"

"More like trouble."

Just what I needed. "What kind?"

"Not sure."

"Let's have it, Bobo. It's been a long day."

"Coupla tough guys from Phoenix. Been on your tail two, maybe three days."

I was going to ask him how he knew that, but decided it was one of the things between us best not broached. Bobo's habit of showing up at opportune times was more than luck. It had occurred to me more than once that he was watching over me. The other explanation would be way too weird.

"What do they want with me?"

"Wrong question."

I thought about it for a moment. Two guys come looking for you, but keep their distance.

"Either I have something they want or they think I'm going to lead them to that something or someone they want."

"Would seem so."

"Who are they? What's down in Phoenix, anyway? Just cactus and golf courses."

"Cactus and something else. Got bigger thorns."

It sort of hit me slowly, as if I'd been operating in heavy fog with my senses shut down. The state that had once refused to honor Martin Luther King, Jr., with a holiday was home for a lot of things besides old-folks condos, overpriced resorts, and Barry Goldwater. The very conservative values and clean desert air that drew retirees and Republicans also had lured a new generation of businessmen. Michael Corleone wasn't the only mobster who was searching for legitimacy.

"I didn't know Vegas had gotten so crowded," I said.

They weren't the same guys, but they shared a similar vision with the Bugsy Siegels and Mo Greens who built America's real-life Oz on a barren section of Nevada real estate previously known as a desert. These guys were a new breed. They had traded those white ties and black rayon shirts for silk foulard and Hugo Boss pinstripes, pink Caddies for midnight-blue Mercedes.

Question was: Why me?

I'd pissed off plenty of people in my two careers. There were any number of coaches, college boosters, and athletes who wouldn't miss a chance to spit on my windshield, and a dozen or so people with whom I'd had run-ins as a private detective. So far, though, I'd managed to avoid any misunderstandings with guys whose idea of corporate advancement was vanquishing their competition to unmarked graves in places nobody goes but prairie dogs.

"Great," I said. "I give, Bobo. What does the mob want with me?"

"Was hoping you knew," he said. "Information I got is they are looking for something. All I know is it's a big deal."

"How so?"

"Guy who drives the Mercedes, name's Morofsky. Otto. Ever heard of him?"

"Rings a bell," I said, thinking a minute and coming up empty. "Name like that is pretty hard to forget. Who is he?"

"They call him Ten-Eighty."

Clang. "This is not good." And it wasn't. Ten-Eighty Morofsky. I knew I'd heard the name before. There's a whole bunch of different guys running their own shtick down in Arizona, but nothing went down without Mo Goldman giving it his blessing.

His word was carried out, often in violent ways, by Ten-Eighty Morofsky, his top enforcer. A guy you didn't want to mess with, not if breathing was important to you.

He'd gotten his name from his particular method of murder. Ten-eighty was the manufacturer's laboratory serial number for sodium fluoroacetate, your basic rat poison. The stuff was lethal in any dose, but the way Ten-Eighty used it you were guaranteed the kind of death that was so slow, it was said you could feel your organs disintegrate in phases.

If you were lucky and he was in a hurry, he'd just dissolve the powder in a little bit of water and inject it into a vein in your neck.

I absently rubbed my own neck, a little bit of a shiver working its way down my back.

"Well, shit, Bobo, this is not good. Not at all."

"Maybe a good thing, this trip to Fresno. How long you plan on staying?"

"Long as it takes to get what I need. Hopefully no more than half a day."

"Might want to stay up there awhile. Take a vacation."

"Can't. Got responsibilities." I was beginning to sound like Bobo. "Got a paying client, and I promised Sam I'd look into Danny's murder."

"Promised Sam, huh? That all?"

Everybody was a fucking shrink these days. "Yeah, well,

I guess I don't have to tell you anything. You obviously got the whole thing figured out already.''

"Down, girl. You forget who you're talking to. Nothing goes on in that head of yours I don't know 'bout a day b'fore you even think about it.''

"Fuck you, Bobo.''

"I'm here to help if you need it,'' he said, getting up to go. "I'll try to watch your back. Best be careful.''

"I will Bobo. Thanks, man.''

"You know where to find me.'' He was at the doorway now, having slipped off the black leather, showing the holster and the oyster-bar T-shirt. When he turned around, I could read what it said on the back. "One shell of a place to get shucked up.''

Bobo trying his best to ease my tension.

I was still smiling long after his footsteps had faded into the hallway.

SEVENTEEN

I closed up shop and headed back home, stopping along the way at my local health-food market to pick up a couple of things for dinner. Maybe I was turning over a new leaf after all.

I wasn't much of a cook, but when I did, I tried to stick to a lot of the stuff you were supposed to eat, like fresh vegetables, pastas, and my favorite, beans and rice. I never cooked red meat or pork, not because I was avoiding it, but the fact was I wouldn't know what to do with a side of beef if it died at my front door.

Now, put it before me on a table with a steak knife and I'd be perfectly at home. It was one of my codes of life that some things, like taxes, are best done by someone else.

I was looking forward to a nice mixed green salad and a good night's sleep. Fresno was a good three-hour drive and I wanted to get going before dawn so I could be back home by sundown. A day in the California heartland was just about all I could stand.

No suspicious Mercedes appeared in my rearview the whole trip. Maybe Mr. Ten-Eighty had found what he was looking for and done a 180 back to Phoenix. Hope was a good thing.

I parked my car in the garage behind my house and walked around to the front. The pet cemetery was quiet as usual, the winter cold having settled in for the night and the rain taking a break, leaving only menacingly dark clouds battling for space in the black sky with stars, faraway planets, and other celestial matter. The moon was nowhere in sight, which meant slow going up my walkway. My block's only streetlight was several houses down from mine.

I had my key almost in the lock when something made me stop.

Looking back, I couldn't say exactly what it was—a feeling, an intuition, voodoo? It didn't matter. I knew, without knowing exactly why, that something was wrong, even though a quick inspection of my small porch and doorway had turned up nothing unusual.

I went still, straining to listen for any sounds melting into a perfect silence. I let my breath out slowly before drifting into the meditative state I used to take naps when I'm too anxious to fall asleep. I followed the sounds of my breathing: in, out, in, out, in, out, until all I could hear was the not-so-distant whoosh of traffic passing on Pico, the drip-drop of water falling from rooftop drainage pipes, and the power lines humming overhead.

My door was shut, but the heavy-duty lock had been bent out of shape and turned slightly upward, a tad off center. Even in the insufficient glow of my outside light, I could see where it had been jacked out of place, leaving a tiny sliver of my door where the paint wasn't weathered. Not many marks. Very professional.

I grabbed one of the more manageable logs off my woodpile outside the door and stood to the side, holding the "weapon" over my head. I gently placed my bag of groceries on the landing and then, with palm barely touching the door, I pushed. It swung open.

I held still, trying not to breathe, relaxing only after being satisfied I was alone. The place seemed empty, but whoever had been there hadn't bothered to camouflage his presence. Very few of my worldly possessions were left standing and many were no longer intact. The only thing apparently untouched was my bike, which I kept hung wheel-end up from two ceiling hooks. I was glad it was there, even though I didn't need to see my $2,500 investment to realize the break-in hadn't been a burglary.

My CD collection was strewn all over the floor, many of

the discs separated from their protective jackets. My stereo had been yanked from the wall and every cabinet in the kitchen was open, the various contents spilled about. The last time my place had looked this bad was after the Northridge earthquake. Or was it Nat's fortieth birthday party? Hard to say.

Every room in the house had been ransacked, including the bedroom. My bed was slashed open. A white foam blood-bath. Looking at it, with the stuffing pulled out, my surprise and dismay turned to anger. I didn't have many things, but what I had, including the bed, which I'd bought specifically to cushion a chronic back problem, were all expensive, well-thought-out purchases. They could not be replaced without some effort, and now I was expending too much of that effort trying to keep from using a baseball bat on somebody's midnight-blue Mercedes.

For I was all but certain this was my introduction to the man they called Ten-Eighty. A pleasure it wasn't.

I was certain also that this wouldn't be my last encounter with Ten-Eighty. I was pretty certain I didn't have whatever they were looking for, but they didn't know that. It was obvious they weren't going to be slowed down in their search, not by a measly Harvard dead bolt, and certainly not by a small-time private detective.

I went into my office, stepping over the debris that used to be my personal papers, and saw that the combination lock I'd put on the bottom drawer of my metal file cabinet had not done its job either.

The face of it had been pried off and a good-sized hole drilled right through the center. Who needs safecrackers anymore when there were cordless power drills?

Most of what was inside the drawer was still there, which meant the mob wasn't interested in my social security card or my final divorce decree. But what they were interested in was much more important, and its theft much more ominous.

I found a space in the middle of my cluttered floor, cleared one, actually. Where was Mary Poppins when you needed her?

I'd always liked people in general, but most of the time I didn't care too much to be around them. There had been low points in my life when I saw only one or two people on a regular basis, preferring the company of my cat, my tunes, and four walls over anything else human.

But lately, even when I was by myself, nothing seemed quite in balance. My own inner electricity was at war with itself, using my head like a squash court until the only things I could feel were the ricochets.

I hadn't felt it as strongly as I did now, sitting on the floor of my office in the middle of what was left of everything I owned and contemplating what I would do to the guy who'd ripped my thousand-dollar futon into a pile of black cotton strips and stolen my handgun.

I didn't much like guns, didn't trust people who did, but Bobo's insistence and the nature of my job had forced me to join the fray reluctantly. I kept two identical Walther PPKs, one at my office and one at home. Both of which I'd learned how to use, both of which I had licenses for, and now one of which was gone.

I needed a drink.

Lucky for me I was mad as hell and Sam and I had already polished off my last bottle of Scotch. I called Frank, my locksmith, instead.

It was still early evening, but he was on call twenty-four hours a day, so I paged him. Ah, modern technology. He called back moments after I'd hung up the phone. In my business, you called your locksmith by his first name and you kept an account.

I told him what had happened.

"Jeez, Zen. I don't hear from you for—what has it been, like a year or something—and you call me with this? This ain't no business for a lady like you." I could hear him popping his gum. It sounded like firecrackers through the phone. "But I guess it's okay so long as you keep sending me business. Did they mess the place up bad?"

"Yeah, Frank," I mumbled. "It looks like an earthquake and cyclone combined. When can you fix my locks?"

"I got one small job in Venice I'm on my way to. Can you believe it, man? Prime time and I'm still out on the job. Man, I'd be up shit's creek without a car phone, you know?" Pop, pop, pop-pop. "Anyways, I'll be over in about forty-five, okay?"

I told him it was.

"Listen, my brother Mike, you know him, right?" He didn't wait for me to answer. "Well, he's got this new business, cleaning up offices and stuff, and well, I figure I could send him over to your place tonight to fix it right back up. Whad'ya say? I'm sure he'd give you a good rate, you bein' my numero-uno client and all."

"That's a fine idea." And it was. "But say, Frank, why don't you send him by tomorrow? I'll be out of town on business all day. He can take his time. Do it right."

"Whatever you say." He popped his gum again and then the phone exploded in a whir of hisses. After a moment he came back on the line. "Shit, these things . . . hello? . . . Shit, *hello?* . . . You there? Zen?"

"Yeah, yeah, Frank, I still hear you. Not so loud, huh? I'm starting to get a headache."

"Sorry, sure, so, um, okay, we're square on Mike comin' by, right? Cool. It'll work out great. I mean, you don't even have to leave him the key."

He was still laughing at his little joke as I recradled the phone.

EIGHTEEN

Frank kept to his word, arriving closer to thirty minutes after my call rather than forty-five and only his constant jabbering made him miss the land-speed record for replacing a dead bolt.

For a change, though, his chatter had a point to it, and by the time he handed me my new set of keys, he had talked me into an electronic security system.

Two hours later Frank had the newfangled thing installed, which was basically infrared sensors in each room, all controlled from keypads at my front and back doors.

Frank had to explain how to set and disarm the thing a half dozen times before I got it down right. I had had training in high-tech equipment, but never bothered to learn anything but the basics, like on, off, and, if applicable, trigger.

I was a simple woman and I was most comfortable with the simple life. Gadgets made me dizzy. Still, Frank was right. It was about time I upgraded my security system.

Now if anyone tried to invade my personal space, they'd get their eardrums blasted off for their trouble, not to mention a visit from a blue-and-white.

Funny, I didn't *feel* safe as I drifted off to sleep on what was left of my bed, one of my golf clubs at my side. Just the opposite.

I got an early start to my day for plenty of reasons besides wanting to get in and out of Fresno as soon as possible. Ten-Eighty was likely still out there somewhere, and having him on my ass all the way to Fresno was like taping a "Kick me" sticker to my back.

It was still dark when I pulled my bike off its hooks and silently sneaked out the back, a change of clothing in my black knapsack.

Living next to a pet cemetery has its advantages. It's quiet most of the time and the creepy things that are associated with human graveyards somehow don't apply to the final resting grounds for little Fifi. For the most part, it didn't attract grave robbers or devil worshippers either, though around Halloween all bets (pets?) were off.

For that reason, the place never had much in the way of security, which made it that much easier to cut through the cemetery's grounds, which I found helpful on occasions such as now.

I had a heavy-duty lock cutter weighing my pack down, but it was the only thing that would cut through the chain that was wrapped around the back gate. I always keep locks around the house for various uses and, because I am a good citizen, used one of them to replace the lock I'd cut once I was inside. I had put one of the two keys (the other I kept for future use) in an envelope which I dropped in the mailbox at the main building, a one-story imitation colonial affair where the bereaved can have their loved ones embalmed, cremated, or even viewed in an open casket.

I was on my bike and on Pico Boulevard moments later, heading for my office, all the while trying to imagine some rich widow's poodle lying in state.

When I was sure I wasn't being followed, I slowed what had initially been a frantic pace, coming to a stop at a light, and pulled my car phone out of my knapsack. Now here was something I never thought I'd ever be caught dead doing.

I called a rent-a-car company I use occasionally and arranged to have a nondescript vehicle delivered near my office. I made two more calls, put the phone back and continued to my office, trying to appreciate the invigoration of an early-morning workout.

At the office, all was still quiet. It was early even for the architects downstairs, who tended to be on their second double-latte by the time most people were falling out of bed. All this meant I had the building practically to myself. A good thing.

I showered, changed into a pair of black jeans, a roomy white oxford shirt and a black leather jacket that I keep in my office (along with a variety of other everyday necessities) for those times when I have to sneak out my back door.

I picked out a pair of Timberland lace-ups for this particular trip. I'm sure I looked as if I'd just come out of an ad for The Gap, but up north I'd fit right in. Just another coed from Fresno State, except for the Walther. For once, I was glad to have it along for company.

The car was waiting in front of a garage a couple of blocks' walk from my building. The universal rent-a-car: a white Chevrolet Grand Am. No wonder rentals were easy targets. Might as well rent 'em all with neon signs. "Look, thief! Cash-rich tourist inside."

At the moment, I didn't really give a damn. Blending into the background was just want I wanted. I had to smile a little as I turned onto the 10 Freeway, speeding out of Santa Monica, the sun rising before me and no sign of a blue Mercedes behind.

NINETEEN

A little less than two hours, miles and miles of stunted hills and carbon-copy farm fields, and two crop-duster buzz-bys later, I was rolling into the raisin capital of the world.

The sun had tried to peek through a mostly overcast sky the whole trip north, but the closer to San Joaquin Valley I got, the bleaker the weather became. By the time I made Fresno, blues were blackened gray.

I hadn't spied any notable German sedans in my rearview mirror, which calmed my nerves a good deal. Nothing much happened at all, actually, except a weird coincidence. Both times I stopped, once for coffee in Bakersfield and the other time for a fill-up before veering off on 99 North, the same black Chrysler just happened to have the same idea.

I eyed the driver both times, but he seemed normal enough. Some suit on his way to a meeting or a salesman hawking his wares to the gullible masses in the hinterlands, but something about him bugged me. He had on these Oak-ley sunglasses, the kind that cyclists and skiers wear. With dark, angled plastic lenses that partially wrap around the face, they had the aggressive look of someone looking for trouble and hoping to find it.

A lot of guys thought they were cool and they were kind of hip now, but they didn't match this guy's off-the-rack department-store threads. Perhaps not great reasons to feel distrust toward someone, but the way things were going for me lately, I wasn't about to dismiss my intuitions.

I was happy to see him fade out of view behind me in the morning rush of traffic into Fresno.

I exited near the small city zoo, cut up Blackstone Avenue through what serves as the town's center and on out past Fresno State toward the eastern end of town. On my way I noticed the new additions to town: several outlet malls had recently been constructed on the outskirts, promising bargains galore. The consumer revolution run amok. Somewhere someone was upstairs laughing at us, or perhaps just vigorously shaking his head in disbelief.

All I had on Harry Winchester was an address in an old section near an air-freight terminal. It took me two or three passes around it before I found the right street and another twenty minutes or so before I pinpointed Harry's former residence.

It was down a long, partially paved residential street of Rube Goldberg houses, many that had begun their lives as house trailers and had been dragged kicking and sagging into some kind of mid-life architectural crisis. Most had generous front lawns, gone brown at best, to seed or sand at worst, and backyards that could double as junk shops. The street was lined with American-made cars from another era, pickup trucks with foreboding front grates and massive fenders, and Nissans that were so old, they were still called Datsuns.

Harry's place was almost at the end of the block, on a stretch of road that had turned to gravel or never been paved over. It was hard to tell. The winter rains hadn't yet found their way up north, and when I bumped off the end of the paved portion of the road and rolled to a stop in front of a rumpled pink house, the Grand Am kicked up a good tail of dust.

The outside was faded, with peeling shutters that had once been brown or dark red. The sun had blurred the difference long ago. The lawn was patchy with brown spots, but someone had started a small flower garden by the entrance, surrounding it with a tiny white picket fence that was no higher than my ankles.

It was a pitiful sight, really, those few bright plants straining for attention, stems going brown and flowers barely open, as if they were embarrassed by their pallid condition. Not enough water and too much sun. From the looks of the neighborhood, they weren't the only things being neglected.

I stood looking at the sad blooms for a moment, then pushed the doorbell, hoping my business here would be quick, fruitful, and inexpensive.

I waited a good long minute before trying the doorbell again and then, after another moment, knocking on the misshapen screen door before giving up.

I began to walk back down the front walk, wondering whether I should wait for someone to show up or try another research tack, when I heard a muffled scraping: the sound of a door bulged by heat and dry weather to where it was dragging against the doorframe.

I turned back, my best public servant's smile on my face, pulling out my white business card. The door swung open, revealing a woman behind it who seemed to have suffered through the same climate changes as the door.

Even through the screen, I could see here was a woman who'd been around a few times, had gone back for more, and decided to go for good once she'd realized it was the best she'd ever get.

She had the look of the terminally impoverished: a little bit indignant and a whole lot defeated. Her blond hair, gone dry and white by too much sun and too many chemical-laden beauty products, was piled in loose strands in a mess atop her head. Her nose was straight, a ring through one nostril. Her eyes were glazed over, and she had a ring through one brow. Her lips were a little swollen, the butt of a Camel cigarette caught indelicately between them.

"Whatever you're sellin', we don't want none." She said this like a dare. Rehearsal for Donahue. Women with nose rings and attitudes.

I waved my card in front of the screen, trying to find a spot where she could read it without taking her eyes off me. Zen doing her best to put an interviewee at ease.

"I got nothing to sell." I let her see the card:

ZEN MOSES
Private Investigator

A little sometimes went a long way.

"I'm up from LA looking for someone. I was hoping you could help."

She looked at the card, back at me, then repeated the whole thing again. I waited. "A private detective."

A smart one, this one. "Yep."

"No shit?"

"No shit."

"Well, fuck me," she said, opening the door just wide enough to fling out the cigarette butt. We both watched it burn itself out in the middle of one of the few patches of grass still visible on her front yard. "What do you want? If you're lookin' for that asshole Bill, I ain't seen the fucker since Thanksgiving. He stole my mama's turkey. Can you believe that shit? Spend twenty bucks at the Safeway and you can get the bird for free. But no. Not ol' Bill. He has to take the fucking family turkey. I mean, the guy's got shit for brains. I hope he choked on a leg and died."

"Sounds like Bill's a piece of work," I said. "But actually, I was wondering if you knew the guy who used to live here."

"You mean Sparky?"

"I don't know." I was digging an old picture of Harry Winchester out of the pocket of my jacket. It was a good fifteen years old, a scraggy blue-collar guy with a forestry logo on his baseball cap and a faded work shirt. He had the skin of someone used to being outdoors and the forearms of a guy who'd been weaned on hard labor. "This, um, Sparky?"

She immediately shook her head, a snide smile swung into place on those battered lips. "Now, what do you want to know about him for?"

The truth was always the best policy, even if it meant embellishing it a bit. "Actually, his daughter is looking for him. Seems someone died and left him money. I'm trying to find him so he can collect his share."

"Well, now what do ya' know? Don't that beat all? He always said he had some famous relative." She eyed the photo another beat longer, taking a lifeline drag of her new Camel.

"You know the guy?"

"You could say that." She was getting that look of someone about to ask for money. "What's in it for me? Bet there's some kind of finder's fee. I heard about that stuff on 'America's Most Wanted.' "

"He's not a fugitive," I said.

"Now there's a shocker," she snorted.

"What do you mean? Was he in trouble with the law?" If he was, it might help me track him faster. He'd have had to give the cops some kind of address.

"Not exactly," she said. "But he was a real strange guy. Liked his women young, I mean real young. Know what I mean? I wouldn't leave my kid alone with him if you paid me."

I doubted this, but didn't say so. So Harry was a lech. Well, Latisha had said he wasn't a model citizen.

"So I think you were about to tell me where I could find Harry."

"Sure. And you weren't sayin' you couldn't pay me for the information, right?" A detective's work is never easy— or free, not in a world where people thought they were owed just for being born.

"Depends on how much help you are."

She frowned at this, folding her arms behind the screen door, which still separated the two of us. I was feeling kind of silly standing out there on her stoop, talking through the door. The neighbors would be gossiping by lunchtime.

I reached into the pocket of my jeans and pulled out a twenty-dollar bill I'd stashed there just for this purpose. I waved it near the handle of the screen door. She opened it a crack and reached out, but I yanked the bill away.

"Information first, Andrew Jackson later."

Another frown, this one bordering on hostile. A woman I wouldn't want to mud-wrestle. "Na-uh," she said. "I get the money first. That fucker Bill, he took everything."

I wasn't in the mood to argue with this woman and it

wasn't my money I was giving her anyway, so I decided to relent. I just hoped she wouldn't disappoint me.

I slipped the bill through the crack between door and doorway and she snatched it up, folding it quickly and tucking it into her jeans.

"I dunno where Harry is," she said and I was suddenly sorry I didn't believe in using weapons as interview props. "I know how you can find out, though."

She had me for a moment there. I had to smile. My second one of the day.

"Wait here and I'll write down the address to this shit hole he used to hang out at." She was gone less than five minutes, returning with yet another cigarette and the promised address.

"Ask for Sparky. He owns the joint. Guess I should warn you, the place is a real dump. Not many women go in there, not unless they're looking for trouble." She gave me one last once-over, lighting up the Camel. "Guess you look like you can take care of yourself okay."

"Thanks for the warning anyway," I said. She was still in the doorway, looking out on her miserable neighborhood when I turned the Chevy around and headed back toward town.

Asshole Bill's ex-girlfriend sent me to a bar well-hidden in a maze of grid streets even farther out of town than Harry's old neighborhood. Actually it was a condemned building that was masquerading as a bar.

The small brick-and-wood square of a place looked as if it had been on its last legs fifty years ago. Most of the brickwork had crumbled or was being held in place by a haphazard schmear of concrete, and part of the wood-slat roof had caved in, leaving a hole in the ceiling.

Hanging over the entrance was a burned-out neon sign: "Cold Beer." Below it, a hand-lettered one: "Sparky's Shack."

I parked in front beside a collection of early-model pickup

trucks (the car of choice here in the San Joaquin Valley) and got out, tucking my Walther in the pocket of my jacket. Just in case.

The inside of Sparky's made the outside look like Buckingham Palace. A heavy oak bar ran the length of the small place, a pissing canal along its base. Here in Fresno, it was a remnant of the past that was still, unfortunately, in use. A patron, weaving with too much booze and not enough sleep, was using the canal with one hand, starting a new Bud with the other. Chalk one up for efficiency.

Besides the guy relieving himself, there were four other patrons in the bar, all sidled up in front of well-used glasses, half staring up at a grainy television behind the bar that was showing, of all things, "The Regis and Kathie Lee Show."

Behind the bar, a hawk of a guy stood, leaning against the back wall, running his finger along a newspaper and soundlessly moving his mouth. Your basic remedial bartender.

The bar's door was open, allowing me to slip in without drawing notice. The bartender was the first to see me and the stunned look on his face caught the attention of his patrons. In a matter of seconds, I had six sets of eyes staring at me with thoughts I didn't want to begin to imagine.

"Hey, fellas," I said as matter-of-factly as I could, moving slowly toward the bar and trying to ignore the smell of urine in my nostrils. I picked a seat toward the end, managing to avoid the piss stream below me and hooking the heels of my shoes on the last rung of the stool.

Miraculously, one of the drunks awoke from his slumber, pushed himself away from the bar and walked over to where I was sitting, a shit-eating grin smashed against his face.

He wasn't as old as he first seemed. I put him somewhere around my age, though his sludge of a beard, bloodshot eyes, and sagging gut made him a sure bet for an early death.

"Now I told my buddies here that this felt like a good morning," he slurred through breath as foul as a junkyard dog's and in a voice beaten into submission by too many smokes. "And then you just walk in here. Looks like my lucky day, don't it now?"

The Walther was burning a hole in my pocket, but I kept it there, knowing from years of working with Bobo that there were many ways to deal with life's unfortunate situations short of shooting someone's foot off. Even if that seemed like the most appropriate action at the time.

"Unless your name is Sparky," I said evenly, "then maybe you should try the lottery." I was eyeing the space between me and him in a way I hoped would convey a little menace. I didn't want to give him any invitation to step closer. I didn't want to hurt him.

"Now a pretty little thing like you shouldn't be messing around in a place like this." The guy's temper was rising, but I noticed he stood his ground. That meant I made him uneasy. I hoped it stayed that way. "Women don't come in here lest they're looking for some good times. I'm here to see you get what you came for."

He advanced a little and I stiffened. I had one hand casually in my pocket, where the Walther was resting. Thankfully, I was spared from using it.

"Back off, Bill," said the bartender, who got Bill's reluctant attention. I wondered if this was the turkey thief. He stood his ground for a moment, then relented and took a seat one barstool away. Still too close for my taste.

I shot a glare at the gaunt bartender, who'd been watching the scene develop, waiting, I suppose, for the moment when things were about to explode before deciding to mediate. Already I didn't like the guy.

"You must be Sparky," I guessed and he nodded, walking toward me and leaning on the bartop to ensure a private conversation.

"Yeah," he whispered. "Excuse me for saying, but what the fuck is a woman like you doin' in a place like this, 'cept asking for trouble?"

I pulled my card out. He picked it up, turned it around a couple of times, then leaned over and dropped it into the stream of piss. "So? What do you want from me?"

I showed him Harry's picture, giving him the same spiel I'd given the woman earlier. I didn't wait for him to ask, pulling a twenty-dollar bill out of my pocket and laying it on the bar.

"Harry will be thrilled," Sparky said. "He can buy more magazines."

"You know where he is?" I wasn't interested in the guy's lifestyle habits, just his location.

"Sorry, can't help you," he said, staring longingly at the money. "Whoever sent you here got it wrong."

"Probably that bitch Rita." It was Bill from down the bar, trying his best to be a tough guy, only I noticed he wasn't interested in looking at me. "I'll show that bitch."

I got up from the stool and walked over to Bill, who continued to curse under his breath, keeping his eyes focused on his beer mug in front of him. I advanced too quickly for a drunkard to even think of reacting, in one motion yanking him off the bar stool by his earlobe.

I nearly pulled his ear off of his head, squeezing as hard as I could until he fell to his knees. The smell of piss was making me feel faint, but I was enjoying Bill's suffering too much to think about it.

"Awww. Ouch!" He was screaming now and while he had gotten his buddies' attention, nobody moved. Sparky looked like he was going to say something, but thought better of it. Maybe he was smart after all.

"Awww! Let go, you cunt!" Bill cried.

"That's it," I said, whipping out the Walther and pressing the end against Bill's temple. "Maybe it's time you stopped referring to women as bitches and cunts."

I'd finally gotten his respect. He was shaky and I noticed he had pissed in his pants.

"He's just a stupid drunk," said Sparky, finally coming to the guy's rescue. With friends like these . . . "We don't need that stuff in here."

I looked at Sparky, then back at Bill, who was practically sobbing, then back at Sparky. For a brief, fleeting moment,

I actually thought of shooting the guy. But thankfully the thought passed.

I leaned over so only Bill could hear, still pressing the gun against his head. "Listen up, asshole," I whispered. "I'd like to shoot you right here and now and put you out of my misery, but a piece of shit like you isn't worth it. However, if anything happens to Rita, I'm gonna come back and kill you. Kill. You. Understand?"

He nodded and I let go, letting him crumple to the floor in a heap.

"Look, Sparky," I said, turning my attention back to the proprietor. "I agree with you. I don't know why the fuck I am in a bar that smells like a public toilet with a bunch of leering assholes with double-digit IQs and hundred-proof breath, but I have a job to do, and today, that's to find this guy. It's a simple way that works. Maybe we can start this over again. Where is he?"

I still had my right hand in my pocket. Sparky's eyes moved toward it.

"Yeah, all right," he said, turning around and banging a hand on his old-fashioned upright cash register. The drawer slid open and a bell went off. He lifted up the cash drawer and pulled out a photo, which he handed to me. "Turn it over."

A much older, much thinner Harry Winchester, leaning against what looked like a Winnebago, his arm around a tiny Mexican teenage girl, smiled up from the snapshot. The trailer wasn't new, but it shone white in the picture, a blue-and-green stripe ran down the side, and someone had painted a hawk, wings splayed, just below the driver's compartment. On the other side was a post-office box in Calexico, one of California's southernmost border towns. The middle of fucking nowhere.

"This where he is?" I asked Sparky, as Bill got up, propped himself against the bar, and added to the urine stream.

"Not exactly." He was pointing downward, looking at

me as if I'd be sorry I'd ever asked. "A few clicks south."

Sparky had lost his resolve to keep his pal's secret. It didn't take much before he gave me an earful about his buddy's doings in Fresno.

TWENTY

Harry's Fresno years had been fairly productive, ac-cording to Sparky. After a few minutes of conversation, we were old buddies.

But what he told me about Harry made me wonder why his daughter even wanted to find him. I would understand if she changed her mind.

Harry was a whiz when it came to finding jobs, but he didn't have the same luck holding them down. He was still a legend in the underside of Fresno for a screw-up that happened when he was driving a street cleaner for the city.

Seems he got so drunk on duty one night he veered off his route, ending up at Chandler Airport, where he drove around in a circle for hours. They say the tiny commuter airport was never more pristine.

He was a regular at Sparky's and the town's only two strip joints, but his taste in women was pretty much as had been described to me: the younger, the better. He managed to hook a succession of teenage girls of low standing and even lower self-esteem, the latest the Mexican girl in the picture Sparky had given me.

She couldn't have been older than fifteen, but her family was too gullible to notice and too poor to care that their daughter was shacking up with someone old enough to be her great-grandfather.

Her name was Frieda and she had left Fresno with Harry almost a year earlier, when Harry got tired of civilization, as Sparky had so succinctly put it.

"Soon as Clinton got elected, he was puttin' all his shit

in that Winnebago and talkin' about leaving the country to all them fags and hippies and feminists," Sparky had said. His words exactly. "He sold most everything he owned. Shoot, that's Harry's old TV set up there."

Harry sent word via a postcard shortly after, instructing Sparky to send his mail to a PO box in Calexico. They hadn't heard from the guy since.

I thanked him and walked out, passing Bill on the way. He was trying not to look at me, and I could still see the red marks on his ear where I had grabbed him. A little revenge for Rita. Fuck 'em. As far as I was concerned, she deserved it.

Time for other things, though. I was at least another day away from returning home—and keeping my promise to Sam and Danny. Seems ol' Harry or Hawk or whatever the hell he was calling himself wasn't to be found without a struggle. Next stop, Mexico.

Calexico was about as close to a real border town as you could get, sitting about a stone's throw from the California-Mexico line, a few miles below El Centro, California. I'd never been there, but was certain it was no bigger than a Greyhound bus station, which is about what it was anyway. A stopping point for one last gander at the U.S. of A. before crossing into the Mexican version of the Third World.

I was thinking about the times I'd spent as a student traveling through Mexico, certain that where I was headed now wasn't going to be any vacation. Times had always been hard south of the border, but recent economic troubles had depressed an already impoverished nation, relegating a once-proud people to suicidal dashes across a few miles of borderline that must seem like light-years.

I had managed to pry myself away from Sparky and his cohorts shortly before noon, leaving me plenty of time to ditch the rental and get a seat on a commuter flight leaving later that afternoon for California's southernmost big city.

I checked in with Vivian, who reported all was quiet, left

a message on Bobo's pager where I was heading, and then called Latisha to report my progress.

She seemed indifferent to my news, even when I told her the added travel would pad the expenses she would owe me. She seemed in a hurry to get off the phone, which was okay with me. The woman still hadn't endeared herself to me.

My flight was scheduled for about an hour, which was too long by sixty minutes for me. I'd done a lot of flying in my days as a sportswriter, but instead of easing my concerns about air travel, my frequent flier miles only added to my fears.

Matters were made considerably worse by the small size of our plane, a typical two-prop commuter job that sloped backward when it was resting on the tarmac. I got on with the eleven or so other passengers, took my seat over the wing and closed my eyes, hoping sleep would rescue me from reality.

We took off with a hop and a rumble. And that was only my stomach.

When we landed in San Diego, I picked up another cookie-cutter rent-a-car, then made the two-hour-long drive down the barren, bumpy, two-lane road they called Route 8 on my way to El Centro.

El Centro is a big city compared to Calexico, which is essentially a post office, general store, honky-tonk bar and a whole lot of farmland. Population varied considerably depending on the season and even the time of day, as Mexicans and Americans alike criss-crossed the border in search of work or even a little pleasure.

Another well-placed Andrew Jackson passed to the guy who ran the one-man town post office got me an address of sorts for Harry. Seems he'd parked his camper somewhere east of Mexicali, a northern state capital city of Mexico, and set up house. I was told it'd be hard to find, except for one unusual characteristic: Harry had recently bought and installed a large satellite dish. Seems Harry didn't cotton to Mexican television.

I never left town without my passport, for a lot of reasons, some actually practical. It didn't matter I was waved through the border crossing with a wink and a leer from a guy who looked a lot like Pancho Villa.

The border crossed directly into Mexicali, a city of nearly one million, a good many of whom are among Mexico's poor. I stopped at a taco stand just over the border and got a tamale and an orange soda.

I drove west on a narrow, newly paved, shoulderless road that ran toward Abasolo, passing fields of cotton, wheat, and various vegetables, all showing more brown than green. It was still months from picking season.

Fifteen miles outside of Mexicali, a half-fallen billboard advertising some long-abandoned golf-course resort marked the spot where I'd been instructed to turn off. I almost missed the entrance. It was a road that hadn't been a road for quite some time, having been filled in by the land-hugging growth of the desert.

A jeep would have been better than my Ford Escort rental, but it would have to do. I bounced around for a quarter mile before the road dropped at a sharp angle, into a valley exposing a rolling hump of hills ahead. Atop and completely out of place with its surroundings sat the black screened satellite dish.

Around that hill, I was certain, was Harry Ford Winchester.

TWENTY-ONE

I pulled the Escort off the road, grabbed my jacket, and followed what was a well-worn path around the hill and down another slope. There, in what passed as a clearing out in the middle of nowhere, was the Winnebago from Sparky's picture.

It was a massive machine sitting on several cinder blocks, canopied by an ingenious contraption of poles and what looked like parachute material. Once white, the trailer was colorless now, the green-and-blue stripes now a broken dotted line, and the bird had faded in the oppressive desert heat.

There was a fair-sized garden off to one side that, surprisingly, was flourishing, unlike the one at his former Fresno residence.

A dull, banged-up motorcycle lay on its side out front, along with two ratty lounge chairs, a small table, and a grilling pit. Everything was nice and tidy. A regular family camping trip.

The only signs of life were a scrawny black cat stretched out under the table and the sharp odor of fried cooking coming from inside the trailer.

I guessed the Winchesters weren't used to having people just drop in. This was one case where surprise might be dangerous, even fatal. People who sought this much privacy didn't normally take kindly to intrusions. I opted for the welcome-wagon approach.

"Hello," I called out cheerfully. "Anybody home?"

I heard movement inside the trailer immediately, a couple of heavy feet walking across the floor. The cat approached lazily. It was small, all black, with expressive green eyes and one white whisker. He was rubbing himself against my leg when the door swung open and I was face-to-face with Harry Winchester. The cat took one look and scurried under the trailer. Smart.

Harry's hair was bleached white, his skin wrinkled and permanently sun-scarred, a sagging chest and gut making his ample tank top seem two sizes too small. He had the look of a guy who never shaved but still couldn't manage a full beard. His was gray going white, exposing his reddened skin in patches.

He wore uneven cutoffs and unlaced workman's. He was smoking a cigarette, dangling it from his mouth the way the woman I'd met in Fresno had, and he was wielding a shotgun.

I wasn't close enough to smell his breath, but I was certain if I lit a match in his direction, it would start a fire.

"What the hell do you want?" he said. "Gimme one reason why I shouldn't blow your head off and lay you out for the coyotes."

He said coyotes as Westerners do, pronouncing just the first two syllables, cay-oats. I started to put my hand up, but the click of him cocking the rifle made me think better of it.

"I'm waiting."

"Listen, Harry." The fact that I knew his name got his attention. I wasn't sure if that was a good thing. "I just need to talk to you. I don't want a thing."

"You must want somethin'. Nobody comes all the way out here for nothing. You might be from the IRS, for all I know."

"Well, shit, are they after you, too?"

He looked at me for a second, then a smile ran over his face.

"I like that," he said. "That's damn funny."

"Does that mean you're not going to shoot me?"

"Don't be too sure," he said, the rifle still pointed in the wrong direction. "Why don't you tell me what you want. I don't much like being bothered."

"Well, I'm trying to and I don't much like having a shot-gun pointed at me," I said, almost beginning to like the guy. He reminded me of a lot of old men I'd come to know. Guys who'd taken the hard road of life either by choice or predic-ament, only to come out the other side with nothing to show but pain and scars. They had every right to feel bitter—beaten, even cheated—but had long decided to keep playing the hand they'd been dealt.

"You're a feisty one, ain't ya'?"

"You don't know the half of it." I raised my hands slowly, turning around as I spoke. "Look, I'm unarmed and it's taken me a long, tiring day to find you. All I want to do is cross the border before sundown and go back home. Couldn't you humor me for a moment?"

He gave me one more once-over and, apparently deciding I was harmless enough, lowered the rifle, beckoning me to take one of the lounge chairs.

He plopped down on the stairs that led up to the trailer's front door, calling inside for a couple of beers. A moment later, the woman I knew as Frieda appeared with two bottles. She, too, had aged since the picture was taken but still looked a long way from high school graduation.

"You a beer drinker?" he said and I wondered not for the first time what it was about me that made even misog-ynists like Harry treat me like one of the guys. Must be my innate charm. "I don't usually like to see women drink, but I ain't responsible for you."

I thanked him, looking over at the trailer. He had pasted a haphazard pattern of right-wing bumper stickers on its side, including "Rush in '96," a couple using an unflattering eu-phemism for the President's wife, and another that read: "Support the Republican party: kill a liberal."

Who said Americans had lost their convictions?

"Don't much care for 'em, do you?" It was part a chal-lenge, part what-the-fuck-do-I-care. I didn't say anything, watching as he tipped back the brew, inhaling the entire bot-tle with one sip, then wiping the little bit he'd missed off his mouth with the back of his hand. He concluded the whole thing with a belch that echoed through the desert so loudly it probably sent someone's Richter scale into overdrive back in San Diego.

"So you gonna tell me what you've come to this shit hole for?" He was smiling and then he stopped and gave me a real good long look, as if he had seen me before and was trying to place me in his mind's vision. "Hold on a minute now; you ain't one of my daughters, are you?"

I shook my head. This guy was pathetic. "Nope, sorry. Figured a father would know his own kid."

He grumbled at this. "Their mother kicked me out years ago. I ain't seen either of 'em must be more'n twenty years now. Fuck 'em all. I don't need 'em."

Whatever. "I am speaking with Harry Ford Winchester, is that correct?"

"Yep. You got him. You ain't from the IRS? What are you, a cop or something, a Fed?"

"No. Nothing like that. I've got some good news for you, Harry. Seems like someone died and left you some money."

"No shit? How much?"

I noticed he hadn't asked who. This made it easier to snow the guy, not that I couldn't find other reasons to ease my conscience. A few more minutes and I was sure to have my own personal top-ten list. "That's to be determined. I was hired to find you so that the lawyers could give you your share. I don't think it'll be all that much once the suits are done with it."

"Fucking lawyers. That's why I left the country." He was shaking his head, turning a bit red in the face in the process, something I didn't think was possible, considering his already ruddy complex. "Why the hell would I be out here in the middle of these fucking dumb-assed mongoloids for? I mean, white people in America, they are the minorities now. Fucking niggers and spics and feminists and God knows what else. And I ain't even talkin' about those fairy faggots and slanty-eyed cheapskates. No, sir. I got this here dish just to keep tabs on what's going on and it's just all gone to shit."

I listened to his spiel with half an ear, glad when he was through ranting and happy I had the restraint not to egg him on more. I wasn't broken up over his desertion. America didn't need people like him anyway. Maybe some of his "heroes" would follow, too.

I stayed a bit longer, though, listening to Harry rave like a lunatic about weak-kneed liberals and the decline of family values and trying to hold my tongue. He even talked himself out of his "inheritance." Something about not wanting part of any "blood money." Whatever that meant.

It was getting dark when I got back to my car and started slowly out toward the main highway. The sun was setting in front of me. All I was thinking about was Mexicali and the border.

In a few hours I'd be back home in Santa Monica, sipping a cold Anchor Steam and taking in the ocean air.

I was tired from travel and from listening to Harry drone on, but happy to have quickly wrapped up a paid assignment. My first in ages. Zen was back.

I was working hard to keep my weary eyes on the road. There is nothing blacker than night in a place where the nearest artificial lights are glows on the horizon. It makes drives like this disorienting. The roadsides are lit up only momentarily as your headlights pass over them, but fade quickly, making it seem as if the world comes to an end all around you. It gave me the creeps.

I was glad when two round lights appeared far ahead of me. I hadn't seen any other cars the whole trip from Mexicali to Harry's place, so I felt better.

Probably a local on his way through or an American tourist heading south toward the little-known resort towns on the eastern coast of the Sea of Cortez. It was a dark sedan and he had his dome light on, so I could just make out a figure. He was looking down and away from me, as if someone smaller than him, a child perhaps, was sitting in the passenger seat. Maybe he was checking a map.

As he faded in my rearview mirror, he hit his brake lights just before disappearing completely. The first thing I thought was an animal had run across the road, but the duration of the bright-red glares and their movement off the road put another, much more awful, thought in my head.

Seconds later I had a déjà vu, as if I'd seen the driver before, and the twinge in my gut suddenly meant something. Then I remembered. The guy at the gas station on my way up to Fresno.

I slammed on the brakes, almost toppling the Escort in the process of a full-speed U-turn. I hightailed as fast as I could back to Harry's trailer, my phobia of the dark the least of my fears.

At the rocky entrance to Harry's road, I slowed to a stop and turned off the lights. I wasn't about blindly to rush in. For all I knew, what I thought I had just seen was a figment of my imagination, the result of not enough sleep and way too much stress.

Still, I made sure the clip of my Walther was jammed in secure and the shiny metal gun was snug in my hand. I was planning on a silent approach. Maybe I was out of mind, but there was always the possibility Harry might come out shooting this time.

I scrambled up the hill toward Harry's satellite dish, a climb much harder than it looked. The surface was dry, hard and rocky and dotted with prickly hazards. I thought I heard a rattle in the now pitch-blackness, but didn't stop long enough to find out if the sound actually belonged to a snake on the slither. I didn't want to know.

From up top I could see why Harry had placed his dish here. Even in the darkness, I could see the glow of Mexicali in the distance.

Down below, the dark Chrysler was parked, engine running. I could barely see its outline in the low light emitting from the trailer. All was quiet. Painfully so. Maybe it was my imagination run wild again, but even the desert suddenly seemed too still. The calm before the storm.

The lights suddenly went out inside the trailer, taking all visibility with it. My eyes hadn't yet adjusted to the darkness when someone came out of the trailer. I could hear the thump of his shoes, small and quick steps—somebody in a hurry.

I held my breath, feeling vulnerable under the moonlit sky, though they would need night goggles to see me. I could hear the crunch of the shoes on ground and then a car door opening and slamming shut, followed by muffled voices. I couldn't understand what they were saying, but from the pitch it sounded as if the two were arguing. As much as I strained, I still couldn't hear particulars. It could have been a tape of myself talking and I wouldn't have been able to make it out.

Somewhere in the distance, I thought I heard someone sobbing. It was so quiet, so terribly sorrowful that it made my heart stop. The sound of fear.

The click and cringe of a car door opening again was followed by more steps, only these were lighter and tapped on the ground in measured deliberate paces, like someone tiptoeing in metal shoes. The trailer door banged open and there was a hollow pop and my heart sank. Then another in quick succession. More footsteps, the crash of the trailer door swinging open, then closing, the car door again, an engine whining in reverse, and the whoosh of gravel under tires.

As soon as I was sure they were on their way, I slid clumsily back down the hill. I tried to keep silent, but my fight to keep from tumbling head over heels was noisy.

Too noisy. The crack, ping, thap of ricocheting bullets came at me, robbing me of my breath and balance. I rolled the rest of the way down the hill, trying to protect myself with my hands.

I came to rest at the base of an agave cactus, which imbedded a good amount of its tiny, sharp thorns in my right forearm. I would have yelled out from the pain, but fear of giving up my location kept me suffering in silence.

I lay curled up in a fetal position, my right side howling. Somehow, I was still holding the Walther in my other hand.

I wasn't sure how much time had passed when I heard the rear wheels of the car spitting up dust. I counted to one hundred before actually moving. My right arm was a mass of tiny pain dots. I felt for some of the prickers, but they were nearly impossible to pull out in total darkness. I yanked out the ones I could, but ended up pushing most of them deeper into my arm.

I made my way back to the car, opening the door so I could use the dome light to see the damage. There were rug-burn-like scratches from my elbow to my wrist. I wasn't bleeding a lot, but it would take weeks to remove all the needles.

The rental was in far worse shape. Two tires had been punctured and the side panel was full of bullet holes. There was only one spare, of course, which left me with zero options.

I got my stuff out of the rental and went toward the trailer, feeling my way like a blind person. It occurred to me then that in all the commotion, none of it came from inside. No noise, no calls for help, no Harry with his shotgun. No nothing.

I knocked on the trailer door, stepping to the side in case somebody was still alive and came out shooting. But there was no sound.

I tried the latch and the door swung open. Inside, the odor of chilies and cooking oil, cornmeal and some sharp kind of spice tickled the hairs inside my nose and made my eyes water. The trailer was bigger than I'd imagined and it took me a minute before I was able to get my bearings. I was getting used to the darkness finally, though I still couldn't see for shit. I found a light switch and clicked it on, hoping the guys who had shot at me weren't still outside waiting for the idiot detective to turn the lights on.

There would be no reason, I saw, as Harry and his teenage bride sat side by side on a couch against one wall, new holes in their heads. Frieda's was in the side, up close and very direct, gang-style. I could see the powder burns on her temple. She had fresh tears on her cheeks.

Harry had got his between the eyes, which were still open, staring ahead, a look on his face that I couldn't quite put an emotion on. It was weird. Not surprise, not fear. Something else. Unfortunately, it was between Harry and his shooter, and at least one of them wasn't talking.

I looked around the trailer. Master bedroom at one end, kitchen in the middle, a table for eating and the couch at the other end. The remains of their last meal lay on the table, untouched. Some concoction of meat and rice. Harry's shotgun was lying next to the door. Harry either knew his attackers or they were pros. It isn't easy to sneak up on the paranoid.

I was starting to get pissed off. Besides the two dead bodies, something wasn't right about this scene. From the looks of things, I was guessing this was some kind of mob hit, which might explain why Morofsky had been tailing me. He must have been looking for Harry. Those two in the Chrysler must've been his boys, but something didn't sit right.

Leaving was paramount on my mind. I made a quick search of the trailer looking for any family mementos. This information would have to be delivered to Latisha personally, and I hoped bringing something of Harry's with me might ease her pain. Talk about your bad breaks. It takes me twenty-four hours to find her long-lost father and less than an hour later he winds up dead. This would not help my rep at all.

I felt more sorry for Frieda. What was she doing with this foul old man? By all accounts, she had gone both willingly and happily. Still, she was young enough perhaps eventually to have had a change of heart. Now we'd never know.

There wasn't much of Harry's personal effects, but I was surprised to find a box of photos of his two daughters. They were both darling little girls, pig-tailed and all smiles. Another time long ago, when family was family and everybody was happy and horrible secrets were yet to be known. Sentimentality ran deep with all kinds of folks, even bitter old Harry.

My search was cursory; I didn't want to be here if the shooters decided to come back and make sure they'd finished the job and I certainly didn't want to run into any Mexican police.

My Spanish was good, but it wasn't *that* good.

There was the problem of how I was going to get out of Mexico. The rental was useless on two wheels, and even if I did find a gas station in the middle of fucking nowhere's-ville, I wouldn't know how to explain the bullet holes to the border guards, much less the rent-a-car company. Harry didn't have a car, but then I remembered the motorcycle out front.

It was a small Honda, a 450 with a ripped seat, a straw basket on the back, and questionable shocks, but the tires were inflated and it only took a half dozen cranks before it started up, the vrooooom of the engine as it cut a hole through the quiet of the night music to my ears.

Harry had left his helmet on the seat, and while it was a little bit big for me, at least it wouldn't raise suspicion at the border. I shut the bike off, went back in, and had one last look around. I heard a noise behind me and whirled, Walther pointed and ready, but it was just the cat I'd seen earlier. She was licking Frieda's dinner off her paws.

We stared at each other for a minute, then she let out a meow that was half howl. I put my hand out and called her over, but she leaped off the table and through an open window. I felt bad for the creature. In a day or two, she'd be food for a coyote.

I left Harry and Frieda as I'd found them, wiped away whatever fingerprints I'd inadvertently left, threw my knapsack over my back and started up the Honda again. I had to work the choke a bit until it found its purring equilibrium, but I was happy to see the thing could still haul ass.

And that's exactly what I did.

TWENTY-TWO

I had little trouble crossing back into California.
When I got to the border, they just waved me through.

I went straight to the airport, paid an obscene amount for a late flight back to Los Angeles, and spent much of the waiting time at the rent-a-car company trying to explain what had happened to my car.

I told the smiling kid behind the counter that the car had been in an accident and wasn't drivable. He argued, but my appearance must have dissuaded him. One look at my swollen and scratched-up arm and my general dishevelment and he was pushing a form across the desk for me to fill out. I could tell he'd heard the same story a million times and didn't much care what I'd done with the company car. It was no skin off his back, and that's the way I wanted it to be.

I left the bike in the rental lot for some other poor soul who needed a ride. The lot was aglow in the artificial light and nearby, I heard a cat meowing. It was a minute before I realized it was coming from the motorbike. I turned to see Harry's cat poke her head out of the basket strapped to the back of the bike.

She crawled out and jumped down onto the pavement, where she went through a brief stretching routine, then shook herself all over like a dog. She meowed a couple of times and then advanced toward me, slowly at first, as if she was expecting me to run.

She got to my feet, rubbed against my legs, and I bent down to give her a pat. She was a bit worn at the edges, but other than that seemed like a healthy animal. I thought about

Ira and wondered if I could take on another feline. Even if I wanted to.

She made the decision easier, hopping up on my shoulders, where she began clawing at my knapsack. When she found a route inside, she took it. I was amazed. She had made her intentions quite clear. It didn't appear as if I was going to get a say-so in the matter.

Just before boarding, I called the border patrol. A Sergeant Lopez answered the phone and I told him about the two bodies, explaining how one was an American national. Then I gave him the location.

"And you are?" He was gruff and unfriendly. Nights on the border patrol can do that.

I gave him my name. It wouldn't be long before they'd find out I had been there. For one, there was the rental. When and if the rental company found it, they would track it back to me.

"What were you doing there?"

"I'm a private cop out of LA," I said. "I was on business for a client."

"What business?"

"That's confidential. I can tell you that I spoke with the man who was murdered shortly before he was shot." I went on briefly to detail what had happened, leaving out the part about seeing the guy in Fresno and my suspicions about mob involvement. "There were two assailants, but it was too dark to get a look at them. They shot at me."

"I see. You are still in Mexico, then?"

"Actually, no. I didn't see any reason to stick around and I am expected back in Los Angeles this evening."

"It would be best if you reported this in person," he said. "I am sure you are familiar with the procedure. They'll want to question you in person."

"They" meant the Mexican police. "To be perfectly honest, Sergeant, that's why I didn't stick around. It would be

a waste of everyone's time. I'm not leaving the country. I'll
be in Los Angeles. You can call me there.''

I hung up, not bothering to give him the number. He could
look it up.

It was pushing midnight when I walked out of the United
Shuttle terminal at LAX into a cold, cloudy Los Angeles
night and looked around for a cab.

Instead I found Bobo leaning against his custom black
Range Rover, a cigar in his mouth and baseball cap on his
head.

I didn't say anything. I had called him from San Diego
and filled him in on the details of my adventure, but we never
discussed his meeting me at the airport. This was Bobo's
way and I loved him for it.

I took my knapsack off, reaching in for the cat which had
slept the entire plane ride, not once making a sound. She
stretched and made some babylike coos when I removed her
from her hiding place.

Bobo just gave me one of those looks he reserves for
people who actually go to movies billed as tear-jerkers. I held
the cat up to him but he shrank back. She didn't seem to be
sure about him either. A match made in heaven.

We drove pretty much in silence. Every few moments he
would ask me about a detail and I tried to help, but the day's
adventure had worn me out. He did crack a smile at the part
about Zen and the man-eating cactus.

It occurred to me in my weary, dreamlike state that shooting people wasn't Morofsky's MO and told this to Bobo.

"I know," he said. "Tell me about it."

"I did."

"No. How were they shot?"

"In the head, Bobo. In the head."

"Front, side?"

"I don't know why this is so important, Bobo. The girl
got hers in the temple. Harry was shot . . . wait."

"What?"

I was thinking of Harry's face, that strange look he had the very moment he ceased breathing. "Harry took one right between the eyes, but it was weird, Bobo."

"How so?"

"I don't know, the look on his face. I still can't put a finger on it."

"Surprise?"

"Yes, and no. More like, I don't know."

"The world's greatest detective at work."

Bobo the comedian again. I was picturing Harry again, his mouth pierced, his eyes even in death saying something. Then it hit me. "This is gonna sound crazy, Bobo, but it was like he was impressed or something."

"Impressed? You're sayin' the guy was in awe of his killer?"

"Yeah, I guess I am."

"Maybe he had a hard-on for mobsters."

"Whatever," I said as we rolled up Lincoln in the obscene luxury of the Range Rover. I had no idea how they had become so popular in a city where it never snowed and where off-road meant parking on the front lawn.

"I'm probably making too much of it."

"Whatever."

Bobo dropped me off in front of my place. Stepping out of his seventy-thousand-dollar urban assault vehicle felt like jumping out of a plane. My arm was still sore and my mind was playing pinball with the day's events, trying to piece something recognizable out of them.

"Zen, girl," Bobo said to me as I thanked him for the ride.

"What?"

"Ever consider the possibility that you're being set up?"

"What do you mean?" Just then his meaning hit me. "That Harry was killed just because I was trying to find him?"

"Something like that. What do you know about that client of yours anyway?"

Now there was something I hadn't considered, not consciously, anyway. But there was something about Latisha I didn't trust.

"I guess it can make sense on one level,"· I said. "But why would she want her father killed? He wasn't doing her any harm, hidden in the middle of nowhere."

"Hey, you're the detective."

"Thanks a lot, Bobo. You're a big help."

"I try." His parting words were said quietly, as if he was trying to give me a warning without insulting me by saying it aloud.

I didn't linger outside my place, not any longer than it took to look around my quiet street for suspicious characters. None showed their mugs.

I took my new tenant toward her new home. She was purring in my arms, trying to push her nose into the crick of my elbow.

It was a miracle I remembered my new security code. Inside, the place was cleaner than it had been in years. I was going to have to call Frank to commend him on his brother's talents.

My massive CD collection had been put back together and now was neatly stacked on my bookshelf, along with all the books that had been strewn on the floor. My futon had been replaced with one that looked remarkably similar, as was my big stuffed chair and the bed.

The cat seemed to like the surroundings and immediately began clawing the futon. Breaking it in, I supposed. I still had some cat food around and rustled up a can and she went at it as if it would be snatched away at any moment. Maybe she didn't care much for Mexican food.

The answering-machine light was blinking wildly, but I required some personal hygiene first. There's nothing like a shower after a long day or a good workout. I always dreaded showers until I was underneath a hot stream of water. My form of meditation.

I put on the replica " '51 Giants" jersey (number 24, of course) that I sleep in, hit the "play" button on my answering machine, and crawled under the covers.

Mostly bill collectors, though Nat had called three times and the IRS wanted to confirm our Friday meeting. As if I'd forgotten.

I was listening to Nat's third message when I closed my eyes. I remember the cat jumping on my bed and curling up beside my head. After a few moments, the only sound in the room was her purring and my breathing.

TWENTY-THREE

Nat's voice woke me up first thing, way too soon, before I had any plans of greeting the new day. All I had to see was the dull way daylight shone through my blinds to know it was early morning. I liked to say that I wasn't a morning person, but the truth was I wasn't an LA morning person.

Give me a sunrise on a clear day in San Francisco and I was sure to be among the first one up to see it. But in LA, I was content to put off morning until it turned into afternoon.

I was always surprised to find someone in this town who was enamored with the first few hours of the day. LA was a night lover's paradise. Hollywood always shone brightest when there was a black sky full of stars in the background. It wasn't too deep and it wasn't too real by most people's standards, but it was LA, and that was good enough for me.

By my bed I kept earplugs and one of those black satin masks that shrinks use, so I could put off daylight and the sounds of a new LA day as long as possible.

When my place was put back together, my sleep aids had somehow gotten misplaced, so I was forced to turn to my pillow for a shield against both elements. It lasted maybe fifteen minutes and two more calls, one from Vivian and the other from Nat again. I was going to have to find some way of prying Nat's fingers off that phone of his.

I showered and dressed, made coffee and read the morning paper, all to the musical accompaniment of one of Sarah Vaughan's 1950s recordings. The cat seemed to dig Sarah's deep, resonant vocals. She made noises of unhappiness when the record ended, stopping only when I put it on again.

"Okay, kid," I said to the cat. "Your new name is Sassy." That had been Sarah Vaughan's nickname, and besides, this cat had an attitude. It fit.

My arm was still sore and I cleaned it again with disinfectant, using a pair of tweezers to pull out some more prickers. It was a slow, painful process, and though the hurt subsided somewhat, I was pretty sure I'd pushed some of them farther in.

I finished just as the sun made one of its rare appearances. It felt like a good omen. I hoped it was.

When I was sure I was awake enough to face the world, I rang up Nat. He'd been whining into my machine about needing to talk to me and I had figured it was his way of trying to pry more information out of me about Danny's murder. It was no doubt the topic of conversation at Father's Office and it wouldn't do well if the proprietor himself was uninformed.

Turned out, though, Nat was having problems with my friends at the police department. Seems they had roped off the crime scene, forcing Nat to close down. He couldn't get inside the walk-in to replace the kegs.

I promised to stop by later and see what I could do to help. This was hardly altruistic on my part. I was thinking of myself and of losing my favorite beer bar. Besides, I wanted another look myself. Something had been nagging at me ever since Victor had discovered the bodies. Maybe another look around, under better circumstances, would jog loose whatever it was that was stuck in my cobwebs.

I dialed Latisha Maxwell's number, thinking of how exactly I was going to deliver the bad news. I wasn't going to give it over the phone; there were some things best done in person. But I wanted to let her know I was coming by.

She wasn't home, but I left a message on her voice mail, a disconnected, robotlike female voice that sounded like the computer on the old "Star Trek" episodes. "Leave. Your. Mes-sage. After. The. Tone." The wonders of technology simply never ceased to amaze, and frustrate, me.

I left my beeper- and car-phone numbers, hoping I could get to her before she found out about her father's death from someone else. I tried the studio where she taped her show, but they were in re-runs this week and nobody knew where to find her; at least they weren't giving that information to me.

The car phone rang as soon as I gunned up the car and I thought, for not the first time, how much I hated the thing. It was, to my surprise, Leah Steinbeck, friendly neighborhood reporter.

"Are you going to tell me what this Latisha Maxwell thing is all about?" She wasn't one to waste time on mere greetings.

"What?" I said.

"You promised me a scoop on whatever it is you are doing for Latisha Maxwell." She sounded hurt. "I'm calling for payment."

I had no idea what she was talking about, but I had an awful thought that word of Harry's death had leaked and someone had made the connection between him and Latisha. Not good.

"What are you talking about? Has something happened?"

"You tell me."

"Come off it, Leah."

"Sorry, Zen. Sometimes my reporter instincts overtake my manners."

"That's okay. Look, there's nothing to tell yet. I'm still working on a case and it's all confidential, as usual. You know I'll call you as soon as I have something."

She was silent for a moment.

"So what prompted the call?"

"I saw your woman a few minutes ago. At the Beverly Glen."

"The hotel?"

"Yeah, she was with some guy in the Arroyo Grande." That was one of the city's better bar/restaurants. It had become quite the hip place for the in crowd. "They were having a, how shall I say it, heated discussion."

"Oh, yeah?" For not the first time, Leah's big ears and reporter's love of gossip were serving me well. "Did you overhear any of it?"

"Nah," she said, and I could feel her disappointment. Like a child standing over the spot where he has just knocked off the top of his ice-cream cone and it's melting away on the sidewalk. "Only that it was definitely some kind of argument. The guy was a real sleaze, though. Slicked back hair, ponytail, the works. Ugh."

"Where are you now?"

"I'm in the lobby," she said. "Somehow I thought you'd want to know."

"And you hoped I'd know what they were arguing about, right?"

Her silence was my answer. Job title aside, she was a reporter at heart.

"Don't worry, I won't forget you, Leah." I had planned on going by to see Nat, but had already pointed the Alfa toward the Beverly Glen Hotel, in hopes I could catch Latisha. "Now I really owe you one."

"Don't you forget it," she said and hung up the phone. No goodbyes either.

TWENTY-FOUR

It was just before noon, making the road to Beverly
Hills rife with lunch-hour traffic. I was happy not to see any
blue Mercedes on my back. Maybe they got what they
wanted from Harry. Maybe they had switched cars.

Both thoughts made me shiver.

Despite the traffic, I managed the drive to the hotel in
twenty minutes, pulling into its ivy-covered circular drive
with the rest of the luncheon crowd.

Renovated more times than the Gabor sisters, the Beverly
Glen Hotel has managed to retain the charm and glamour of
old Hollywood. Tucked in a quasi-residential neighborhood,
the Art Deco pink stucco structure had become a favorite of
the rich and famous who wanted a break from their adoring
fans. Its history made it a popular tourist spot, but it was so
hard to find that the regular Instamatic-camera crowd didn't
descend in droves. So much for maps to the stars.

It was a great place to hide, and for someone in my profession, it was worth knowing about.

I valeted the Alfa and arrived in the lobby bar dry-
mouthed and, I thought as I passed by a gilded mirror at the
entrance, looking the part of the hipster. Fortunately, I'd chosen black linen pants and a black silk shirt. Dressy, but casual. Quintessential LA garb.

The bar of the Arroyo Grande was starting to fill up when
I walked in and looked around for Latisha. It was a moment
before I spotted her, sitting by herself in a corner of the small
room.

She was paying rapt attention to the drink before her, a

short glass. She held it in her hand, swirled it around, took the smallest of sips, then returned to the swirling.

She hadn't seen me yet, so fascinating was her drink, and since the bar was closer to the entrance, I stopped and ordered beer. They didn't serve Anchor Steam, but I felt in the mood for something darker, so I got a glass of Guinness instead.

I watched her across the room, wanting to make sure she was drinking alone before approaching. There was also the weight of what I had to tell her. I didn't mind putting off the inevitable, even if it was only for a moment.

A few people went up to Latisha and extracted her autograph. One guy even tried to take a seat at her table, but she was clearly not in the mood for company. This was surprising in a room that seemed mostly full of Hollywood's young and hip—just Latisha's type, I would think.

I'd really come to like LA and found that a lot of the stereotypes about it were untrue. I loved the town's playfulness, a wide-open "anything goes" attitude that influenced everything from clothes to architecture. It was a tough town to meet people, but, like Cleveland and Philadelphia, it could be cruelly underrated. I'd spent a summer in New York and fell for the Big Apple as every young kid does, but although I'd get shot on both coasts for saying so, I truly believed that southern Californians and New Yorkers were more alike than either would care to admit.

Of course, the differences were huge. Here in LA there was a superficiality, bred from a wide-spread refusal to admit to the passage of time, that I despised. I found people here to be unable to deal with the ugliness of life with anything more than a talk-show host's pop psychology. Perhaps that's why people like Latisha and her ilk had achieved celebrity status. After all, they do say we get what we deserve.

I was looking around at the well-bronzed, terminally skinny and mostly sockless crowd drinking Zima and pricey tequila and talking about joining AA and being snubbed by David Letterman. There's an old joke I'd heard once about the difference between Los Angeles and New York City:

When a New Yorker says "Fuck you," he means "Have a nice day," and when a Californian says "Have a nice day," he means "Fuck you."

How true.

I was halfway through the rich dark beer when I decided it was time to interrupt the brooding talk-show host. I got one of what she was drinking from the bartender—a Wild Turkey on the rocks, which I thought quite suited the Southern girl that she was—and made my way across the room. She checked her watch as I approached, something she'd been doing frequently since I'd walked in. An appointment at the hairdresser?

"Please, I'm waiting for someone." She didn't look at me when I cast my modest shadow over her table. "I really don't have time now."

I put the drink down next to the one she'd been working on. It was nearly empty. "Not even for a trusty servant?"

I swear she registered surprise.

"Ms. Moses—"

"Zen," I reminded her. "Mind if I join you? I won't take up much of your time. After all, it's your time I'm working on."

She seemed to shake awake, the way people do when they are talking to you about one thing and thinking something entirely different. "Certainly, I'm sorry." She waved her hand à la Norma Desmond from *Sunset Boulevard*. "I really am waiting for someone. I only have a few minutes to spare, but I wanted to talk to you."

"About?" I sat down and leaned in to ensure just the two of us were privy to our conversation. Just in case a Leah or two was lurking in the background.

"Well, I was thinking I won't be in need of your services anymore," she said. "I must say I'm amazed you found my father. You are certainly a woman of your word. But as we discussed, that was really all I wanted to know."

"That sounds fair. But don't you want a final report? I did go to see him."

She shook her head. "To be honest, I've had second

thoughts. I'm glad he's alive, but I don't think I want to open all those wounds again. My mother was wrong, you know. You can't start over again. Y-y-you can't forgive.''

I was losing her again. She had that faraway look some people get when they are lost in painful memories they don't often think about, though they always weigh heavy enough not to be forgotten.

I knew about those things all too well. But I realized then that Latisha was the kind of woman who wore her emotions on her face, like a layer of Revlon. Hers was more refined than most and she often was able to cover her worry and pain and anguish, but she gave into it too easily and this made me very uncomfortable.

How she ever made it in television was a mystery to me. But then so were a lot of things about that living room centerpiece most people practically genuflected in front of every evening come prime time and often also all those hours in between.

I was getting a little ticked off at her attitude, which, it occurred to me, might be just acting.

"I understand." I tried to soften my words, letting her know I was about to say something important. "But there's something I think you ought to know."

She checked her watch again. "I really am in a hurry. Couldn't we finish this conversation later?"

"It's about your father," I insisted, wondering whom she was waiting for that would make her want to get rid of me and why she had paid me a lot of money to find someone she now didn't want to find. "He's . . ."

"Please. *Please!*" She added just enough volume to her low whisper that some heads in the rising din around us turned our way. "I am no longer in need of your services. Send me your bill."

"Fine," I said, grabbing a pen out of my pocket and writing, "Your father was killed last night," on the napkin that her drink had been sitting on.

I took her hand off the glass and pressed the folded napkin into her cold, wet palm. "Call me later if you want to talk about this. For all I know, you may be in some danger.''

She snatched her hand from mine and closed her hand into a fist. I walked away from Latisha and my beer.

The valet had ransomed my Alfa for six bucks and when I had paid up, I U-turned and parked across the street. I slumped into my seat and prepared for what I hoped would be a brief wait. I slid my pullout radio into its sleeve, slipped in Billie. I was in one of those moods. I reached under my seat for the box of Trivial Pursuit cards I keep there for the express purpose of killing time.

I waited an hour and a half for Latisha to emerge, but when she didn't appear, I finally decided to chance a return to the Arroyo Grande. The bar had cleared a bit, leaving only the professional drinkers and a few touristy-looking folks who should get points for finding the place. There was, alas, no Latisha.

I left the hotel a little dazed by my churning gray cells. It wasn't Latisha's covert departure that had bothered me so much as her apparent need to do so. Surely, this hotel was used to leading stars out with the minimum of interference. No, I would give good odds that Latisha had other reasons for slipping out unseen. I just wished I knew what they were.

TWENTY-FIVE

I was feeling uneasy on the drive back to Santa Mon-ica, and even the funky new Los Lobos CD I'd slid into my car player wasn't helping to lift my spirits.

I should have been pleased. I hadn't been asked to protect Latisha's father, just find him. And find him I had, hadn't I? A job completed. Right?

I wasn't going to convince myself that was all this was, no matter how many times I patted my own back. This is what getting shot at does to a person. I wasn't going to walk away from this case, even though I knew I should, even though I didn't much like the client, even though, from here on out, the bills were on me.

No wonder I was always broke. I wanted to kick my no-good, kind-hearted soul in the ass. I wanted to be cynical, Philip Marlowe cynical. I wanted to be able to shake my head, walk away and have a knowing laugh about almost getting my head blown off in a Mexican wasteland.

But I couldn't. Too nice, too easy, too fucking stupid.

The sky, which had been growing darker with every stop-light toward Santa Monica, opened up again and the rains spilled out, causing immediate flooding and washing down my windshield in sheets. It fit my mood.

I drove all the way back to town, weaving in and out of traffic like a madman, my hands clenching the steering wheel until they ached.

*   *   *

I pulled in back of Father's Office and took one of the two spaces out behind the bar, parallel to Nat's storage garage. I parked a little too close and had to slide out ungracefully, trying to keep as dry as possible.

I took my knapsack and pull-out radio with me.

There was a yellow "Do Not Cross" police tape on the back door, so I had to circle around to the front, torrential rains or not.

Nat opened the door after a couple of knocks. He had the cordless pinned to his ear and put a finger to his lips.

After a moment and a brief conversation I didn't bother to listen to, he clicked off and looked me over.

"You look like hell." He wasn't laughing, but his eyes were and that in itself lightened my heavy mood. At least someone was taking all this in stride.

Being back in the bar was a little spooky for me. I didn't need a shrink to tell me I was still struggling with my grief. I knew I was trying to put all those feelings about Danny and Sam and me aside to deal with at a time when things were clearer, when I could give some meaning to my cousin's death. But these were things I knew I couldn't regulate. I wasn't tough enough.

Sooner or later, I was going to break down in tears or haul off and deck someone who might or might not deserve it. I could only hope the feeling would hit me at a time when I could have the experience in private.

Nat, though, knew me better and reached out a hand to squeeze my shoulder. He didn't say anything. He didn't have to.

"Thanks, Nat," I said.

"How 'bout a beer?"

"Thought you were all out?"

He raised an eyebrow. "You ought to know me better than that."

"I should," I agreed, watching as he poured me a Jamaica Red ale, one of my favorite microbrews. It was a smooth beer the color of molasses that had a lively flavor just this side of bitter.

The phone rang as soon as he put the beer in front of me and I drew my hand across my neck—our sign that I wasn't taking phone calls. It obviously wasn't for me, as Nat took the phone and a beer he'd poured for himself back to his office.

Besides being the proprietor of Father's Office, Nat was also a local politician of sorts. He served on a couple of city commissions, generally hobnobbed with city officials, and was on a first-name basis with the mayor.

I rarely talked politics with him, but I respected his efforts to contribute to his community. The call obviously had something to do with official matters; I could hear intermittent mention of things like rezoning, off-site improvements, and building permits.

I went back to his office, leaned in, and quietly shut the door. He hardly noticed.

The police had yellow-taped the walk-in, too, putting a seal on the door. I looked at the warning tape stuck firmly where the door met the doorway and felt slightly offended.

It was like a silent message from Brooks. The guy didn't trust me. Imagine that.

Well, my friend Brooks was no fool. The good detective is always prepared. I reached into my knapsack for my Swiss Army knife and cut a neat slit through the seal. I sprayed both sides with a solution I'd gotten from a mail-order catalog and the adhesive came off like peeling paint.

The chill of the freezer washed over me and I shivered involuntarily. The sense of death and loss the room now held for me didn't help quell the goose bumps that tickled my neck and spine.

Here was one place I didn't want to be in for long. Nat still hadn't come out of his office and I hoped his call would last long enough.

I had every intention of making this quick. I flipped the light switch but nothing happened, so I fished in my sack for my flashlight.

Waving the tiny beam into the corners of the freezer, I felt as if I were still in the dark. I didn't know what I was looking for and I was convinced that if there was anything important to be found, Brooks and his boys would have discovered it already. But that inner voice of mine, the one that called out like a hungry child, was speaking to me.

I accidentally kicked over an empty keg. It tumbled over, banging so loud I nearly jumped out of my Nikes.

Nat opened the door and looked in, one hand on the cordless. He spoke into the phone and then clicked off, shaking his head at me.

"I should have known," he said, putting the phone on one of the shelves near him and rubbing his hands together. "So what are we looking for?"

"We are not looking for anything," I scolded. "Get the hell out of here. It's bad enough I'm breaking the law. You don't want to get involved in this."

For a moment he didn't budge. "I'm in this as deep as you," he was arguing, but it was halfhearted. "It's my bar, for Christ's sake."

I shook my head. "Please, Nat. Let me do what I have to do here. Please. Wait . . ." I said. "Tell you what. It would be helpful if you could keep a watch out."

He looked at me, still clearly unhappy, but shrugged anyway. "Now that I can do," he said.

When he left, the sound of the metal barrel clanging to the floor had pretty much subsided. But in the ensuing silence I heard something besides metal on concrete.

It was like a tire losing air and then a click, like the sound a baseball card makes when you put it in the spokes of a bicycle. Only this noise sounded so far away, it was barely audible. I waited, listening and holding my breath and feeling my teeth chatter. The sound was more regular now, had been all along. I just hadn't noticed it until I tuned in.

I waved the flashlight around the room, the beam glancing off the metal racks and kegs putting on its own laser show. I couldn't find what was making the sound, now keeping time in my head like water torture.

I saw it then, almost by accident, and knew immediately why the cops hadn't noticed it. At the back of the freezer a trio of fans whirred away, blowing the thirty-seven-degree air onto the kegs. When the beam of my flashlight passed over one of them, I could see a flicker of dark on every turn of the blades. With each pass came the slap of something on hard metal.

I reached up gently and felt around, standing on my tiptoes and feeling the temperatures begin to settle in under my skin. I felt something hard and plastic and pulled it down.

It was a tiny cassette tape, the kind used to store computer data, a rubber band holding a letter-sized envelope in place around it.

The envelope was covered in beer stains, was sealed, stamped and addressed, but its owner had never mailed it. He never had a chance.

I had the flashlight between my teeth shining on the envelope but nearly dropped it when I read to whom it had been addressed. There, under the narrow beam, I read it over and over again.

From the first to the last, it didn't change: It was addressed to me.

I left the walk-in and closed the heavy door, shaking off the chill. Nat came up behind me, but I had already tucked my find into my knapsack.

He watched in silence as I pulled out a sticker identical to the one I'd peeled off the door. I pasted it back in place and turned toward Nat, expecting a frown. Instead, he was smiling, shaking his head.

"You never cease to amaze me, Zen," he said. "Where did you get that?"

I reached into my knapsack and pulled out a pile of the stickers. Enough to invade every sealed-off police scene in all of Santa Monica, and still have some left to stick on the refrigerator. "Sometimes it's good to have friends in low places," I said.

"I wouldn't know." He winked back at me. The hurt he'd shown earlier had faded already. That was Nat. He didn't have the capacity or the patience to hold grudges, or any other emotion, for that matter.

"Look, Nat. I'm sorry. I just don't want to get you in trouble."

"Forget it, Zen. Sometimes I push too hard. So . . . what now?"

"I think I'm ready to call it a day," I told him. "Some things I gotta do and I'm beat."

"Will you be all right? Want someone to stay with you?"

In a big way, but I knew it couldn't be Nat. Not anymore. "Nah, I'll be all right. Thanks."

"I know that much."

We sat at the bar and finished our beers. Then I kissed Nat good-bye on the cheek and made my exit. It was still raining when I got outside and hurried back to my car with my head down, trying to keep myself and my radio as dry as possible.

The ocean breezes had whipped up and slapped a chill into the evening, that, along with the rain, made me think the walk-in might be more comfortable.

I was squeezing in between the driver's side and Nat's garage when two sets of hands grabbed me from behind and yanked me backward. I slipped on the loose wet gravel and heard the screech of my car radio, which I was still clutching in my left hand, as it scraped across the hood of the Alfa.

One of them slammed me up against the garage doors, elbowing me in the mouth, and I felt the heat of blood and bruises on my lip. Then he went to my ribs, the blows opening new pain centers in my gut and around the scars from my surgery. I coughed violently and got boxed so hard on my ears, they started to buzz.

I knew I was in trouble when a strange heat began to filter through my body, the cold rain the only thing that kept me from passing out completely.

Bobo had taught me well, but I was tired and hurt and a fog had settled into my head; I couldn't arrange my nerve endings to follow my instincts. So I leaned against the garage doors for support, searching for a handle on my senses again and taking too many blows in the process. For a moment the beating stopped, and I caught a glimpse of my attacker. A fullback. Short, squat, all muscles; no neck, no hair.

I was hot, but shivering, and when he grabbed at my neck again his hands were dead cold, his fingers like ice picks digging into my skin.

A lump of dry air formed in my throat, the flavor of beer mixing with the acid building up in my empty stomach and threatening to come up. The spooky warmth returned and I could saw a picture of me floating above myself winning over my hold on reality.

Rain and the bite of wind beat at my face. I felt the flimsy, slick plywood of the garage door behind me, and something else. It was cold. Solid. Metal. The handle in the still-closed grip of my left hand seemed out of a dream. But when I focused feeling on my fingers, I realized it was real: my car stereo.

I swung the heavy metal box, aiming for his legs, but it landed several inches higher.

He threw his head back and grabbed his crotch, staggering backward. His scream brought me back momentarily, and when he came at me again, I threw a head-butt in his direction. It connected, the hard part of my forehead with the soft cartilage that supported his nose. I lashed out wildly with the radio, and on the second pass nailed him on the side of the head. I could feel the dent it made in his temple, the crunch of bone.

He went down at my feet. "I hope *your* ears are ringing now," I mumbled through pain and confusion and a fat lip, as a tiny pool of liquid in my mouth dripped down my chin.

I bent over, sucking wind and gasping and choking and hacking up blood. Then I felt a sharp sting in my lower back. The last thing I heard was someone calling my name.

TWENTY-SIX

I was flailing in the water, a heaviness weighing down my arms and legs, a dull ache hammering inside my head. I was swimming upward, feeling the air pour out of my lungs, leaving a baseball-sized knot of pain in the middle of my chest.

I rose higher and higher, but the water got deeper and darker. I could see the surface, but the harder I swam, the farther it seemed to get. I could make out faces in the murkiness. There were Nat and Sam and Brooks and Harry and Latisha and Danny floating in the pool, spinning around and around, close enough to touch, but I couldn't bridge even the short distance between them and me.

Gasping for air, I turned and saw Danny hanging there, his face bloated black and blue, his features decaying. He reached out to me, his wrinkled hand dripping pieces of skin. He was mouthing something through his fraying lips, but I couldn't make it out. Something made me lean closer and an air bubble suddenly spurted out of his mouth. I realized suddenly we were both drowning. But when I motioned to him to swim to the surface he remained still, a look of pain and anguish on his face. I was failing him again.

I yelled at him to follow me, taking in gulps of salty seawater each time I opened my mouth. Finally, when I could stand it no longer, I set out for the surface. But my body was heavy and my breath was gone. We were both dead. I tried to scream, but the water rushed over me and I awoke gasping for air.

Whiteness. I opened my eyes to the glare of fluorescent

lights, the bright pattern of pimpled squares staring back down at me, surrounded by pocked, white acoustic tiles. Like me, the lights flickered every so often, as if they needed a rest from too much electric current.

The walls were white, so was the sheet pulled over me and the quarter-roll of surgical tape that I could feel, but not yet see, on my left side. Another scar, no doubt. And this one on my up-till-now pristine side, the one that had been undisturbed by my recent surgery.

That, and the rotting smell of antiseptic and mildewed laundry that hospitals reek of, reminded me of the eight days I'd spent waiting to be released after my operation. Something my nose would never forget. Now, every time I walked into a hospital, I felt like throwing up.

I wasn't really in a room, more like in a berth with a curtain dragged across to keep me separate from the rest of what I was sure was Santa Monica Hospital's emergency-room patients.

I could hear a baby crying somewhere nearby and the serious tones of a doctor probably breaking lousy news to someone. The low buzz of medical equipment, those goddamned lights, and the occasional beeps and hisses of the police scanner were the only other sounds. It was quiet time in the ER.

I lifted my left hand to check my watch, sending a dull ache into my side where the bandages were. It was a few minutes after one in the morning. I'd been lying here all evening.

Long enough for me. I got up on my elbows and swung my legs over the bed. I was still wearing my jeans. I tried standing. My head hurt, my side was sore, but I was obviously pumped full of some pretty good pain relievers, so I was fairly certain I could make it the few blocks home.

My shirt was nowhere to be found, but my leather jacket and knapsack were hanging over a chair in the corner. I took them both and peered out through the curtain.

There was a long doctor's station to my right, manned by a female doctor and a male nurse. Times, they were truly achangin'. They were busy with their work, paying no mind to me. I tucked my hospital gown in my jeans and put on the jacket, then crept down the hall and out through the ambulance doors.

I traded good-nights with the oblivious rent-a-cop outside and gingerly walked the half block to the Quality Inn on Santa Monica Boulevard, holding my hand to my side, as if I was keeping my insides from falling out. For all I knew, I was. They had a popular nightly karaoke special in the hotel bar and I knew it would be one of the few places in town where I would have no trouble finding a cab.

All I had in mind was going home and sleeping at least until the NBA playoffs started sometime around May, but the fog in my head was lifting and I felt well enough at least to retrieve my car.

It was still parked behind Father's Office and looked its shabby self, but even in the dim light of the street lamps I could see the nasty scar that my car radio had carved across the hood. A jagged line that reminded me a little of the way Mulholland Drive snakes through the Hollywood Hills.

I ran my finger over the scratch. It was deep, cutting through the red paint all the way to the metal. Would require a new paint job. Hell, so would the whole car.

I drove home slowly, trying not to move too much, but the effort of working the shift and the clutch at the same time caused pain in places I had no idea existed.

My house was still tidy—no one had yet violated my new security system. I slumped down in a chair and pressed the blue "play" button on my answering machine.

The first few were everyday calls from various creditors and someone calling to inform me of an unbelievable time-share offer in Vegas. I was certain the salesman was right: it was completely unbelievable.

Nat and Brooks called as well. Nat, who had no clue, to say he was surprised I'd checked out of the hospital and wanted to know if I needed anything. Brooks, completely clued in, was giving me hell for leaving without hospital permission. I couldn't tell if he was concerned for my well-being or mad he hadn't gotten a chance yet to interview me. Either way, I was inclined to take his advice and go back to the hospital.

But in between the two gentlemen and the time-share salesman was a familiar voice I didn't quite get the first time around. It was soft, feminine, and rushed. I had to play it back three times before I got the message down: it was Latisha. She'd called around 11 P.M., asking me in a quiet whisper to get over to her place as fast as I could. "You must come here at once," she said breathlessly into the phone. "Come to the house immediately. It doesn't matter how late. I'll be up."

I tried Latisha's number but got her machine again, so I called a dispatcher I knew who worked out of the Beverly Hills Police Department. There had been no calls to Latisha's neighborhood. It didn't exactly quell my concern, but I wasn't about to race over there either. Many a time I have been called to the aid of someone with enough money to think everyone owed them their undivided attention, even the cops and EMTs. Even small-time private detectives.

Still, I showered, pulled on a clean pair of jeans, basketball sneakers, sweatshirt, and my favorite black anorak.

I pulled into Latisha's cul-de-sac a little after 2 A.M. and got no answer when I buzzed from the driveway intercom.

I looked up at the house. It was dark, save a subdued glow of security lights on the front lawn. I backed out and found a spot to park beneath a strip of eucalyptus trees, and waited. Thirty minutes later, she had not shown. I should have left, but curiosity got the better of me.

Latisha's lot was at the center of the cul-de-sac, farthest from the intersection, which would make what I intended on doing a little easier. It was very calm, eerily so, as if somebody were in the background holding up a "Quiet, please" sign.

I thought I had remembered from my initial visit that Latisha's security was, if not lax, at least lacking, and I found my recollections more than accurate. There was a ten-foot wrought-iron fence around most of the property, except for closest to the dead-end side of the street. There, a swath of heavily shrubbed landscaping, roughly a yard and a half wide, stood between a waist-high chain-link fence and the entrance to the backyard.

It was rough going, the growth beneath me was a combination of ground-covering ivy and some kind of flower that kept catching the shoelaces of my Nikes. It was also very noisy in the dead calm of the night, like stepping on Styrofoam.

Normally, the fence would have been a simple hop for me, but I wanted to be extra quiet, and there was my tender left side to think about. I decided to scale it in two steps: pull myself up to sit on the top of the fence and swing my legs one at a time—slowly—over to the other side.

Once I got a good foothold in a link of the fence, yanking myself up was easy. But the top of the fence was narrow and slippery from all the rain. I was sore all over, so I had to do the maneuver almost in one move. I hit the ground harder than expected and lost my breath for a moment in a wave of pain and exhaustion.

I squatted, leaning against the fence for several moments, trying to right myself again as I listened for unpleasant sounds: humans, sirens, or dogs barking.

When I was reasonably sure I was alone among potential hazards in Latisha's backyard, I got up and made my way down the side of the house and around to the front door.

They had a typical alarm, the kind that summons a private security company first, cops second. I wouldn't know how to disarm it, but it appeared I didn't have to. The blinking green light indicated it hadn't been turned on.

Or it had already been disarmed by someone else, though I didn't see any obvious signs of tampering and there were no cars in the driveway. I was about to test my newfound knowledge of alarm systems, when I heard a buzz like a timer ticking off and several tastefully aligned halogen lights came on in front of the house, illuminating the perfectly trimmed lawn, the brilliantly colored floral landscape and me.

I quickly ducked into the shadows and rolled, not without a great deal of pain, onto my stomach.

After a few moments, when I was certain I hadn't been seen, I crouched and crawled my way round to the back of the house and easily jimmied the lock on the sliding glass doors. The pool motor was quietly purring in the background and the smell of chlorine settled in the air, a sour smell in my nostrils.

A shiver abruptly hit me, a strange chill teasing at my neck like a draft, a spooky thing at a time of night when the wind had died to a whisper. I shook it off, looking back at the dark water of the pool and feeling as if I was being watched. It was either the painkillers or my imagination, or a little bit of both.

I ducked into the house quickly, going through the dark living room to the front door, and peered out, again making sure I was alone inside and out. The whole process, from fence to foyer, took no more than eight to ten minutes. So far, so good.

The pile of mail on the table in the hallway was still there from my last visit, but it had grown larger. Half a dozen at least were from various credit-card companies, but other than that, nothing seemed unusual.

The lights were off and I used my flashlight to pave my way through the empty house. If Latisha was in the house, she was either a sound and trusting sleeper, or she was incapacitated. I hoped she was lost in dreamland.

I looked all over the house, which wasn't as big as I'd expected it to be from the outside. Upstairs were two big bedrooms, three smaller ones, two full baths and a covered sunroom, and in none of them was Latisha, or her sister. Or anyone, for that matter.

I went back down stairs, plopping down on the leather couch, puzzled. She could have left in a hurry, but then why not leave me a message *not* to come?

I was tired and in pain and the drugs were wearing off, but I wasn't one to squander opportunities and right before

me was a grand one. I started to make a search of Latish'a
house, hoping something would shed light on the woman's
recent behavior.

I crept back upstairs, and after going through the smaller,
well-appointed bedrooms, I inspected the two larger rooms.
One, I surmised, was Sara's, a simple French country design
with a wrought-iron canopied bed and a thick pine desk. It
was a spare room, not many knickknacks, a few stuffed animals, and what looked like a journal on the desk. It was
locked, but even if it were lying open I wouldn't have
touched it. Sara wasn't my client. Her things were none of
my business.

Latisha's room obviously was meant as the master suite
of the house. Unlike her sister's, this one had Latisha's im-
print all over it. The room was bigger than my whole house,
all windows and open space. A dark-stained wood floor was
covered in places by intricate Persian-like rugs scattered
about, purposely haphazard.

The ceiling was pitched in one corner and the canopied,
baroque poster bed and the wall-to-wall railway ties gave the
room two contrasting styles—kind of Victorian versus rustic.
At the time it seemed weird, as if the original decorator had
been fired in mid-design. But I'd recall later how this strange
bastard of a room would so remind me of its occupant.

There were several fine art paintings on the walls, one I
recognized as an original Frida Kahlo, a Mexican painter
whose life is said to have been much more exciting than her
paintings. Her work had become very hip recently, ever since
Madonna started collecting it.

She had two other works by lesser Latin American artists
I had heard about, but never liked. In the corner, however,
was one of my favorite prints. It was a stick figure of a man
with a skeleton's head, and a cane in one hand. He was in
mid-stride, walking across the painting with an ominous purpose. *La Muerte Camina*, or *Death Walk*.

There was an original oil hanging over her bed that also
caught my attention. It was an amateurish work, but its

subject—two young women sharing a laugh over a croquet game—was oddly compelling.

It was a moment before I realized the women were Latisha and her sister and the landscape around them Latisha's backyard. What the artist lacked in drawing talent he had had made up for in insight, catching Latisha as she stood a head above her younger, more fragile sister, appearing to demonstrate a croquet technique.

Latisha had one arm draped over Sara's back as the two were bending over a mallet, Sara's face turned back at Latisha, giving her a look of affection that could only pass between two siblings. It was a poignant moment, Latisha's almost motherly gaze and strong hand of support and protection and her sister's obvious and tender response.

I sat at the desk staring up at the juxtaposition of the Toledo hanging over it and the croquet painting on the opposite end of the room. I quickly rummaged through her desk, which was neat and tidy and mostly empty.

The bottom right-hand drawer was locked, but it would be an easy one to jimmy open. Fortunately, I always check the obvious first, and this time I was not to be denied. In a delicate ceramic dish shaped like a bunny rabbit I found the key underneath a pile of paper clips.

Inside was a folder filled with medical records for someone named Jane Bodoni Winchester, who had been under constant treatment for various psychiatric problems for the past six months.

According to the records, she had first been admitted to a private mental hospital in Century City after a violent episode where she "attacked her guardian and threw objects." From what I could surmise from the mumbo jumbo the doctors had scribbled down, she had some kind of repressed memory syndrome that had been brought on by an unnamed event.

Another Winchester? From her age, Jane would've been younger than Latisha by several years. It made sense, of course; there could've been three siblings. But in all the pictures I'd seen of the family, there were only two sisters.

The only other thing in the drawer was a sheaf of letter tied up with a piece of string, all addressed to Latisha's sister, Sara. They were all typed on what looked to me like a manual typewriter. The letters were long, rambling declarations of obsessive love from a sick and twisted mind.

I read them over quickly and was surprised to see Latisha's name mentioned a few times. The guy probably had a hard-on for both sisters. America, I'd learned, had no shortage of lunatics.

The letters were not signed and there were no clues as to where they had come from.

A light went on suddenly, stopping me cold for a moment. I listened. There was just the same silence of the night and I realized it was those damned timed security lights again, keeping faithfully to their silent schedules.

I'd been in the house no more than twenty minutes, but I was beginning to get jumpy. I grabbed one of the letters, shut the drawer and locked it again. After quickly checking the bathroom and Latisha's impressive closet space, I went downstairs and let myself out, exiting into the backyard.

Two green-yellow lamps were now shining over the pool—the backyard security lights that had just timed on—making me feel like a naked alien target in the artificial light. They gave the surface of blue water an eerie, surreal quality. It didn't help my nerves to see, in that new, weird light, someone floating, fully clothed, in the shallow end.

I went up close to the pool and looked down.

I was thanking myself for taking the precaution of wearing gloves when I'd made my search of the house.

I grabbed the straining net and with the pole end steered the body closer to the edge. My left side was pretty useless, the drugs having lost their effectiveness. After several long moments, with a dense sweat on my forehead and under my arms, I managed to flip it over.

I nearly stopped breathing as the corpse made a 360-degree turn, showing its front side long enough for me to identify the man I thought I had seen twice yesterday. The everyman look on his solid face was not so attractive anymore, due in part to a neat dark hole about where his right eye used to be. A heated pool certainly wouldn't have done much for his complexion, either, though at this point I'm sure he didn't care.

Behind me, I heard a loud pop. It was probably just a backfire or a fat squirrel breaking a branch. I didn't want to wait around to find out.

I stupidly took off running and, in the throes of an adrenaline rush, hopped over the fence, using my hands and arms as a springboard.

It was only when I landed, first on my feet and then spilling over to my knees and onto my ass, that I started questioning my sanity.

I managed to get my heart rate down to very, very, very fast by the time I hit the street and walked, oh so casually, over to the Alfa.

I slid into the seat, sweating and panting and battling off a strong desire to throw up, while at the same time I was trying to hold my left side from coming apart at the stitches. I willed myself to relax and pull myself together. After some moments of this, I drove off.

I waited until I was well into Century City before I dialed 911 on my car phone.

"I'd like to report a murder," I said, trying to sound like someone else. I gave Latisha's address.

"Can I have your name, please?"

I shut the phone off.

"Bad connection," I said.

TWENTY-SEVEN

I stumbled into my place a little after 3 A.M., feeling as if I'd been away for weeks. I felt my way through the darkened rooms, went straight into the bathroom and sat on the edge of the tub. There was a scarlet circle bleeding toward the edges of my bandage, and I set about trying to peel it off.

I heard the creak of the floorboards too late to do anything about it except turn toward the door and grab the nearest object I·could find. It was a bar of olive-oil soap.

But the shadow that appeared in the doorway was the familiar bulk of Bobo, a grim look on his face and a black duffel in his hand.

"Jesus, Bobo. Don't you ever knock? How'd you get by my security system anyway?"

"Always a way in," he said, tossing the bag at my feet. "Figured you might need some things."

"There'd better be a bottle of Scotch in here."

I leaned over, keeping my shirt, which was half off, from falling to the floor, too. With one hand I unzipped the nylon bag and dumped its contents on the floor. A couple of rolls of white medical tape, plenty of gauze, some kind of disinfectant, and a prescription bottle of Percocet.

I was too tired to laugh, but I flashed my old friend a smile anyway. It was always strange to find him reaching out to me like this because I knew him to be a man of very few words and even fewer emotions. The fact was that he felt things deeply. He just was able to put those feelings in his own specific places, deep, personal recesses he only called upon on the rare occasions he felt they were needed.

Beyond that I knew he had a code based on old-fashioned tenets like honor, loyalty, and family. I guess I was as close to kin as anyone to him and he took the responsibility seriously. It was not without a biting irony that I realized just then that Bobo was the brother I'd wanted Danny to be, and I guessed I'd been the sister to him I should have been to Danny. Now I felt sorry for holding that against him.

"Let me." Bobo was in the room, squatting down next to me, and helping to remove the dressing. He examined the stitches closely, poking a finger at the sore spots and making me flinch. "Hurts?"

"You could say that."

"Should've stayed in bed."

"Now you're my mother?" I winced when he touched another spot.

"Hell, you need one." He was still prodding my flesh.

"Ouch. That hurts; what the hell are you doing?"

"What the doc would've done if you'd stuck around a little longer. Checking for damage. You wanna hang on to that other lung of yours would be my guess. They was gonna let you go anyway."

I just shrugged at this. I didn't feel like making a joke, though the moment seemed to call for one. Plus I knew leaving had been stupid and that my friend was right.

He had a new bandage on my wound and made me take one of the pills. "You left these behind."

I swallowed one. I wasn't much for drugs, but the way my side was aching, I decided to make an exception. Bobo was looking at me as if he had something to say. Normally I'd let him take his sweet time, but I was so tired my eyelids were drooping.

"What?"

"You need to get to bed, girl." I let him help me into my bedroom. He turned away to let me slide the rest of my clothes off. Bobo the gentleman. If he weren't for real, nobody could make the guy up.

"So, Bobo," I said once I was comfortably between the sheets, "tell me what's on your mind."

He started to say something, but stopped and shook his head. "It can wait." I was going to say something, had formed the thought in my head and was waiting for it to come out of my mouth, but nothing happened. The last thing I remember is staring at his mismatched eyes and wondering why the blue one wouldn't stop moving.

When I awoke, Sassy, whom I'd forgotten in all the commotion, was purring loudly beside me. My clock radio flashed 9:30 A.M. in its irritating fluorescent green.

Bobo was sitting in the big chair in the corner of my bedroom, his massive hands flat on the armrests, his feet stretched out and his head rolled all the way back. His mouth was partly open, and even from across the room I could see his nostrils flare with the rhythm of his breath. It was almost comical.

He hadn't removed his gun, it was strapped into his shoulder holster. His T-shirt read: "Life's not a dress rehearsal."

I'd been lying on my back and felt the soreness of last night's fight in just about every spot on my body. I tried a gentle roll, finding any movement at all slightly easier than when I'd last had my eyes open.

I thought about it for a good fifteen, maybe twenty minutes before I gingerly raised myself up, pausing for a few moments to sit on the side of the bed and calm the movement in my head. Slowly I stood up and padded into my bathroom, a chunk of nausea rising up in my empty stomach. Thank God it was empty.

I supported myself on the sink and took my first look in a mirror. There was a broken line of red around my neck, in the pattern of stubby fingers like the hand turkeys I used to trace in grade school. My upper lip was swollen, a tiny reddish-brown scab sat in the middle and a mild blue bruise ornamented my right cheekbone. Other than that, the face seemed to be intact. The few broken hours of sleep had been good for me, and although I was drained of color, the lines and bags had receded around my eyes and mouth.

After showering I was greeted by the intoxicating odor of strong coffee and voices in the other room. Bobo must be peering in at a morning talk show. He was one of those people who couldn't bear too much silence. It made him nervous. I slipped on some jeans and a comfortable old white oxford shirt. The room was heavy with mildew and the rain had returned, pounding again over my head.

I went into my kitchen, getting a whiff of a muffin or something, along with the coffee. The TV was off, but the voices hadn't stopped. I recognized the other even before I saw Brooks sitting across from Bobo at my breakfast table.

The two men seemed like old friends, which partly pissed me off. It felt as if Bobo was a traitor. I scowled at them.

"Well, well, well," said Brooks, a funny look on his face. Was it concern?

I leaned against the counter, took a deep breath and managed, with considerable pain but only a very slight grimace, to lift myself up so my legs were dangling against the cabinet.

"Feeling better?" Brooks asked. Bobo was sitting back, watching the interaction of the two of us. I was going to have to give him shit for this later. He always said he was a born observer of humans and I would be the last one of them to contradict that, but I just wished he wouldn't practice on me.

He seemed to get the hint of my quick glare and got up.

"Gotta go," he said in his own special succinct manner. He almost grinned at me on his way past. I nearly kicked him for it, but the effort wasn't in me.

"So," I started after we heard Bobo shut my door. "You guys friends now?"

"You owe him a lot," he said and continued before I could say he was telling me something I already knew. "He chased that guy away before he could put more holes in your back. That puncture wound in your side, it was deep as hell. You could have bled to death in that alley, easily. He was there through the whole thing. He told me you're working on a case together. Lucky he was looking for you.''

"You mean following me," I said.

"What?"

"Nothing. You're right. Bobo is solid gold."

"You guys go back a ways?"

"You could say that," I said. "So, to what do I owe this visit, Detective?"

"Jonathan, remember?"

I nodded.

"You look like shit," he said. "What's the matter, no hospital insurance? They were going to let you go in an hour or so anyway.''

"I have this thing about hospitals, what you might call an aversion. If I'm hooked up to anything less than life support, I'm out the door.''

"I understand that's what you told the doctors last night," he said.

"I don't know what I said. I can't remember that part. I've felt worse, but I guess it comes with the territory."

"Are you really tough, or this some kind of act for my benefit?"

I just shrugged. Truth is I felt like I'd been stuck in the spin cycle for a week.

"Then nothing bothers you, huh? Man, you are something else.''

I didn't answer. I wasn't in the mood to dissect my psyche for him.

"The silent treatment?"

"Hey, give me a break here. I'm tired and I'm hurting and I have a big day ahead of me. Can we just get to the point here?"

"I'm just conducting an investigation."

"Conduct, then."

"Do you have any idea who those guys were?"

"I barely remember what day it was."

"You know it might have helped if you'd kept me informed."

"About what?"

"The Moses case, that's what."

"There's nothing to say."

"Somebody wanted to shut you up, or send you a message, anyway."

"Now, now, Jonathan. What would make you say that? I have other cases, you know." The thought certainly had occurred to me that the two guys had something to do with Danny's death, but I couldn't be sure. They could just as likely be involved with the other dead bodies I'd discovered lately.

Which made me think of Latisha. Surely, the guy in the pool last night had been after her. He had already taken care of Harry. But what he was after was beyond me. I was only hoping Latisha had managed to get away.

"Care to enlighten me?"

"On what? My other cases? C'mon, Jonathan. I know it sounds like I am deliberately being obtuse, but you know as well as I do that I can't tell you what I'm working on. Besides, you're the cops. How come you haven't got anything?"

He looked back at me, surprised and a little hurt. I was sorry I'd said it as soon as I had opened my mouth.

"Sorry," I said, though it barely filled the vacuum my comment had left in the air. "I'm, what can I say? I'm hurting and upset. Forgive me."

He nodded and just then his beeper went off.

"Can I use your phone?"

I pulled the handset off the wall where it hung next to my fridge. From where I was sitting, it was an easy reach. He passed by me and took the phone.

"I hope you aren't offended. Even though you are a pain in my ass, I'm glad you're all right," he said as he was dialing. "The guy you took down might give us some leads."

This was news to me. "You got one of them?"

"Man, you really are in bad shape." He stopped to say something into the phone and then cupped one hand over the voice piece. "One got away and the other, well, he's got 'SONY' imprinted on the side of his head. My guess is he'll be listening to his own kind of music for a while."

His look was one of real respect. "Man, using a car stereo as a weapon, that's fucking inspired. Where did you come up with that?"

"It's in the private detective when-all-else-fails manual," I said. "Under chapter heading 'SYA.' "

He looked back a question.

"Save your ass."

He broke into a belly laugh, which he quickly stifled. His demeanor suddenly changed and I could hear an excited voice on the other end of the phone. But before I could make out what they were talking about, Brooks took the phone into the other room, scratching a tuft of hair on his chin. Either he was cultivating a new beard or I wasn't the only one not getting much sleep.

I slipped off the counter and poured some coffee. It was good and strong, just as I liked. I said a silent thanks to Bobo. It was for more than the coffee.

TWENTY-EIGHT

It was a good five minutes before Brooks came back into the kitchen and hung up the phone, a serious look on his face.

"What?"

He just looked at me, shaking his head.

"Got a cell phone?" he started to look around the room as if one of those things would be lying around.

"Yeah, in the car. Why?"

He took me by the arm. "We're going for a ride."

"What? Now? I can't, I have things to do." But he was already dragging me to the door, and by his demeanor I could tell this was not something I could say no to.

"Don't you think now's a good time to go over some mug shots? Maybe I could identify one of my attackers."

"Later," he said, clearly miffed.

"Don't tell me I'm in trouble with the boys in blue again?"

"Now you're going to have to tell me," he said. "We got the whole ride to Beverly Hills to find out."

He said the Beverly Hills part with emphasis, as if it was supposed to tell me something. A hint.

"Wait," I said. "What's going on?"

"You should know," he said. "You're the one who keeps stumbling over dead bodies."

The *s* meant more than one. Oops. "Who's dead?"

"I thought you knew."

I hung my head. Latisha was merely a client and I didn't

even really like her, but if she was dead, that meant I'd failed her. Just like Danny.

"You look like you just lost your best friend."

"I, er, I knew her."

"Her? What the hell are you talking about?"

"Latisha Maxwell."

Brooks laughed. "Latisha the talk-show host? How close did you get to the body anyway? She's still alive. The body is a man. Fine detecting, Watson."

I thought my heart stopped for the briefest of moments and I actually felt a smile coming to my lips. "I misunderstood," I said. "I thought you said bodies, as in more than one."

"I did. There was that body in the bar, remember?"

I just shook my head and followed him out the door.

We were in his unmarked cruiser, a white Chevy. Neither one of us talking. He was waiting me out, but I wasn't about to make this easy on him. The whole thing was too hard to explain anyway.

I broke the silence. "So do you have anything on the guys who hammered me?"

He didn't seem to be in the mood for anything but what was on his mind, but he played along anyway. "Nope. Sony's still out."

"Is he going to recover?"

"Do you want him to?"

"Jesus, what kind of thing is that to say?"

"Sorry." And I could tell right away that he was. "The doctors think so. Just might take a few days."

Then we were quiet again and as I could see by the twitching of his jaw and the muscles pulsing on his neck, I knew he was stewing about something. The air in the car was heavy with his foul mood. Another time and place, I might have had a laugh at his expense trying to set him off, but now was the wrong time.

I couldn't stand the silence—even his police scanner wasn't making a hiss—so I flicked on his car radio, finding my favorite classic jazz station. Dinah Washington was in the midst of "What a Difference a Day Makes."

He glanced over at me.

"Not all black people like jazz," he said.

"I know, the others are busy playing basketball."

He tried another glare, but I answered by singing a line from the song.

"Everybody knows that one," he said.

"What would you prefer? Should I whistle 'Autumn Leaves'?" I mimicked an old-time radio announcer, " 'How about an old ditty from yesteryear,' " and, when the song ended, launched into "Blue Moon" over the radio deejay.

I hammed it up, sitting on the phrases like a bad lounge singer until I could hardly contain my snickers. I'd always harbored a fantasy to be a cabaret singer and still thought about it sometimes, ready to give up everything for a smoky hotel bar in New York, a red dress, and a piano. For now, though, I was like ninety percent of the rest of the world, singing at Christmas parties, in showers, and while driving down the highway.

"Okay, okay," he said. "So you know the standards. Must have had a lonely childhood."

"Not exactly," I said. "Just loved my dad's old seventy-eights."

"Know what you mean," he said.

We continued in silence. He had taken Santa Monica Boulevard and it was backed up. On the radio, they followed Dinah with a big-band tune and another, even older, thing from the twenties and then with Rosemary Clooney singing "When October Goes."

I sang along with that one, too.

"You'll never believe who wrote this song," he broke the silence.

"Want the lyricist or the composer?" I asked.

"Mmm. You're pretty good, but people ought to know it. It's common knowledge." He almost laughed.

"Once again, the mysterious private eye impresses the cynical cop," I said.

"Me? Cynical? Au contraire."

"Hey. I resemble that remark."

"Now *that* doesn't surprise me."

"Oh, come now, Jonathan. Don't tell me you have survived your years in blue as an idealist."

"Hell, everybody's cynical sometimes."

"Sounds like a slogan."

"You can have it. You've made it into an art form. No one can touch ol' Zen in the cynical department."

"Ouch. What's bugging you?"

"Lots of things."

"Like what?"

"Well, there's this late-night cell-phone call, for one. Then there's this nagging question, like why would someone who is cooperating with the police leave the scene of a crime and call it in anonymously?"

This didn't come as a surprise, but I wasn't sure I was going to be able to explain my way out of it. The funny thing was I'd left two crime scenes and broken into another, all in the last forty-eight hours. Zen's life of crime.

Shirley Horn was singing "Isn't It a Pity?" A sad song no matter how performed, but with her deep breathlessness Horn turned it into real deep-in-the-night music. The kind of sound you imagine comes out of those smoky after-hours jazz clubs that seem to exist only in old movies, the ones that attract both happy lovers and lost ones. In the overcast sky of the day and with the light groggy feeling that had settled into my bones, the music seemed to echo my mood.

Even Brooks seemed to be affected by it.

"Well?" He was waiting for a confession. I wasn't giving any.

"We have a record of your call, Zen," he said. "Why are you playing with me? Unless . . ."

"Unless I killed the guy?"

He looked at me.

"Now I know you don't believe that."

"You carry, I know that. You know how to use 'em. I've heard you're an expert."

"I don't use guns unless I have to," I said forcefully.

"Listen, are you going to charge me with something?"

"I should, goddamn it. You left the scene of a crime."

"I had my reasons," I said. "And while we're into the third degree, tell me something. Why is SMPD interested in a crime over here?"

"I can't tell you that."

"Touché."

"This isn't a joke, Zen." He said this through his teeth, a vein in his neck threatening to pop out right there. I felt bad not for the first time about putting him through this. But even if I could tell him everything, I was certain it wouldn't shed light on anything.

We had pulled into Latisha's cul-de-sac. A circle of reporters had gathered on one side of the street, kept behind wooden sawhorses by a line of Beverly Hills cops. I could see Leah in the foreground, chatting up some cop. I ducked down in the seat and Brooks smiled at my attempt to stay out of sight.

The gate recoiled across the driveway just as Brooks turned into the apron. There were cops everywhere as he pulled up to the carport. Latisha Maxwell's Ford Explorer was tucked under it. The Chevy was nowhere in sight.

He stopped the car. "Anything you want to tell me before we go in?"

"Off the record?"

"Oh, sure, why not?"

"It's important."

"All right, between you and me then."

"Maxwell is a client of mine."

"What did she hire you for?"

"I can't tell you. It's privileged."

"Great. I said this is off the record."

"I know, but I can't say more than that. I've already broken one rule by telling you who I was working for. I just wanted you to know why I was here last night."

"Just trying to cover your ass?" he said, not kindly. "I didn't know they had rules in your profession."

"I have them," I spit it back at him. For two people who

apparently liked each other and had a good deal in common, we were pretty good at irritating each other.

"Did she ask you to meet her?"

"Yes, she called," I said.

"And you met with her?"

"Not exactly."

He eyed me suspiciously. "Was she here at all?"

I kept silent. I'd already said too much.

"Did you see who killed the, er, guy?"

"Whoever he was, he was already dead when I got here," I said. "I didn't see anyone."

"Should I add breaking and entering to my list?"

"I plead the fifth."

Thankfully, he smiled.

I followed him, then stopped at the doorway.

"One more thing," I said. "The alarm was disengaged when I got here."

"How would you know . . . oh, never mind." He waved at me with his hand and I followed him inside.

Latisha Maxwell was sitting in her living room, perched on the edge of her white leather couch, in danger, I thought, of sinking into its cushioned depths. I looked around the room at all the absurdly soft furniture.

She looked up at Brooks and me, her slightly reddened eyes registering surprise when they passed over mine. I managed a wry smile. Brooks introduced himself.

"This is Zen Moses, a . . . ah, private investigator helping out with the case." His tact was appreciated.

"Actually we've met," she whispered, surprising me. What happened to discretion? She was dressed simply in black silk pants and a high-necked top with gold buttons down the front. I moved over to her; she was trying to tell me something, but I cut her off.

"I know this is a bad time," Brooks began, "but I need to ask you a few questions."

"Yes, of course," she said. "My manager and lawyer are upstairs. Do you mind?"

"You're welcome to have them here." Brooks was a charmer who, I noticed, was clearly aware he was talking with an attractive woman. I liked what it brought out in him. He managed to give her a once-over without leering. Talk about having the gift . . . Latisha was enjoying the attention. "But we're not interrogating you. Just a couple of questions."

"I'd feel more comfortable, Detective . . ." She waited for Brooks to repeat his name and then continued. ". . . Brooks. This whole thing has me rather shook up."

He nodded. "I understand."

She sent a small Hispanic woman I had not seen before to fetch her mouthpieces, and after a few minutes, they walked into the room, carrying suitably solemn looks on their faces. It was almost comical.

Latisha introduced us all around, surprising me by including me. Philip Sloane was the lawyer, a white-haired, diminutive guy who reminded me of a far less handsome version of Spencer Tracy. He had the authentic scent of old money: the tailored cut of his blue-gray suit, the suspenders exposed by his expanding gut and shrinking jacket, and the Foulard bow tie neatly knotted under his drooping jowls.

When we shook it was like touching a reptile. I shivered, hopefully unnoticed, when he gripped my hand with his rough flesh. He had to be somewhere on the far side of eighty.

Kay gave me the evil eye in that patronizing way I'd become familiar with, and greeted the two cops as if they belonged to the same gym. When it came to my turn I put my hand out, leaving him in a position where he had to shake or look like an ass. He let his hand drop to his side. Round one to Lar.

"Nice seeing you again, Larry." I winked at him and could see his fury building. What a jerk.

Brooks turned my way, but I just shrugged. He couldn't help smiling and I liked being the instigator of it. Of course, the distaste of keeping him in the dark only made me feel bad again.

As they all sat down, an extraordinarily well-dressed man walked into the room, his sleeves rolled up businesslike and his jacket under his arm. He had a badge clipped to his belt.

He appeared to be no more than twenty, but I was sure he was much older. His face was pale, milky-smooth, and he had blue-black eyes that could pierce ears.

"Detective," Brooks said, rising to greet the man, then going through the introductions again. When he got to me, the guy frowned, giving me a look of complete distaste. I didn't sense a dinner date from this one. "This is Detective Harold Lime, Beverly Hills PD."

"The Third Man," I said with a smile. Everybody looked at me as if I were drooling. "Harry Lime. The Third Man. That was the name of Orson Welles's character in the movie."

Lime just gazed at me. It was South Carolina Highway Patrol minus the aviators. "You mean nobody ever pointed that out before? Even in this town?"

"I'm new to the area," he said, his voice in the James Earl Jones range. "I don't really go to the movies. The name's Harold."

I was about to say something, but a glare from Brooks cut me off. I needed to be on his good side, so I kept my mouth shut.

"There's some cross-jurisdiction here," he said mostly to Brooks and the lawyer, who looked half asleep to me. "Detective Brooks will be running point. My department will serve as backup."

Brooks went through a list of questions with Latisha Maxwell and she patiently answered them. I stood and listened quietly in the background, having convinced the housekeeper that I was important enough to merit a cup of coffee.

"Where were you last night?" Brooks was asking.

"You don't have to answer that." It was the first question that got the lawyer's attention. I thought the old man had been taking a nap. I wasn't alone, everyone jumped when he spoke.

"She's not being charged with anything," Brooks said. "It's just routine." He looked from Sloane to Latisha. "You don't have to answer if you don't want to."

"That's all right," she said. "I can't actually say much, but I was handling a family emergency."

Now this was interesting.

"Can you give us any more information than that?"

She looked at the two cops, her lawyer, and, for a long moment, at me, then shook her head. She leaned over to Sloane and whispered something to him I couldn't hear.

"If it comes to it, we'll be completely forthright," he said. "But at this point, Mrs. Maxwell refuses to answer that question except to say she was forced to come to the aid of her sister."

"It was of a medical nature, the emergency," Latisha cut in, quieting her lawyer's protest by placing her hand on his knee. "I can't explain. You saw for yourself outside. The press can be so horrible. I don't want Sara's name dragged through the tabloids."

I found this enlightening, though not a bit useful for my case. I hadn't seen her sister around, which made sense if she was ill. But something else was bothering me and I couldn't quite get a focus on it.

Latisha claimed not to have known the body in her pool and that seemed to satisfy the cops. But while she did a good job acting as if we didn't know as much as we did about each other, I could tell by the way she caught my eye every so often that she wanted badly to talk with me.

I tried to keep focused on the moment at hand, putting her off with a look my father used to give me when he was in the middle of a conversation and I was standing nearby, bursting with something to tell him.

I had watched some tapes of her show that Leah had sent me and was getting a better feel for her mannerisms. Even magnified in only the way television can, they were obviously hers, no matter how affected they seemed.

She was in her public mode, the way she sat just a tiny bit slumped, the big white leather couch making her seem smaller, more vulnerable, one hand grasping a tissue and the other resting on the seat as if she needed it for support.

She was playing the room. And her audience was duly paying her mind. For not the first time, she made me think of Norma Desmond. How fitting then, to have found a corpse in the pool. Ah, Hollywood.

TWENTY-NINE

When Brooks was through with her he let Lime in to
ask some questions of his own and beckoned me to a quiet
corner of the room, near one of her shelves of gadgets. We
were standing by the room-wide glass door, the pool in view,
a yellow strip of police tape now reflecting off its surface.

The sun had poked through again, but only enough to cast
bright spots on her yard. It was the kind of light that might
form a rainbow over the Hollywood Hills. I wished I could
go find one.

"Looking for something?" It was Brooks catching me
glancing upward.

"My pot of gold," I said.

"What?"

"Nothing." Brooks had the Tavern puzzle in his hands
and was working his way through it, trying to pull it apart
with brute force. What was it with men and those things?
Too much testosterone? I didn't have the heart to tell him
he wasn't getting it.

"Ever see one of these?" He waved the puzzle at me and
the click-click made me think of ghosts dragging chains. Zen
getting morbid.

"Yeah," I said.

"I forgot, you've been here before." He almost smirked,
but held back. "Don't suppose you know how to solve it."

I nodded. "What's the fun if you don't figure it out yourself?"

He was tugging harder at the horseshoes, trying to separate the center ring, and it looked like he might actually do

it. I reached out my hand and he handed it over.

I was about to show him the secret when Latisha walked over to us. Her look was clearly directed at me. To his credit, Brooks once again caught on even before I did.

I followed her in silence as we weaved around the remaining cops to poolside, near where I'd found the body. It was creepy to be standing there, but if she felt the same way she didn't let on.

Instead she stood looking at the water for several moments, deep in thought. I let her be. Kay, as usual, was nearby, lingering a few steps behind us.

"I suppose you are wondering what happened last night." She was looking everywhere but at me, I noticed.

"You could say that," I said. "You left me hanging." With a corpse.

"I didn't know he was dead."

"Excuse me?" Her words had stopped me. Up until then, I'd thought she wasn't near her place last night.

"It's not like I killed him," she said. "My housekeeper called me. She was on her way home when she saw him pull into the driveway. She called me when she got home."

"She knew him?"

"He's been to the house a few times, mostly when my housekeeper has been here," she said. "She doesn't understand much English, so she has no idea what he wanted. He came by once when I was home but I refused to let him in. He gave me the creeps."

"You didn't ask who he was?"

"I did. I just didn't believe him. He said he was a friend of my father's and wanted to pass on some information to me. I, of course, told him my father was dead and that he must be mistaken. He got a little upset, said he would be back. I don't know why, but the way he said it scared the shit out of me."

"You didn't call the police, I suppose?"

"What for?" she asked. "What would I have told them?"

"The same thing you told me just now," I said. "Maybe

they wouldn't have done anything, but at least there would have been a record of it.''

"It didn't seem that serious,'' Kay said, moving closer to us. "Not worth getting people involved in.''

"I guess you mean the press,'' I said. "You spin guys are all alike. Weren't you at all worried about your client's safety?''

He shrugged. "We get enough hate mail and threats every week to fill your living room,'' he said, a bit indignant. "It was handled appropriately. And anyway, after that, he didn't come back.''

"Until last night,'' I said. "Raise your hand if you know how he ended up with a hole in his head in this here swimming pool.''

Neither made a move. "No volunteers, huh? That's just great,'' I said. "Why did you call me?''

"I panicked. I didn't know who else to call.''

"The cops, remember?'' I said. "But no, there was the press to consider. That the same press in front of your house and hovering over our heads?''

"You don't understand,'' she told me.

"That doesn't matter, Latisha. You should've told the cops.'' Like me, I thought, not without a good dose of sarcasm.

She shot a glance at me that, if looks could kill, I'd be pushing up daisies right where we stood.

"I had my reasons for not saying anything now,'' she said. "And nothing's changed.''

She was starting to piss me off again. "Well, I can say something,'' I hissed back at her, pointing at my chest for emphasis. "I'm the one who found the body. I'm the next person to be questioned here.''

She waved me off. "That's your problem. I'm sorry you were put in a bad position, but it couldn't be helped.''

Kay jumped in. "You can't say anything anyway. Even private detectives have to respect client confidentiality. I recall you said as much in our first meeting.''

That's the second time that day it was implied that PIs

were supposed to be loose in the ethics department. I was going to have to find a support group. PIs Anonymous.

I kept my eyes on Latisha. She was still looking for something to focus on. Anything not to look at me.

"You fired me yesterday. Remember?" I said.

Kay shook his head. A negative.

"What? Did I misunderstand you?" She was still trying not to look at me and I grabbed her wrist. Kay made a move toward me, but I put my still-bruised and scratched hand in his way. He stayed put, to my surprise. Maybe he wasn't as dumb as he looked.

I turned back to Latisha, still clutching her wrist. She was fighting, but it was halfhearted. We were far from the milling cops' carshot, but I didn't want to draw any attention. I leaned toward her and tried to bury my rising rage between my teeth.

"Does 'I'm no longer in need of your services, send me the bill' mean you're actually keeping me on? Is the earth flat? What the hell is going on, Latisha?"

"I'm so sorry," she said triumphantly, pulling her hand out of my grasp. I let it go. "I can't recall seeing that final bill. I suppose you haven't gotten around to posting it yet." She gave me the smirk Brooks had kept hidden, amplifying the differences in style and maturity between the two of them. It made me feel even worse for treating Brooks so badly.

She turned away, dabbing her face with her well-worn tissue, as if she was putting on a show for whoever might be spying us. Kay stepped in between us, putting his arm around her. She hugged herself as if trying to fight off a chill. Despite the recent trend, it was almost shirt-sleeve weather, warm for December.

Technically, Latisha was right. She was still my client until we had a paper saying otherwise. I wasn't happy about it, but there it was nonetheless.

"There's one more thing you should know," I said. "The dead guy. I think he murdered your father. I saw him there that night."

She seemed genuinely surprised, so much so that she took a step back. "No." She said this quietly. No tears, no sighs, not much emotion at all in her uncharacteristically vacant eyes. She looked at the pool and I followed her eyes, looking for answers in the depths.

It's amazing sometimes how water, like fire, can be so mesmerizing that it seems to be hiding something important.

Latisha was still shaken. Kay tried to comfort her again, but this time she pushed him away. "Please, Lawrence," she said, whispering something into his ear I couldn't hear.

He looked at me, then back at Latisha, then back at me again, before reluctantly moving away. The way he showed his teeth at me when he passed, he could've been a dog protecting his territory. A big dumb one, no doubt.

I waited until she regained her composure. "Why was your father killed?"

"I don't know, I don't know," she said.

"You must know something."

"What do you want from me?" She seemed exasperated and preoccupied all at the same time. It was quite the feat.

"The truth would have been nice."

"I've told you all you need to know."

"What did your father do to you to make you run away?"

"None of your goddamned business," she snapped. Then the violent lines on her face softened, leaving the old Latisha staring into space. "I just wanted things to be right again. Now it's all ruined." She was drifting off again.

"Well, you're on your own," I said. "You will have my final bill this afternoon."

"Fine, fine," she said. She was still in her ethereal mode, as if she were floating. It was eerie and somewhat disarming.

Suddenly she threw her hand up and cried: "My bougainvillea." There was a commotion across her yard by the fence I'd hopped over the previous night.

Several LAPD cops were standing knee-deep in the green and red foliage lining the edge of her yard. One of them held a shiny metal object in his gloved hand.

Though caked with mud and debris, it was clearly a handgun. It looked a lot like my missing Walther. Despite the grime, the low-light cloud covering made the shiny stainless-steel weapon practically glow.

Latisha suddenly found an interest in her shrubbery and seemed to forget about me. I guessed my audience was over. I waited long enough to watch her cross the yard and engage one of the cops in conversation before I casually walked back around the house.

The press corps were on the other side of the street, and when I was certain no one was watching, I cut across and found Leah leaning against one of the barriers.

She started to say something, but I put my finger to my lips, grabbed her arm and pulled her down the sidewalk. "Where's your car?" I whispered. Behind us, some of her colleagues were slinking forward, sensing a story. I thumbed back at them and gave Leah the "cut" sign. She understood completely, turning quickly and putting her hand up.

"Back off, fellas," she said. "She's just my mother's cousin."

I could hear a couple of beefs and someone mentioned my name, but even they had enough decorum to stay back. Leah's reputation commanded it.

We quickened our gait; I could see Leah's blue Honda Accord at the end of the block. She started whispering questions in my ear along the way, but I waved her off.

We got in the car and Leah put the key in the ignition, but didn't turn it over.

"What are you waiting for?"

"We're not going anywhere until you tell me what's going on." She was pouting. "I've been out here all morning and they won't tell us anything."

"Just drive, Leah. I'll fill you in later." She looked doubtful. "Look, if you don't go *right* now, I might be telling you this story from behind iron bars. It might make a great story, but by then it won't be an exclusive anymore." This seemed to get her attention and we left Latisha's block in a hurry. Two minutes later, we were speeding back to Santa Monica, the Honda lost in the crunch of lunchtime traffic on Sunset Boulevard. I stared out the window, thinking of dead bodies in swimming pools, broken families, the ache in my side, and a missing handgun. Life, it seemed, had taken a turn for the worst.

THIRTY

I swore Leah to secrecy with yet another pledge to let her have the story when I was able to hand it over to the Fourth Estate and told her as much as I could without compromising my ethics.

I even told her the most damning thing of all—that the gun they had fished out of Latisha's designer shrubbery was my stolen Walther.

"Are you sure?" It was the first time she had said anything since I began the story. We were parked on my street a few buildings down from my place. I was paranoid, and for good reason. Seemed that the cops were about to join with the mob in pursuit of me. I guessed I'd won the jackpot.

"It could just *look* like your gun, you know."

I shook my head. "Even from where I was standing, I could tell it was mine. I don't know why, I just knew."

She shook her head, crinkling her brow.

"Something wrong?" I asked.

"Besides that country-club mobsters are on your tail for something you have that you don't know about, that cops from at least two jurisdictions are likely to put out a warrant for your arrest anytime now, and, to top it off, that you look like your cat after his accident? You mean, besides all that?"

I nodded, managing a thin smile at her attempt at levity. That's what friends were really for.

"Actually, yes." She was serious again. "Something is bothering me. You would see it too if you weren't so close to it."

"I give." I was feeling tired and slumped down in her

front seat. A drizzle began, and tiny, silent raindrops started covering her windshield. The car smelled like a combination of all the cars I'd ever been in—part mildew, part the particular odor of heat-stroked vinyl and plastic and the remnants of that dirty-sock smell that pours out of air-conditioner vents when you first turn the cool air on.

"It's all too neat, as they say in the movies," she said. "If I had an imagination, which I don't, according to my shrink and my mother, then I would think someone was setting you up."

"You're the second person to say that. But who and why?" I said. "I mean, sure, you could make it work with the guy in the swimming pool, assuming he was murdered with my gun, but the couple in Mexico . . . unless . . ."

"Unless they were killed by your gun, too. Just like your boy in the swimming pool."

"Jesus, Leah," I said. "This is not good. Not good at all."

"What are you going to do?"

"Get out of town," I said, reaching for the door handle just as the sky opened up again.

"You can't run." Her look was sisterly. As far as I was concerned, that's what she was to me. "That's ridiculous, Zen, and you know it."

"I know, I know." I patted her hand, which was resting on her well-worn stick shift. I realized then how lucky I was to have the small, but very loyal and loving circle of friends that graced my life.

Latisha seemed to know this in a strange way I was only now beginning to make sense of. It was what she seemed to cling to. It was evident in the photos she kept in her house and the painting she'd hung over her bed.

It seemed Latisha had missed her opportunity, whether it really existed or not. I didn't want to miss mine.

"Can you write with what I gave you?" I said. "I know it wasn't much."

She nodded. "Are you going to tell me what you're up to or just run back into the night as usual?"

"This thing is personal, Leah." And it was that and more. "I've got something I have to do that I've been putting off."

"You're going to have to face up to the cops sooner or later, you know."

I climbed out of the car and into the downpour, using my leather jacket to shield my head from getting soaked. I had to yell through the rain so Leah could hear me.

"I have to face something else first."

I swung her door shut and hurried across the street to my house, detouring through my neighbor's yard, a private detective with a purpose.

THIRTY-ONE

All was quiet inside my house, though when I looked out my living room window, I could see a dark Mercedes parked across the street. I hadn't seen it a moment ago, which meant the occupants, if they were still in there, had probably not seen me yet. Coming by for a gander, no doubt.

Maybe they were just waiting for the rain to stop.

Sassy was curled up asleep between my bedspread and sheets. I could see her shape and the quiet rise and fall of her breathing under the covers. It seemed like the sanest place to be at the moment.

I poured myself a cup of coffee from the little that was left over from that morning.

I took a cigar out of my humidor, noticing that my stock was getting low. I'd found that the size of my cigar supply was roughly tied to the level of stress in my life. The more stress, the more cigars I smoked, and vice versa.

I picked a Gloria Cubana out of my collection of robustos, which were short, wide cigars. My friend called them doggie walkers because one would last just that long.

I left a message with Bobo's state-of-the-art paging service that probably made no sense to the operator who took it, but would be crystal to Bobo. We always had our own way of communicating.

It was just then I remembered that I still had Danny's envelope and tape in my knapsack.

It had been a long time, but the writing was clearly familiar to me. Danny's messy scrawl had always been a joke around the house. My dad used to say he should be a doctor because nobody could read their handwriting either.

I held it in my hand for a moment, this last concrete link between Danny and me, not wanting to rush. In all likelihood, whatever was inside represented what would have been our first conversation in more than dozen years. Now I knew with certainty it would be our last.

There were many things about Danny that stood out in my memories when I thought about him, and a lot of them were vignettes I'd rather forget. But just then, sitting in my living room, worried about the trouble I was in and hypervigilant about the trouble that might come knocking at my door at any second, I was thinking how much alike we were, how important he was to me and how much I really missed him.

Whatever it was that linked my father and Sam and Danny and me was stronger than even I had realized, perhaps even more than any of us had been willing to give credit to. And in the end, that was probably our biggest sin, one we were still paying for, both the living and the dead.

Of course, the living were lucky; we could still do something about it. We couldn't go back in time and change what had already been done and we certainly couldn't make the pain go away, but we could ease it and we could make a difference for the time together we all had left on earth.

You had to start somewhere. I ripped open the envelope.

THIRTY-TWO

*If I was expecting some magical revelation, some in-*sight into my cousin's last days, perhaps a critical clue from the grave, it wasn't obvious when I pulled out the envelope's contents: a well-worn sheet of paper that looked as if it had been rescued from the garbage and uncrumpled. It was a letterhead; printed across the top was: "High Cliffs Ranch, Pescadero, CA. FOR INNER PEACE AND THE PERFECTLY RE-ALIZED BEING."

On it was a brief note in Danny's hand, though from the sharp lean of the script and the way some of the words were almost attached to each other, I could tell it had been written in haste.

Dear Zen:

    If you're reading this, I'm probably dead for real and I'm sorry I couldn't tell you everything in person. There was a lot of shit going on back then. I had to do what I did. You must believe me. There was no other choice. When it all comes out, I know you'll understand. I pray you will.

    All I can do is say I'm sorry. I wanted so much to be with you and Father again. It's so unfair. But I made mistakes and if I've learned anything in my short life, it's that you have to own up to your responsibilities.

    I can't say much more. They're on to me and if they get this . . . I don't want them to get it. The truth is there. It's hidden, but it's there. You're going to have to look hard for it. If anyone can find it, I know you will.

This tape is very important.

I always loved you and Dad. There hasn't been a day when I haven't thought about you both and what might have been. I was mad at you back then, but I didn't do this to cause you more pain. I did it because you were right. I hope you'll understand. I'm sorry for the pain I caused.

"Let these matters that I command you today be upon your heart. Teach them thoroughly to your children and speak of them while you sit in your home, while you walk on the way, when you retire, and when you arise."

Sei gesundt,
Daniel

I wiped away a tear, not yet ready to cry my eyes out. I didn't know what the quote meant nor why my cousin had chosen to close his poignant note with it.

I picked up the tape, turning it over in my hands. I'd need the right equipment to read what was on it.

High Cliffs Ranch. Words I hadn't heard in years, hadn't ever wanted to again. It was the exclusive commune where Guru Tama Tai catered to his well-heeled flock, contemplated his next grand vision for finding the perfectly realized person inside us all, and made, according to some unconfirmed press accounts, a shitload of money.

No one had yet nailed down the amount or the source of the Guru's wealth, estimated on the right side of a billion dollars, though plenty had tried. The Guru had powerful followers, including the head of one or two *Fortune* 100 companies, but his major base of support was among the Hollywood elite. All that juice could be quite the insulator.

Tai's commune had not been the only one targeted by government investigators, but it turned out to be the most difficult to infiltrate. All kinds of horror stories came out of the place: alleged slave labor by Tai's faithful, curbed freedoms, and enforced rituals, from strict water-and-bread diets to arranged marriages.

The suicide of thirteen members of his flock should have opened at least a small hole in the Guru's Teflon coating, but if everyone knows you can't fight city hall, imagine fighting the money that had built that very city hall you were up against. Tai had constructed his own city southwest of Pescadero, a small town with a mayor and one high school and a nice, touristy downtown named Tamaville.

But the Guru had safely ensconced himself behind the wall of religious freedom and battled authorities in northern California for years to retain his status as a religious institution, thereby paying no taxes. He had won enough rounds to earn a reprieve from the government auditors, but nobody would have been surprised, least of all the Guru himself, if state officials came back tomorrow for another round.

I was beginning to think Sam was right after all, and that the only way I was ever going to find out what Danny had been up to was to find out where he'd been.

That meant, of course, going back up north, to the place I least wanted to go, but probably most needed to be. Danny had left me no other road to follow, nowhere else to go.

The phone rang and I waited for the machine to pick up. It was Bobo telling me he was on the way and not to worry.

"What, me worry?" I said, picking up the receiver.

"You'd better, girlfriend."

"Why's that?"

"Heard you might make the hour's Most Wanted list."

"Shit, already?"

"One of us knows what's going on."

"You don't want to know," I told him. "Just come get me. I'll explain later. And, Bobo . . ."

"I'll call you from the phone booth on Pico." He'd read my mind. "Cut through the pet park. Be there in fifteen."

"You mean the cemetery."

"That's what I said." He rung off. Sometimes a man of

few words was good to have when you were in a hurry.

I checked my watch and called Sam. He answered on the first ring, his voice anxious, on edge.

"It's Zen," I said. "You okay?"

"Are you? I was worried."

His concern was sweet and I should have welcomed it, but my stubbornness surfaced again and I couldn't help feeling a little annoyed. I tried to hide this.

"No problems," I said. "Just the usual. Same shit, different day."

He laughed, but his cautious and placating tone only reminded me of his distress.

"So," I said, filling in the empty gap of our conversation. It was as if we were talking again for the first time, jockeying like two prize fighters feeling each other out before the first punch. "What's up? Sorry I didn't get back to you. Things have been hectic."

"That's okay," he said. "I just found something you might be interested in."

Just then the doorbell rang and I nearly had a heart attack. No way it was Bobo. Probably wasn't the mailman either. Even Sassy, who had come out of the bedroom to sit in my beat-up easy chair, wasn't waiting around to find out. On the second toll of the bell, she was scooting back to her spot underneath my bedspread.

"Sam," I whispered, "someone's at the door. I gotta go. Bobo's coming by. We're on our way to your place just as soon as I can get out of here. Can you wait?"

"Of course," he said. "Will you be all right?"

"Don't worry." I hung up the phone, grabbed my knapsack and Danny's computer tape and headed into my bedroom, where I quickly stuffed it with some clothes and a few other things I thought I'd need later.

I heard the doorbell again and then some knocking, followed by a muffled female voice calling through my door. I stopped to listen.

"Ms. Moses? Are you there?" The woman's enunciated tones hit me in pieces until I began to put a name with the voice. I almost laughed out of relief. I sneaked up to my front door to look out the peephole: there on the stoop, standing under a red umbrella, was a very staid, very businesslike woman who could only be Marcia Atwood, my friendly neighborhood IRS agent.

She was right on time for our scheduled appointment, proving that some people could actually be in the right place at the worst of times.

It also put me in a bit of a quandary. Poor Marcia was not only getting soaked, but was possibly in harm's way if the guys in the blue Mercedes decided this was a good way of getting to me.

I peeked through my front window blinds at the Mercedes. One of the doors opening made my mind up for me. I pulled out the Walther, flicked the safety off with my thumb, took a deep breath and in one swift action opened my front door and pulled a stunned Marcia Atwood into my house.

She was about to say something, but I held my finger to my mouth and shook my head. "Trouble." I pointed toward the door behind her and mouthed the words. "Men. With guns."

"Come," I said, leading her to the back of my house and making her leave the bright-red umbrella behind. I punched my code into the keypad at the back door, took another good, long, deep breath, and flung the door open, setting off the blare of my alarm, which even in the steady rain could probably be heard clear across Santa Monica.

Marcia, like a few million other white-collar employees of her gender, was not wearing the kind of sensible shoes necessary for things like running away from gun-waving mobsters. But her knee-high, stacked-heel boots wouldn't slow her down too much, either.

She was a small woman with red hair, pale skin, and wet green eyes that twinkled like sparklers. She was dressed in a dark pinstriped skirt suit and a shiny white blouse with a bow at the neck. Right out of a Talbot's catalog. She wasn't a kid anymore, but seemed stout and had more than kept up with me as we stumbled down my back stairs. Maybe it was the fruit of a daily exercise regimen or maybe it was just the heavy thud of footsteps somewhere close behind.

The lock I'd left on the cemetery's back gate was luckily still there and I used my key to open it. We were just through when the shots started, muffled pops in the rain.

I went to the ground, pulling Marcia with me, but she was reluctant to sully that nice suit of hers. I nearly had to yank her arm off to get her out of harm's way.

The ground was thick with mud and we were both soon covered with a good deal of it. She wasn't real happy, but then again, we were both still breathing, and that was worth a helluva lot more than the suit she was wearing.

The rain was still coming down pretty hard, but for once I was happy for the cover it gave us. Soaking and dirty and using the headstones for cover, we began half-stumbling, half-crawling to the other side of the graveyard. Unfortunately for us, the markers in the center of the cemetery were mostly small and modest. Had it been a sunny day, we would have been dead meat.

Over my shoulder I saw our pursuers had gotten through the locked gate. They looked a little out of place, with long black raincoats covering their designer suits and hats—one wore a fedora, the other a baseball cap, with the brims pulled down over their faces.

We were still moving, but the going was slow and treacherous and we were trying to stay out of view. Baseball cap saw us suddenly and waved his weapon in our direction, firing off a couple of shots. I fired my own back, the recoil almost making it slip out of my wet hands, but I couldn't see for shit and doubted I'd hit anything. Probably, I'd just put a nine-millimeter hole in some poor Schnauzer's epitaph.

Marcia was in front of me and I pushed her to move faster, though I knew she was probably doing the best she could. We were almost across when the heel of her boot caught on something and I collided with her, pushing us both to the ground. When we scrambled back to our feet, our pursuers were closing fast enough to make me think we weren't going to make it to Pico in time.

I turned to see fedora pointing an AK47 our way and saw our only protection was in the form of the cemetery's most ostentatious marker. I grabbed Marcia and flung her toward the ground with me, rolling us to a stop behind the black granite stone, the spray of automatic fire whizzing by above us and cracking like thunder into the headstone, yet harmlessly pinging off.

The rapid fire stopped and the rain was beginning to let up. I cautiously peeked around the four-foot-high marker, which had a tasteful line drawing of the deceased on the front (a floppy-eared mutt named Archie) and the outline of a dog bone carved on top.

The boys were still looking for anything that moved. I thought of firing at them, but it would be impossible to hit both at once. If I got one, or worse, missed completely, it would only start off another barrage.

I turned back and sat on the ground, leaning against the stone. There in front of me I saw a way out: a short, clear path to the cemetery's main building. It was only about fifteen yards, a mere hop to clearing the open field of the graveyard and getting to busy Pico Boulevard on the other side.

I gestured to Marcia, using hand signals to explain my plan, and though she looked doubtful, she nodded agreement. We sat up on our haunches. I silently thanked Archie for his help and picked up a stone and tossed it toward another group of taller headstones toward our left.

No accounting for intelligence. They concentrated another burst of fire in that direction. I was thinking those two boys out there didn't watch enough television as we scurried, bent over and shielding our heads with our arms, around the building. We didn't stop until we were out the front gate and into Bobo's Range Rover.

For once, he didn't give me any guff about messing up his leather upholstery.

THIRTY-THREE

"Ms. Atwood, I presume?" **We were both in the back** seat, looking as if we'd been contenders in a mud-wrestling contest. The graveyard and our pursuers were disappearing quickly behind us, Bobo giving his truck as much gas as she'd take.

Marcia was getting her bearings back and started giving me the third degree. I let her rant for a minute and then put my hand on her muddy arm.

"I'm sorry," I said. "I never plan these things. I'm a private detective. Shit like this happens and I'm sorry you were brought into the middle. I didn't want to leave you on my doorstep to fend for yourself."

She seemed to consider this for a moment, looked herself over, fingering a tear on the lapel of her ruined suit. Then she started to cry.

I put my arm around her and told her I'd make good on her lost clothing, which seemed to placate her a little. I got her address, which was in Playa Del Ray, near where Sam lived, and told her we would drop her there.

"You can get your car later, when it's safe. Or, if you like, I'll have someone drive it to your house," I said. Although she had regained some of her color, she still had that rumpled, half-crazed look of someone who has just had a shock. Getting shot at can do that to a person. Truth was, I was trying pretty hard to keep from shaking myself.

"Will you be all right?" I asked her.

"Yes," she said weakly. "I should call the office. But what would I say?"

I thought about it for a minute. "Toll them you walked into a burglary. Embellish as much as you want. I'll back you up," I said. "You'll look like a hero."

She almost laughed at his and I was glad.

"You have a dangerous profession," she said. "It's not for me, I guess."

"It's not usually that dangerous," I said. "Believe me, it's not so easy on me. Besides, you did pretty well for an amateur. I'm impressed."

Another smile. "So tell me," I continued. "Will this reflect badly on my audit?"

This time the laugh came out, though it quickly turned into a coughing fit. "Gosh, I hope I'm not coming down with something," she coughed. "As far as the audit goes, well, we'll just have to see about that."

So much for female bonding.

Bobo broke the news that he'd heard through his police sources that I was wanted for questioning about the murder in Beverly Hills, so after we dropped off Marcia I used his car phone to call Brooks.

I left a message on his voice mail that I needed to talk with him. I had resolved in the last few hours to fill Brooks in on the particulars. I was going to need somebody over there on my side, and right now I doubted Brooks was thinking pleasant thoughts about me. I said this much to Bobo.

"Least of your troubles, girl."

"What do you mean?"

"Got a call from Hector today."

"Hector? Hector Cardoza? What's that have to do with me?" I hadn't heard Hector Cardoza's name in years, and even the mention of him brought a smile to my face. He had been a border cop, moved on to the Coast Guard, and somewhere along his rapid rise to the top gave it all up to operate a charter-fishing business out of Coronado Island near San Diego.

Hector traded in what he considered the traitorous existence of chasing his people along desert arroyos and then coastal waterways for a job hauling boatloads of middle-aged executives and their two-hundred-dollar tackle sets out onto the Pacific to do battle with swordfish, yellow fins and other big-game fish. It was, he liked to say, his way of fulfilling a man's dream.

"He still has friends inside," said Bobo, and I knew he meant the border patrol, which made me feel queasy. I had a feeling where this was going. "They had an interesting story to tell about a Los Angeles private cop. Something about a couple of bodies south of the border and a gun that turned up in Beverly Hills."

"Shit, shit, shit," I said. "Hector say if they talked to the cops up here yet?"

Bobo nodded. "Word is they're coming up here tomorrow, see if the gun is the right match. From what Hector says, it don't look good for you."

"This doesn't make sense, Bobo," I said. "I mean, something is wrong here."

"You've been set up."

"Tell me something I don't know. But for what? And why?" I said. We were in a quiet residential section of the Marina where Sam lived and Bobo had slowed to check addresses.

"Not like you don't have enemies." He had found the right one and pulled up and over the curb to a vacant lot between two houses. Who needs parking spaces when you had four-wheel drive?

"Some guy out for revenge, you mean? This doesn't feel like that," I said, and it didn't. Something about this whole thing was cockeyed. It was obvious, I was sure, and I'd probably kick myself later for not seeing it, but for the life of me I couldn't make sense of anything.

"Something's wrong about this whole thing," I said. "Something's flat-out wrong."

"That we know," he said. "That we know."

THIRTY-FOUR

Sam lived along the canal that runs through the mid-dle of the Marina, a sad, dark waterway lined with an architectural mishmash of new and old, houses and condos, big places and small.

It was a section of narrow streets, gated entranceways, and seven-figure properties.

Sam's was one of the smallest and least noticeable on his block and I could see immediately why he chose it.

Set up over the street on top of a one-car garage, it was more Victorian in style, a narrow, multilevel house with pale yellow wooden siding and dark green trim, both of which had been weathered by the California climate. A thirty-step wooden stairway led up to his front door, a feature rarely found in LA outside of the Hollywood Hills.

It was a charming house, one I thought suited Sam well. I wasn't surprised that he had been happy here.

He opened the door when we were halfway up the stairs and smiled wide when he saw Bobo. The two embraced. It was a moment I didn't expect, but should have.

His look for me was the kind parents reserve for children who have been playing in the mud, which wasn't so far off from the truth.

"You don't want to know," I answered his silent question, passing through his doorway and touching, by rote, the blue-and-white mezuzah he had nailed to the side of the door. I noticed with some poignancy that it was the same one we had had in the house I'd grown up in.

We had never been very religious, but the pull of tradition

is strong, particularly in families like my father's, only a generation or two removed from the old country.

Danny and I got into the habit of touching the ceramic icon each time we entered or left the house. It began as a joke of ours, a way to bring us luck, but later we began to believe in its powers. I think my dad and Sam got a real kick out of that.

"Maybe you'd better wash up," Sam was saying as he ushered me inside. The house smelled of mildew and wood and cigars; odors of my childhood. I used a bathroom off the foyer to clean up, but the mud had already dried on my jeans and jacket and a quick washup wasn't going to cut it.

I found Sam and Bobo in the living room. It was an easy room, with big windows and bookshelves and a big fluffy couch on one side of a thick oak coffee table and two comfortable chairs on the other.

Bobo was sitting in one of the chairs and Sam was sunk into the couch, making him appear even smaller and older, and I felt sad for him.

He was halfway down a cigar, which reminded me that I'd left my Gloria Cubana back home with the cat.

Sam offered me a seat, but I was restless and anxious from too much coffee or too much excitement. Probably both. So I stood by his picture window, staring out at the muddy canal below us and, farther out, the rain-soaked coast. The air was thick with a heavy gray fog and it cast a kind of glow on the horizon, making it seem dirty, as if you could reach up and wipe away the grime and reveal the picturesque blue underneath.

Bobo was trying to fill Sam in on all the pertinent details. Another time and place, I would make fun of the way he was able to whittle down so much into so little. For now, though, all I could do was marvel at it.

Sam waited until he was through and leaned back, shaking his head in disbelief. He was just doing what everyone was thinking.

"Not good," he said. "Not good at all. What will you do?"

I shrugged a little. "I have no idea, Sam," I said. I was in a foul mood suddenly. What with dead bodies and frame-ups, getting shot at in the cemetery, a client with an attitude, and my dirty, wet clothes, I suppose I had reason to be irritable.

Bobo pointed in my direction, eyeing me from the side, as if he was trying to deliver a subliminal message. It came through as "Ease off on the old man." I just smirked at him and turned my back.

"Had a bad day," he said aloud to Sam. "A bad week. Maybe a bad year. Happens."

"Shut up, Bobo," I said, an edge in my voice that surprised even me. As I was saying the words, I knew I had no use for them. "Sorry, Bobo."

I felt the ache in my side and the fatigue of the last few days building up inside of me. I slumped down on one of Sam's chairs and pulled Danny's note out of my pocket and slid it across the table toward Sam.

"What do you make of this?"

I watched his expression as he read over the note a few times, but it didn't seem to change much. Just a father in mourning. I felt the pang again and somewhere inside of me tears were welling, but they were so deep I knew for certain they wouldn't pour out now. I wondered if they ever would.

"That damned Guru," Sam said, his grief now mixed with anger and resentment, emotions with which I too was intimate.

"But what does that other stuff mean?" I asked him. "Make any sense to you?"

He shook his head. "It's vaguely familiar. I think it's biblical. From the Old Testament, but I'm not certain. It's been so long," he looked over the note again. "These last words, 'Sei gesundt,' it's Yiddish for 'Be well, go in health.' "

I knew the words as soon as he pronounced them; my father used to say it all the time to customers. But I'd never seen them on paper.

"I'm sorry I can't be of more help," he said, handing the

1 ZEN AND THE ART OF MURDER

note to Bobo, who wanted to take a look for himself. He was well versed in a lot of things. I wouldn't be surprised if he knew the origin of the words. "I found some things Danny left here. I thought you might want to see them," Sam said.

He crossed the room to a desk in the corner and brought me an envelope similar to the one in which I'd found Danny's note, but larger. Inside was a torn sheet of computer printer paper, the kind with the small holes on each side so it can feed through the machine. It contained a list of forty or fifty names, several underlined, and one in particular Danny or someone else had highlighted with a star. In one corner, Danny had scrawled some letters and "C-4."

"Who's Susan Wolf?" I asked Sam. "And what do these letters mean?"

"I have no idea. Danny never mentioned any of his friends there."

I handed the list to Bobo. He frowned. "You mean to tell me Danny was living up there all this time?"

"I think so," Sam said. "He referred to it a few times as his prison. I got the feeling he was stuck there, but he did say he was close."

"Close to what?"

"Who knows?" said Sam.

It was hard to believe all these years Danny had been as near as a leisurely drive up Highway 1, and it made the pain, anger, and resentment I felt for my cousin and his Guru bubble up in my gut.

I realized then that, with all that I was coming to terms with in these last few days, there was still a whole lot more that would take years to deal with.

THIRTY-FIVE

Bobo had gotten up for a stretch and was looking out at the street when he called for Sam and me to be quiet, waving us over to the window overlooking the garage.

Down on the street, a Santa Monica police cruiser was double-parked and two uniforms were coming up Sam's stairway. I recognized with dismay that the one in front was my old friend Sergeant Lennon.

"Trouble," I said to Bobo, giving him the fast version of what happened between us at the pub.

Bobo just snickered. "Just think of him as beef and me as the meat grinder," he said, wringing his hands. "Baby face is all mine."

"Easy, Bobo," I said. "Why don't we just sneak out the back . . ."

"There's no back," said Sam. "Unless you want to jump off the deck into the canal. I don't recommend it."

"Well, shit," I said for what seemed like the millionth time today.

"Not to worry," said Bobo with a treacherous kind of smile on his face that would freeze a lion in its tracks. He could look downright frightening when he wanted to.

Sam let the doorbell ring a couple of times before going to the door to answer it. He opened it just enough to look out at the two cops.

"Can I help you?" He said it in a way that made him seem old and fragile. Sam the geriatric.

"Mr. Samuel Moses?" one of them said.

"Yes, that's me. What can I do for you today, officers?"

"Mind if we come in?" Lennon was asserting his authority and he pushed by Sam in a way that made me want to kick his ass.

"Well, well, well, look here," Lennon said when he saw me and Bobo. We were sitting in the living room, Bobo making like he was reading *National Geographic*, when all the while he was waiting for the kid to do something stupid. I looked at Lennon and realized it was just a matter of time before that would happen.

"If it isn't the famous private detective." His voice was heavy with sarcasm and confidence. He thought he had the upper hand. "Don't they take showers where you're from?"

"That's Ms. Famous Private Detective to you, comrade," I said, leaning back in my chair and putting my feet on Sam's table. I hoped he didn't mind.

"Get smart with me all you want," he said. "But better save yourself for the trip back to Santa Monica."

"Are you arresting her, officer?" Sam said from behind him. Lennon ignored him. His partner, a quiet kid with dark skin, thick curly hair and eyebrows, was about to say something, but Lennon stopped him.

"I got this, Salazar," he said to him, then looked back at Sam. "No need for everyone to get worked up here. If Ms. Moses will come with us . . ."

"Maybe you should answer the question." Bobo choosing his spot.

"Who the hell are you?"

"I'm her lawyer," Bobo said, uncrossing his legs and dropping the *National Geographic* on the coffee table. It landed with a smack on the oak surface. "And I want to know: Are you arresting my client?"

"Her lawyer my ass," said Lennon, turning toward me. "If you don't mind, Ms. Moses, we're going to have to take you back to the station now. Let's not make this difficult."

I didn't move.

"Well," he said.

"Am I under arrest?"

"That depends."

"On what?" Dobo was standing now, carrying his considerable muscular bulk in such a way he was almost hovering over the entire room. Even Lennon seemed to want to take a step back. But, to his credit, he held his ground.

"On whether you come quietly."

"That's bullshit," Bobo said, taking a step forward. Lennon's hand went to his service revolver. Salazar, having apparently been blessed with more brains than his sergeant, reached out a hand to stop Lennon's progress.

"What are you doing?" he said under his breath to Lennon, but so we could all hear. He had a slight Hispanic accent that made his soft, steady voice seem even quieter. He addressed us with an air of someone who understands both sides of respect. I liked him immediately.

"We do not have a warrant for your, ah, for your client's arrest, sir. We were merely sent here to question Mr. Moses about her whereabouts. I do know that she is wanted for questioning regarding the murder in Beverly Hills yesterday. But of course at this point her compliance is of course voluntary."

Lennon was steaming. A red glow was rising along his jawline and his cheeks were puffed as if he'd made a bet to see how long he could hold his breath. It didn't matter if he was right. He just wanted to get the best of me and he was embarrassed and angry that his lower-ranked partner had undercut his authority.

"Excuse us a minute," he said, walking Salazar back to the foyer. Sam was still standing behind them and Lennon clipped him on the way by. It was a hard shove, knocking Sam back a step or two and it was clearly unnecessary. Even Salazar seemed amazed at his partner's actions.

I jumped to my feet to defend my uncle, but Bobo kept me back with one of his huge hands. I could see from the way the muscles in his neck were wildly twitching that he was as pissed off as I was.

We couldn't hear what was being said between the two cops, but it was obvious that Lennon was dressing down poor

Salazar. He had his face in the kid's kitchen, Marine-style, and he was poking his finger at his chest.

After a minute Lennon, who was red-faced with rage, walked back toward me, but Bobo stood in his way.

"Get out of my way, *sir*." He spit out the last word as if it were rancid. "You are impeding a police officer."

"What's your supervisor's name?" Only I knew how close Bobo was to exploding. He was the kind of guy who would kill you smiling and wonder why nobody could see how angry he'd been.

Lennon didn't answer, just tried to do to Bobo what he'd done to Sam, only harder. He was an equal-opportunity bully along with being a stupid one.

In one motion, he had twisted Lennon around by that same arm and pinned it behind his back. Of course, the sergeant went for his revolver with his free hand, but Bobo got to it first and, in a move that surprised us all, including Lennon's partner, slid the weapon across Sam's hardwood floor to Salazar's feet.

Salazar put out his foot and caught the weapon, but didn't pick it up. He just looked down at the .38 and then back up at Lennon and then at Bobo, deciding in the end just to let things be. Bobo, it seemed, was a better judge of character than any of us.

Lennon was cursing Salazar and me and spraying a few four-letter words around, but he stopped struggling after a minute when he realized Bobo could probably hold him still all day.

I went around to face him and he spit at me, "Now you're under arrest!" He was seething. "I'll get you for resisting and assault."

"Is that before or after I report that you struck an old man and tried to strike my friend here? Not to mention taking me against my will." I had rolled up a copy of *The New Yorker* that had been lying on a side table and was prodding Lennon in the chest with it. "Now, I'm not under arrest, am I?"

"Fuck you."

"I'll take that as a no."

"What should I do with him?" Bobo asked.

"Well, I don't know," I said. "Can't just let him go. He might cause more trouble. Can't kill him. We don't do things like that. Not unless we have to. Mm, let me think."

"Hold on a minute." Salazar had apparently seen enough. He came over to where we were standing. "Can we talk for a moment?"

We went into the foyer to the spot where Lennon had been in his face.

"How can you stand the guy?" I asked him. "Don't you ever want to stuff a doughnut down his throat?"

"All the time." He smiled. He was handsome in an old-world kind of way, solid and sure, every feature in the right place but not bragging about it. "Look," he said, getting serious again. "So far, everything is under control. I mean, it's not as if he didn't deserve it. He can be a real asshole sometimes, but I've never seen him act like this before. He doesn't like you much."

"We had a run-in of sorts," I said.

"Yeah, well, what are we going to do now?"

"Listen," I said. "You've heard this before, but I had nothing to do with the murder in Beverly Hills, or any other, for that matter. I'm a private cop, and sometimes, but not often, we run into bodies. The truth is I'm being set up."

"I know who you are," he said. "Josh Lopez says you were the best, a straight shooter. And that means something. He's not free with the compliments, if you know what I mean."

I did. "How do you know Josh?"

"He's my uncle."

"Wait, don't tell me." I was racking through the cobwebs. "Diego, right?"

"Yes, ma'am, you have a good memory."

"Call me Zen. I'm not that much older than you," I said, though I was sure I had almost a decade on him. "Your uncle talked about you kids a lot. So you followed in his footsteps, huh?"

He was beaming with the pride of family and responsibility. It was infectious and I liked him more for it.

"Well, it looks good on you," I said. "Here's the deal, though. If I promise to get in touch with Detective Brooks, can you let us go? How much trouble will you get into with the brass?"

"Maybe a little," he said. "But I can handle it. The truth is that Vince went over the top. He knows it, too. That might save both our asses."

"Well, I can see you're just as smart as your uncle," I said. "How do you want to work it?"

"Up to you," he said, placing a car key in my hand. "Though, if I were you, I'd check out the new cruisers we got. They got electric locks. Man, very fancy."

"I can't take this. What will you say happened to yours?"

He pulled out another one from a hidden pocket at his waist. "One thing a cop never wants to do is get locked out of his vehicle."

I shared one last smile with him and went back to where Bobo was still holding Lennon by the arm. The sergeant was straining with agony. A few more minutes of that and he might tear a rotator cuff.

I had Lennon's weapon, sans clip, and put it on the coffee table. "Now, are you going to follow us, or will you be a good boy and go play in your own jurisdiction?"

He had a caged animal's rage on his face and I smiled, just to let him know I was in charge and he wasn't.

"I don't know, Bobo," I said. "Maybe we should restrain him."

Salazar came over then and intervened. "We can't follow you. This isn't Communist Russia." He glared at his sergeant. "It's still a free country and you are free to go as long as you agree to go down to the station."

Bobo released Lennon and he tried to soothe his injured arm without letting on what he was doing. I was wondering how idiots like him got to be cops. I caught Bobo's eye and covertly passed him the key to the patrol car. He looked at it, nodded, and left without a word. I could see Sam through the corner of my eye, watching us with a wry smile on his face. He was enjoying it.

"You ought to teach him how to heel," Lennon said after Bobo had shut the door. He was gathering his weapon from the table.

"I noticed you waited until he left to insult him," I said. "You're just a coward and bully, Vince. You were wrong back at the pub and you're wrong now. Why don't you give your juvenile pride a permanent vacation?"

"This isn't over," he hissed at me, then stalked toward the door. "Coming, Sal-a-zar?" He said the kid's name as if it were dirt and then slammed the door without waiting for an answer. I hoped he would be all right, but if he really had any of Josh in him and I was certain he did, then I knew he'd be fine.

I gave Sam a quick hug. "Diego," I said. "Tell me one more thing."

"If I can."

"Did they ID the body in the swimming pool?"

"Yeah, he was one of Mo Goldman's boys. Guy named Blitz, Karl Blitz. Know him? Everybody called him Glitz."

"Glitz Blitz? You're kidding, right?"

He shook his head. "Why is Santa Monica PD interested in a mobster from Phoenix?" I asked.

"He's not from Phoenix," Salazar said. "He's been running some shit for Goldman out of Santa Monica for months now. We've had a special detail on it, but it's on the QT, so keep it to yourself. Course now that old Karl is dead, it screws everything up royally."

"What's in Santa Monica? They cornering the black market on homeless people?"

He smiled at this. "Think bigger, Zen. Think Hollywood."

"Movies? You mean the mob wants to make movies?"

"That's what our guys were trying to find out. Who the hell knows? Makes you wonder how a guy gets a nickname like Glitz, don't it?"

THIRTY-SIX

"Glitz Blitz. I like it. I think." The first words out of Bobo since we'd left Sam's place. I don't know what he did to Lennon's police cruiser, but it must have worked because we caught a call for a tow truck on Bobo's scanner.

"Lucky for us Salazar was there," I said.

"Lucky for Lennon, you mean."

We were making time, speeding up Highway 101 north toward Pescadero in Bobo's Range Rover. Highway 5 was the fastest route up north, but if you were headed to the coast as we were, 101 was more direct.

We stopped once, in Santa Barbara, for some gas and some dinner at this little Mexican hole-in-the-wall that had become legend in the central resort community. We'd been on the road for nearly six hours, the darkness around us starting to cave in, reminding me of the desert. The rain had come and gone by the time we'd hit 101, but the two-lane highway was slick and the air was cold. We had the heat on inside Bobo's well-appointed truck.

"You think there's a connection between Latisha and Glitz?" He almost laughed as he said it. "I can't get over that name."

"Me neither," I said. "What makes you say that about Latisha?" In truth, it hadn't even crossed my mind.

"Don't know," he said. "Seems funny to me. Him showing up so soon after you in Mexico, then ending up a floater."

"He was following me, remember? I saw him at the rest stop near Fresno."

"How did he know?"

"Know what?"

"How did he know to follow *you*?"

Now there was a question for which I had no answer.

It was just a little before 1 A.M. when Bobo nosed the Range Rover into Tamaville and we starting looking for signs that might direct us to High Cliffs Ranch.

Every sign in the tiny town made reference to the Guru and his flock. Restaurants, a café, a gas station and market, a school, even a newsstand. Get your blessed papers here.

All had the same logo of a fat, whited-bearded man releasing a dove into the sky. I had always heard that High Cliffs was secluded and hard to find, but whoever said that had apparently never been here.

There were signs pointing to the ranch all over; it was just a matter of following the arrows. They led us right through the middle of town, a wide avenue dotted with shops, restaurants, bookstores, and tourist spots where you could buy film, a souvenir, or a cheap pair of sunglasses. Then we passed by a series of cozy, old-fashioned beach neighborhoods of rickety clapboard houses and bungalows, all battered into comfortable familiarity by age, weather and the salt of the Pacific.

The residential area was more confusing, a grid of streets that crisscrossed every block or so, most of them paved, a few only gravel and dirt. Bobo had to circle around a couple of times before he found the ranch's main entrance, near a modest and rusted old sign that was fixed to a Western-style crosspost.

Bobo rolled the Range Rover through the gate and onto a narrow dirt-and-gravel road that was marked by deep gashes, gullies and ruts left by the natural course of erosion. While no obvious barriers stood in the way, it was clear by the road and the partially hidden and low-key entrance that visitors were unwelcome here.

The road rose upward a few hundred feet. It was slow

going as it wound, sometimes treacherously, around corners where a few low shrubs and rocks were the only buffer between the road and a hundred-foot drop into the valley.

Bobo's truck, while agile and surefooted, was also clumsy because of its size, and more than once it appeared as if it was too wide for the road. I was holding on so tight, my hand hurt.

Bobo looked over at me occasionally, amused at my fear of heights.

At the top, finally, the road opened into a large open campground with tents lit up from inside like jack-o'-lanterns and bonfires so high it seemed as if the trees were ablaze.

We parked at the edge next to a heavy-duty generator. We could see distant lights through the trees and the motion of a spot beamed across the woods at brisk intervals. Bobo pointed in that direction.

Past the tents we could see the road continued, but at its mouth stood several armed guards: the Guru's own private army.

"Must be the ranch," he whispered.

There was no need to keep our voices down. All around us people in robes of various colors were swaying and dancing to a constant drumbeat, and singing.

A stage set up at one end was darkened, save for a string of lights arranged to spell "Happy New Year."

We found a group of people passing a joint around and warming themselves by one of the fires. It was like the stragglers at a Grateful Dead concert. They were friendly and didn't seem suspicious or threatened. The love in the air was suffocating.

"Let's get out of here." Bobo had a hold of my sleeve like a child following his mother into the doctor's office. "These places give me the creeps."

"I didn't think anything affected you, Bobo."

"All this religion crap. It reminds me of my nana's medicine. Scary stuff."

"This ain't voodoo, Bobo, it's bullshit."

"Wouldn't be so sure if I were you," he said. "People

will lay themselves on the line for any old thing that sounds right to them. The believing part is the thing they most believe in.''

I knew what he meant and I realized how right he was to be afraid. I had seen that look in two members of my family and I was sure I would see it again tonight. The tragedy at Waco was only one example of the power a madman with a God complex and a silver tongue can have on fragile people who can't find meaning anywhere else in their lives.

It's part of the harsh inequities of modern life, but it's also something else, I think, that drives people to become blind followers and walk down a path they might not otherwise consider.

People want order and stability and solid ground underneath their feet. They want to be part of something they can see and feel and pass on to their children, something that's worth believing in. Many find it at home. Some have the ability to preserve traditions, born from years of hauling their culture, sometimes on their very backs, from town to town, country to country, continent to continent.

But Americans, it seems, get lost easily in the maze of this industrialized nation they've created, and many, even the most normal, are left searching for their place in the chaos.

Danny found it first on Wall Street, but when that failed him he had to find something else to fill the void. I could chastise him for not turning to his family, but he wasn't the only one who didn't see that what he needed was right in front of his face. We'd all made that mistake.

I looked around at the people dancing and partying around the fires, like children playing Indians. They were of all ages, races, and backgrounds. The only characteristic they seemed to share was being happy. I wondered how long it lasted and whether finding inner peace was the price of worshipping a man of questionable lineage. Hell, who was I to say they were wrong?

We'd made our way through the celebrants toward the stage, me leading and Bobo still hanging back a bit.

Just when we thought we'd pass through the crowd unnoticed, we were approached by a man in a bright green robe.

He was short, with a gut that stuck out in front of him like a belly on a porcelain Buddha, making him waddle when he walked. He was hairless except for a long beard that was braided and must have been two feet long.

"Ah," he said over the din, which was marked by rhythmic chanting and high-pitched moaning, reinforced by a distant drumbeat that was causing the ground to vibrate. "Newcomers. Looking for the promise of tranquillity and eternal peace. To become the perfectly realized being."

"Are you kidding?" Bobo said.

I agreed. "Sounds like a line from a B-movie."

He spread his hands out, palms-up. "It's what many expect to hear," he said. "Sometimes truth sounds like a cliché. That's because all truths are simple ones."

"Well, I've got about as much inner peace as I can handle," I said. "But you may be able to help me with something."

"We are here to help our fellow travelers," he said and I thought again how they all seemed like Deadheads to me. I was waiting for Jerry Garcia to launch into "Casey Jones."

"We were looking for someone we think lives here. Do you know Susan Wolf?"

"I am sorry," he said and he looked it. "But we don't go by such names here. Once a person pledges our faith, he or she sheds her given name and takes on a new moniker, one chosen by our Father."

"You have no record of their real names?" I asked. "Couldn't we ask some of your, ah, followers . . ."

"Oh, no," he said, still maintaining his good humor in spite of my interrogation. "Such records aren't kept. The whole idea is to break away from the past, to develop the soul and body and spirit in a new, more focused way. To become, as I said, the perfectly realized being. And I am so sorry, but visits are forbidden unless requested by the individual. As you may imagine, many families come here in the misguided attempt to 'rescue' their loved ones when in truth they want to be left alone. Parents often do not know their children.''

''What if I told you this was gravely important,'' I said.

''Unfortunately you will have to wait until you are contacted by the individual you seek. There is nothing I can do about it.''

''Are they free to contact the outside world?'' asked Bobo.

''Despite reports to the contrary, everyone is free here. Look around you. Do you see anyone in chains? No. Everyone is here of their own free will.''

''And the rent-a-cops there? What is their purpose?''

Mr. Pleasantries waved us off again. ''We have long been a curiosity for outsiders, tourists and such,'' he said. ''In addition, the Guru's teachings have drawn many followers who are celebrities in the greater world. They expect and deserve their privacy.''

''I don't mean to be *contrary*''—I was tired and frustrated and the emphasis I put on the word was pure sarcasm—''but I don't believe you.''

''That is to be expected,'' he said. ''It is unfortunate. Followers of the great Tai feel the love and the power and the belonging. And isn't that what people really need?''

I remarked about the fact that donations were required.

''People give up their life's savings to come here,'' he said, ''for one reason: Everyone tells them they can buy happiness, and when they realize that is a tragic falsehood, many end up here and see that material things no longer have value they can relate to. They have no more need for money than a bird in the sky. Donations are modest, but people give because they believe.''

I found it hard at this point to argue with him. It's not easy to tell a man who sees everything through rose-colored glasses that the sky is blue.

''Does your Guru take visitors?''

The man laughed. ''Oh, he is too busy to see outsiders. His powers are fragile and fleeting and he must immerse himself in his meditations to keep them strong. Surely, you understand. The life of a prophet is not an easy one and not fit for just any man.''

"Jesus confronted his people, those who believed and those who didn't," said Bobo. "He did not hide from them. That was considered his strength."

The man seemed to consider this, scratching at a spot on his chin. Even in the flickering light of the bonfire, I could see he was as pale as chalk. "Look what it got him," he said finally. "Imagine what good he could have done had he lived a little bit longer."

Bobo looked at me and I knew underneath his shades he was rolling back those mismatched eyes of his. There was no other response.

"I must go," the man said suddenly. "You are welcome to join our celebration. I am sorry I could not be of more help to you. I bid you peace."

We watched him waddle into the darkness, his long beard swaying like an elephant's trunk. We were left standing in the middle of the campgrounds, the sparks of the fires around us spraying toward the stars like fireworks.

THIRTY-SEVEN

Bobo couldn't stomach staying at a place in town, so we drove up to Pescadero and got a couple of rooms in a roadside at the edge of town.

I had hoped to deal with this thing quickly, but from previous experience we both knew we couldn't leave until we'd found a way inside the Guru's compound. And getting through their security wasn't going to be like picking a padlock, more like breaking into the Pentagon.

The difference between the United States Government and the corporation known as High Cliffs was that the latter could shoot first and ask questions later.

The desk clerk, a skinny, tow-headed twenty-year-old with a face full of zits, braces, the beginnings of a goatee, and the tan of a beach bum, had given us the lowdown on the place everyone hated but no one could stop talking about.

"Dude, it was awful. They fired everyone and hired a bunch of their zombies instead." He had a thin, whiny voice that had the same effect on me as fingernails on a blackboard. "Nobody goes down there anymore. Afraid someone might convert 'em or somethin'."

"You been to High Cliffs?"

"Sure, dude. Me and some buds take our wheels up there. Some gnarly paths up that mountain. Totally dank, man." It was hard to follow the kid, like having to learn a whole new language and besides.

"It was bad?"

"No, dude. Dank. That's good, man. Diggedy dank, that's real good. You should watch more Letterman, dude. Truly."

"So," I said. "You were telling us about the ranch."

"Yeah, anyways, there's some real *good* bike trails up there and we like to go up there, but they got dudes with guns and they always chase us outta there. The rush is amazing, dude. You ought to try it sometime."

Unfortunately, we had no choice.

"So there's no way in, I mean secretly." He looked at me and then at Bobo, lingering on the big man for a second.

"You guys the cops, or what?"

"Nothing like that," I said. "His sister is being held against her will at the ranch and we need to find a way in."

He was beside himself. "No way, dude. No fucking way. You gonna go in with some heavy-duty hardware, or what?"

"This ain't a raid," I said. "Just a small, *quiet* rescue operation." I emphasized the word "quiet" and he fell into his part.

"Hey, that's cool with me," he said. "Guess you want to know where it is, huh?"

For all the problems with the language barrier, the kid was golden when it came to details. He not only knew where the High Cliffs ranch was, but he knew a couple of prime spots where we could sneak in without much resistance.

"Lots of people have tried to get in there, you know," he said in a rare moment of somberness. "Don't know anybody who made it."

It was too late to find Brooks in the office, but I called anyway and got a chipper "hello" from one of the graveyard-shift desk guys.

Brooks was long gone, so I left my number and gave my name as Sarah Vaughan, hoping he would make the connection. I wasn't about to alert the entire Santa Monica police force to the whereabouts of a wanted murder suspect.

I didn't sleep well and awoke stiff and cranky when the sun I hadn't seen in days poked through the flimsy curtains of my room. The bed was too soft and the pillows too hard, leaving me with a crick in my neck and a dull pain in my side where I'd been stabbed. It seemed like months ago. Hard to believe it was only a couple of days ago

Bobo had slipped a note under my door, saying he was going to check out the spot the kid had talked about and find us the necessary equipment. Actually, he only left one sentence: "Checking the spot, be back with the supplies," but I could read between the lines.

We weren't going to hit the place until nightfall, which meant I had a whole day to kill for the first time in a week. It was nice having work again, but I'd forgotten how tired you could get. I noticed a microbrew beer place near the hotel and my plan was to get a little more sleep and then some lunch and a good brew. It had felt like days since I'd had a decent meal and for the first time in a while I was really hungry.

I had just closed my eyes again when the ringing of the phone cut through the room like a fire alarm. Maybe the last guest who had stayed here had a hearing problem.

"Hello," I said, sounding, I knew, as tired as I felt.

"Wake you up?" It was Brooks. I couldn't tell if he was mad at me or not.

"Not really," I said. "You mad at me?"

"Not really," he said.

"How come?" Once again he caught me by surprise.

"Plenty of other people angry at you, that's why."

"Gee, thanks for cheering me up."

"Consider payback for disabling one of my cruisers and roughing up one of my cops."

"He started it."

"So I heard."

Good man, Salazar. I would have to commend him to his uncle.

"Well, what idiot sent that dumb shit to bother Sam? If I hadn't been there, he might have handcuffed him and brought him in."

"What can I say? Watkins has a thing for the kid."

"Well, I knew there was some reason for his promotion. But then, he didn't look too bright to me either."

"Watch it. He's smart enough to be on my ass at this very moment."

"Because of me?"

"Happen to see the paper yet?"

"The *Times*? No, why?"

"I'll let you be surprised," he said, which didn't sound like a good thing to me. "I'd wear a pair of dark sunglasses today if I were you."

"What?"

"Never mind. Just get the paper."

"Thanks a lot. Anything else I should know about?"

"I suppose you'll hear this sooner or later, but you should know the ballistics reports matched your gun with the slug in the dead guy's head."

"Hold on a minute," I broke in. "I didn't—"

"I know, I know. Let me finish here," he said and I was beginning to wonder if I was talking to the same man who a day ago had wanted to haul me into custody.

"It's pretty damning if you ask me," he continued. "Hard to blame the brass for wanting to chat with you. If I wasn't in the picture, you'd already be in handcuffs."

"I reported my Walther when it was stolen a few days ago. You can look it up."

"I did."

"So?"

"No record that I could find."

"That's impossible. I know I called it in." A little bit of dread was sinking in my stomach. "I wouldn't lie to you about that."

"I know," he said this so quietly I almost missed it.

"If you know," I said, "then why are still busting my chops?"

"Look, Zen," he said, "what exactly am I supposed to believe? You've been keeping shit from me the whole time. How can I trust you if you won't trust me, and how can I get to the truth if you won't be straight with me?"

They sounded just like the words I had recently spoken to Latisha. They probably were.

"I'm not trying to be evasive. It's only coming out that way," I said. "I don't really know what's going on either and I couldn't tell you where the truth ends or begins. The only thing I do know is that someone is committing murder with my Walther, and so far I haven't been able to do anything about it."

"I know and I understand," he said. "But that doesn't help me much. It's getting pretty hard to defend you down here, and on top of that, I get the feeling you don't much trust me."

"It's not that."

"Then what is it? You're not the only person to suffer loss, you know."

For not the first time since I saw Danny's face in the walk-in I was close to tears, the anguish in my heart so strong I felt I was drowning in it. If Brooks had been in the room with me then, I would have collapsed into his arms and cried on his shoulder. I would have done it gladly.

"Zen? You okay?"

"Yeah," I said, my voice cracking with the effort to keep the tears to myself.

"I'm sorry," he said. "You're gonna have to come back to Santa Monica."

"Yeah," I repeated. "But I need a favor. I need twenty-four hours to deal with something up here."

"How about a favor for a favor?"

"That's why I called." I had found my bearings again. "You talk to the federales yet?"

"You mean the double murder south of the border? They're due in later this morning. Why?"

"One of the bodies was an American citizen, guy named Harry Winchester."

"Yeah, we knew that already. How did you know?"

"I was there the night they were killed." I waited. Brooks had fallen completely silent. "Still there?"

"Yes, please go on."

"I'm breaking my code by telling you this. I need your promise to keep me out of it."

"Do I have a choice?"

"Nope," I said. "But don't worry. I'll point you in the right direction."

"I'm waiting."

I gave him the details of the night I visited Harry up to and including getting shot at and my impromptu motorcycle dash across the border.

"The guy you followed back to the trailer, who was he?"

"You know the guy I found in the Latisha Maxwell's swimming pool?"

"Don't tell me."

"Yep. One and the same."

"That doesn't make sense."

"I tell you the truth and you rain on my parade. What's a girl to think?"

"If what you say is true, then our talk-show host isn't being straight with us."

"Color me shocked," I said. "Worst part is, she's my client."

He was following my line of thinking perfectly. It was more than a hint, I had practically led him by the shirt collar, but Latisha had toyed with me and I was giving some back. I had my doubts whether she was involved or not, but my instincts told me the answers to a lot of my problems somehow rested with her. Maybe Brooks could get out of her what I couldn't.

"I have to admit it makes sense," he said. "Oh, I almost forgot. The guy who attacked you came to last night."

"And?"

"He won't talk. Asked for his lawyer."

"Great. Why are you telling me this?"

"I told you already he was clean, but he has a very peculiar tattoo. A dove with a 'TT' underneath it. Know it?"

I knew it. "I've seen it. Followers of some crazy Guru."

"Not the same Guru who runs the commune where your cousin supposedly committed suicide twelve years ago?"

"How did you know that?" It was strange hearing it from someone outside the family. It wasn't a secret, but with all the time and distance since Danny had jumped, it seemed like one.

"A police report was filed in San Francisco. Mass suicide. A dozen people hurling themselves off a cliff. It wasn't hard to find."

"It's hard to talk about," I said. "It's personal, a family thing. I wanted to deal with it myself."

"What makes you think I wouldn't have respected that?"

"Your commitment to your job," I said.

"Touché."

"What are you going to do?" I asked him.

"Nothing. Not until you get back," he said.

"Thanks. Take this number down." I gave him Bobo's cell phone. "Call me if you need me. Other than that, I'll be back in town tomorrow."

"They'll want you in here."

"It's New Year's Eve, Jonathan."

"Then make sure you get here early."

THIRTY-EIGHT

I couldn't get back to sleep, so I made a round of calls back to Santa Monica to check my messages and let everyone know I was still breathing.

Vivian was all out of breath when I reached her after getting busy signals for a good five minutes. I had had the Los Angeles *Times* sent up to my room and there in the corner of the front page was a story about the murder in Latisha Maxwell's backyard. Next to the story was a mug of the talk-show host, next to one of me that was at least two years old. My hair was longer and I had lost a considerable amount of weight since then.

Under the mug, the caption read "LA private detective Zen Moses. Wanted for questioning." Great. Not only did I have the cops and the mob on my ass, now I was going to have half of the LA press corps on it as well. If I had my druthers, I would rather take my chances with the cops or the mob. At least they didn't have call-in broadcasts.

Vivian was jazzed by the whole thing, which in a way made me glad. She would stay on top of things for me. So far, there were reporters at my office and my house, but she swore she hadn't said a thing.

"There's nothing to say, Vivian," I said.

"What a shame." She seemed genuinely disappointed. "It might be good for business."

"Having your gun involved in a high-profile murder is not good for business," I told her. "Solving the case would be."

"Oh, you'll do that, bubala. You always do."

This made me smile, proving that blind loyalty could sometimes be a good thing.

"Maybe going on TV will help."

"What are you talking about?"

" 'Latisha Live!' They said on the radio this morning they're having a special show on New Year's Eve so Latisha can answer all the rumors around the murder."

"So what does that have to do with me being on television?"

"You're scheduled as a guest. I thought you knew."

"It's a surprise to me," I said, my fury for Latisha rising.

"You mean you're not going on?"

"Not on your life."

"Oh, doll, I told all my friends to watch. They'll be disappointed."

"They'll get over it."

I took a long shower as hot as I could stand it, taking selfish advantage of the fact that I wasn't paying for the water. I let the spray run over me, trying to make sense of the seemingly conflicting details that were rumbling around my head.

I needed a scorecard to keep track of the trail of bodies and suspects and related cast of characters. The real problem was working two cases simultaneously and not knowing who belonged to what.

The guys in the blue Mercedes, for example. Mo Goldman's boys. They were on my tail for a reason. They hadn't seemed in a talking mood when they chased me and Marcia through the cemetery, that was for sure.

It seemed logical their interests coincided with whatever Blitz was after from Harry and Latisha. What could they want from a sick old man and a talk-show host? Extortion? Possibly, but for what? They could threaten to expose Latisha's public lie about her past, but killing Harry and poor Frieda would be getting rid of the blackmail leverage. I was certain Goldman was a lot of things, but stupid wasn't one of them.

And where did Sara Maxwell fit in? And the lunatic's love letters, and who the hell was Jane Bodoni Winchester?

I called Leah as soon as I got out of the shower. It was time for the great Zen to speak. The rest of the LA press could be damned, but I owed this much to Leah. After all, she'd literally saved my ass.

My faith in her was renewed yet again when the first things she asked was whether I was all right and if I needed anything. I told her I did, but that if she wanted, I'd give her a quick interview first.

I couldn't tell her much, but I laid out how I'd found the body, leaving out the details about breaking into my client's house and rummaging through her personal belongings.

I had promised Latisha I wouldn't reveal that I'd been hired by her, and for now I decided to honor my word to her, telling Leah that, for the record, the name of my client and my reasons for being in the neighborhood had to remain strictly confidential.

"Can you work with that?" I asked her when we were done.

"Are you kidding? It's more than anyone else has," she said. "Those clowns at downtown are going to be eating crow for breakfast. Thanks, girlfriend."

"I got one more thing for you," I told her. "But it has to be on deep background, so you're gonna have to track it down yourself."

"Understood. Lay it on me."

"The guy in the pool is named Karl Blitz. He works for Mo Goldman."

"You mean *worked*."

"What?"

"Glitz Blitz," she said and I was once again floored by the depth and accuracy of her information. Oh, to have her sources. I might never have left the business. "He's a renegade. Goldman's got a contract out on him. They sent him out here to find some movies to invest in, you know, on the up-and-up. But Glitz took to the Hollywood lifestyle and paid for it with the boss's money. My guess is they finally caught up to him in Latisha's swimming pool.''

"Jesus, Leah." I was stunned. "How the hell do you know all this, and how come you haven't printed it?''

"Got a source downtown at organized crime, a close, personal source." She didn't giggle, but she might as well have. "Haven't been able to get anyone to confirm it on the record.''

"You're sleeping with a guy at OCU?''

"Um, you could say that," she said.

"Girlfriend!''

"Hey, I didn't know it when I met him. Guess I just got lucky.''

"Go, girl," I said. "But if what you say is true, the cops must know I'm innocent.''

"There's been communication problems between the Santa Monica cops, who set up a special team to investigate Glitz, and the OCU, who have been tracking Goldman all over the western region. I don't think Santa Monica knows Glitz was on the boss man's hit list.''

"Who's the Beavis running the operation for Santa Monica?''

"A captain named Watkins. Know him?''

"We've met," I said.

"Well, I think he's a big toad. He won't give me shit. Won't even return my phone calls. Maybe you could ease the lines of communication.''

"Forget it. One of his minions has it in for me," I said. "However, I'm surprised anyone can resist you, Leah. You're incredible. I owe you big-time.''

"You've made a good dent by giving me this stuff on the record," she said. "Now, if you'll just let me get off the phone . . .''

"One more thing, Leah.''

"Give 'em an inch . . .''

"Very funny. Know anything about Latisha's sister, Sara?''

"Wish I did. That's the big mystery. All kinds of rumors

that she's deathly ill, but the Maxwell camp has kept the details very hush-hush.''

"Ever here of Jane Bodoni Winchester?''

"Nope. That all?''

"Mind checking those names out?'' I asked.

"What are friends for?'' she said and was gone.

THIRTY-NINE

I managed to get out for a brew, a pleasant salad of mixed baby greens, and a bowl of turkey chili, but it might as well have been astronaut rations. I couldn't concentrate on anything but the thoughts running around my head. I felt like a rat in a maze with no exit.

Word travels slow to most lazy small towns, and Pescadero was no different. I was able to walk the several blocks from my hotel to the bar and back again with nary a sideways glance. To the denizens here I was just another stranger passing through.

Bobo was in my room when I returned and I didn't bother asking how he got in. Doors were minor challenges to Bobo, roads to cross, where the object was getting to the other side. In these endeavors he was a master.

He was dressed from head to toe like a biker, complete with black Lycra tights, padded gloves, and a pair of gray Nike cycle shoes on his feet.

He tossed me a bag which had similar stuff in it and I was surprised he knew my size, right down to my feet. I was about to ask him when he interrupted.

"Mm. Good guess." He was pointing to his temple. "Never underestimate the powers of the Cajun mind."

That brain of his had hatched a plan to spend the afternoon posing as mountain-bike riders and take on the hills overlooking High Cliffs. Come dark, we'd try to sneak in, using a spot he'd found after following the desk clerk's directions.

"Try?" I asked him.

"Place is heavily armed." He shrugged. "Guys with rifles patrolling all over the place. Lots of 'beware' signs. Not real friendly folk."

"Great," I said. "When do we go?"

He looked at his watch. It was late afternoon, meaning we had only a couple hours of sunlight left. "Now's a good time," he said. "Gets dark in a few hours. Enough time to get us situated."

"Ready when you are," I said.

I got my things and left the room to check out. One way or another, we weren't coming back.

"You know what you're looking for once you get in there?" Bobo asked as he closed the door shut.

"Susan Wolf, I guess," I said. "Beyond that, I have no idea."

He shook his head. "Didn't I teach you anything?"

Bobo rented a couple of prime mountain bikes, not a problem in these parts. The sport had practically been invented in northern California, and Highway 1 was dotted with great trails, from San Diego as far up as Portland and Seattle.

"Not to worry," he said when he saw me checking out our rides. "They're borrowed. Just don't crash."

He left the Range Rover at the end of a fire road that ran along a freshwater creek. It was an ideal spot, just below a hill already well scarred by mountain-bike tracks.

We needed all the time we had to find Bobo's spot. The hills were steep and rocky, and recent rains had added to the treacherous footing. The sun was out, but the air was thin and cold, and I was reminded once again of my lung deficiencies.

Whatever Bobo had paid for the bikes was well worth it; they handled the terrain with the agility we needed to keep from constantly falling or slipping back down the hill.

We didn't see a soul the whole ride up the hill, though the signs Bobo had mentioned were peppered all over the woods. They looked at first like typical "No Hunting" warn-

ings, but up close their meaning was perfectly clear: WARN-
ING: YOU ARE ON PRIVATE LANDS PROTECTED BY ARMED
SECURITY. PROCEED AT RISK OF LIFE AND LIMB.

Guru Tai was nothing if not direct. We finally came to
rest at the spot Bobo had chosen a little before sundown. I
was worn out enough to wonder if I had enough energy to
finish the job.

Bobo had packed a couple of energy bars and we each
had full water bottles. I needed both.

We were up on a ledge on the side of a hill that wasn't
quite big enough to be called a mountain, but from our van-
tage point we could see the High Cliffs Ranch roughly fifty
feet below us.

We were shielded by the thicket of woods around us, but
could easily see the compound, some ten thousand acres
spread out almost as far as we could see. Bigger than some
whole towns.

And, in fact, that is what it seemed from where we were
standing. Small unpaved pathways laid out in precise grids
were lined with clusters of small buildings with wooden
porches, like a Western-replica town.

At the far end was a single-story building as long as a
football field. I guessed it to be the ranch mess hall. The
main house seemed out of place. It was built in the Victorian
style of the turn of the century, with pointed roofs and a
widow's walk that at one time, when the forest around had
been younger, might have given a pretty decent view of the
Pacific.

We could see the ocean from where we were sitting as
the sun set fire to the horizon. The ranch had gotten its name
from its proximity to the cliffs that ran along its western edge
and dropped some one hundred feet into the rocky beaches
below.

The same cliffs where, until a few days ago, I'd thought
I'd lost my cousin. I wondered now, barely able to make out
the edge, how many others who had "jumped" that day were
still alive. And what light they could shed on the mystery of
Danny's death.

The rest of the property was divided into small growing fields, and even in the dim light of the setting sun we could see people working the land.

I wondered if Susan Wolf was among them. I wondered if we could find her, and even if we could, if she could tell us anything.

We heard some movement in the distance, a rustling of branches, and we both fell silent. After a moment, Bobo whispered that we ought to get the show on the road. I followed him out of our hiding spot.

He led me down an incline that was so sharp, we had to use a rope to keep from tumbling into the ravine below. The first thirty feet were steep and slippery, but the slope eased and the undergrowth was heavier, making the footing much easier.

At the bottom, I followed him through a dense thicket. It was hard going and the branches scratched at my legs and arms and occasionally caught me in the face.

Bobo may have his brilliant plans, but I have my strokes of genius as well, and as we closed in on the compound, we heard the result of one of my bright ideas.

Far down below us, on the northern side of the Guru's vast property, a crackety-pop-pop-crack erupted in the night. It was the unmistakable sound of firecrackers.

"What the hell?" Bobo had dived for cover and had rolled to his feet, waving his .44 at the dark woods around us. I was standing over him and offered my hand to help him up.

"What you grinning for?"

"Remember that desk clerk?" I said. "He said he wanted to help. I thought about it and called him from the room last night. The firecrackers were his idea. I just hope he doesn't set fire to the forest."

"That would be a diversion, all right."

FORTY

The kid and his friends were apparently making the most of an opportunity to wreak havoc. It was probably something they would have done anyway, and now they were getting paid for their effort, though I doubt the fifty dollars was being passed around the group.

Bobo and I made tracks for the compound, finding a clear path to the barbed-wire fence that surrounded the place. The commotion, which was in full, loud, ear-popping swing, was drawing the attention of the night security.

Fifty bucks was getting off cheap.

Bobo cut the wire and we cautiously crawled through. The ranch was mostly dark, but we could see some people milling about outside one of the buildings, staring off into the distance at the sparklers as they burst in the night sky.

All we had to go on were a bunch of names and a computer tape. Neither one of us knew what we were looking for or if we'd know it if we tripped over it. But at least we were in. Now we would have to be both good *and* lucky.

Sometimes you get lucky. About the time we were crawling through the fence, a searchlight had begun to make its rounds of the compound. It was coming from a rickety tower in the middle of the cluster of buildings where a couple of guards stood watch. We kept having to duck out of its way.

On one of its passes, I pulled Bobo toward the back of a small, dark building that was very close to where we had made our entrance.

As the light crossed us, it illuminated the inside of the building and I could see what looked like an office full of computers. Bobo started to move on, but I stopped him.

"In here." I pointed.

To our surprise, there was no alarm system. They obviously had a high opinion of their exterior security. Bobo jimmied the lock and let us in.

I pulled a flashlight out of my bag and shined it over the room. My feelings about Danny aside, I realized I didn't have any idea what the modern commune would be like. I expected to be transformed back into the sixties, but what I saw surprised me. Inside was a complete state-of-the-art office setup, with rows of desks, fancy computers, a couple of fax machines, a massive copier, several laser jet printers and what looked like a telethon tally board.

"What a setup," said Bob. "The guy's a regular Donald Trump."

"You're telling me. It looks like the telecommunications center for the Home Shopping Network."

"You know your way around those things?" I was already seated before one of the computers and had flipped it on. I have a limited knowledge of computers from my days as a reporter and have even been known to surf the net. Most of what I knew had been gained by trial and error.

The screen automatically asked for a password, something I had expected, and I tried a couple of tricks to see if I could find another way in. I started to look through the drawers in the desk to see if the user had written it down somewhere when I realized I had had it all along.

I pulled Danny's computer printout out of my pocket. He had written a bunch of letters at the top of the page and I punched them in. Nothing. "Shit," I said.

Bobo was alternating between looking over my shoulder and out the window. "No good?"

I looked at the letters again. DOGYMSIIAT.

"Aha!" I said, glad my years of crossword acumen had finally paid off. "DOGYMSIIAT backward is TAI IS MY GOD."

"He's nothing if not modest," said Bobo. "Hurry up."

I keyed it in and still nothing.

"Damn, it didn't work."

I looked at the letters again and the number. "C-4. C-4," I repeated. "What the hell?"

"Time is of the essence." Bobo was not helping matters

"Wait," I said. "I think I got it."

I had sat down at the very first computer, but maybe the numbers were Danny's way of giving me a clue. The terminals were set up in rows, five across and seven deep. I counted three rows deep and sat down at the fourth computer.

I typed in the code.

"We're in," I said as I was granted access to some kind of accounting database.

I went to the search mode and typed in "Susan Wolf" and the screen went dark a minute, then an animated caricature of a wolf appeared with a cartoon bubble that said, "Welcome to Grandma's House, Red Riding Hood. My, what big eyes you have. Punch in the code to hear more."

"What code?" I said aloud.

"Problems?" said Bobo.

"Gimme a minute," I said.

"That's all you got."

I looked over the printout. There were fifty names on it, but only about a dozen were underlined. I typed in the first name, nothing. Tried another and another and still nothing.

I'd been stumped.

"Hurry," Bobo said. "I think your boy is running out of fireworks."

I keyed in another name. Nothing.

"Forget it, Bobo. I can't get in."

"Let me see," he said, now leaning over my shoulder. "Cool graphics."

"Yeah," I said. "Probably Danny's handiwork."

"Oh, yeah," said Bobo, reaching around me for the keyboard and pecking out Danny's name. The screen flickered: "Please enter your password."

"Danny would have made it easy for us," I said. "Gotta be something we know."

I tried his date of birth, then mine, the word "cigar" and Sam's name. Nothing. Bobo was back at the window.

"Try your name," he said.

"I did. Nothing."

"Your full name?"

I typed in "Zenaria" and said a silent prayer to my cousin.

I looked back at Bobo but he pointed in my direction.

"Thank me later. We're running out of time."

The screen was a link to a large database. Danny had set it up so you could type in a word or phrase and the computer would search the raw data.

I typed in one of the underlined names, Jarod Simon. Pay dirt. It brought up a host of information on Mr. Simon, including a rather full bank account. I noticed the computers were equipment to run the tape that Danny had given me, but I knew I was running out of time.

"Bad news." It was Bobo confirming my fears. "Two security guards are coming this way."

I fumbled around for an empty tape and shoved it into the machine and hit the "enter" key so hard it flew off the machine. I waited for what seemed like hours as the information downloaded.

"How much time?" I asked Bobo, who had drawn his .44.

"Zero," he said and I heard him checking his clip. "Now!" he hissed when I didn't budge. The information was still downloading. I held my hand over the eject bottom and pushed it as soon as I the indicator light went off.

The tape flew out and hit the floor. I snatched it up and ran, flipping the computer off as I went by and nearly tripping over a chair.

I could hear voices approaching and my heart was racing as I followed Bobo out the way we came. We were through the fence and rappelling up the hill before anyone knew what hit them. I was tired but my adrenaline had kicked into high gear, and for the first time in days I felt that I was ahead of the game. I didn't have the answers, but I knew Danny had led me toward the light. I hoped, like the bike ride back, it would be all downhill from here.

FORTY-ONE

We made good time getting back to the Range Rover despite the darkness and our fatigue. As soon as I sat in the passenger seat, I closed my eyes and faded off.

It was a groggy, dreamless sleep marked by shadowy figures and the coarse sound of the truck's big tires hitting the highway beneath us. It was just before dawn when Bobo nudged me awake. We were parked in the alley behind my house.

"You leave a light on?" he asked me. I shrugged, stretched and yawned, and shook the sleep out of my head. I was stiff and beat, but I didn't feel as bad as I thought I would; even a bad rest is better than none at all.

"I don't remember," I said. "I had to leave in a hurry. It's quite possible I left the light on."

"You want me to come in with you?"

"Nah." I shook my head. "It's probably nothing. Be hard to sneak by all those reporters camping on my doorstep."

He grumbled at this and let me go. I could see, when I got out of the truck, that the bikes were gone. I'd have to ask him what he'd done with them.

When I saw the door was locked and the alarm still set, I waved Bobo off and watched his truck rumble back down the alley.

I disengaged the alarm and opened the door, threw my stuff on the table in the kitchen. I was still wearing my bike clothes and had my mind on a shower.

I was pulling the bike shoes off my feet when I saw a shadow move across my living room. It was too big to be the cat, too small to be a car passing, and before I had time to react, the baseball cap from the cemetery walked into my kitchen.

He was still wearing the cap, a blue felt hat with a brown rim and POLO written across it. He wasn't tall, but he was wide and solid, with deep-set, shadowed eyes spaced far apart and a jaw that looked as if it could shrug off a Tyson hook. He was leveling a very large gun at me, his mouth fixed in a crooked, demented grin, though I was sure that if you asked him, he'd say he wasn't smiling.

"Didn't your mama ever tell you to take your hat off indoors? Bad karma, tough guy."

He grunted but said nothing, waving me toward the living room with his gun. I didn't see any other choice, noting that my Walther was *inside* my knapsack. I pulled off my other shoe and padded after him.

There were two other men in my living room. One of them was the other guy from the cemetery, who was much shorter than his friend and far less beefy, but, I could tell, much more dangerous.

He had an old-fashioned crew cut which looked even more out of place next to the large round gold ring that dangled from his left ear, and his eyes sat on top of his nose with a ferocity that made an impression even if you weren't looking straight at them. His pupils were dark brown, unfriendly and lifeless, except they wandered to one side as if he were always looking to his right and up.

It was a disarming characteristic and it made you want to follow his line of sight in the way someone with a scratchy voice makes you clear your throat. I had a feeling I was looking at Ten-Eighty Morofsky.

The third man was older, with a correct posture to his slight build that gave him the air of an athlete. His eyes were a soft blue, but I could see how they could harden if he wanted them to, and he had a handsome line to his jaw that offset a nose that had been broken more than once.

Like the other two, he was well-dressed but wore his threads with the bearing and confidence of someone who wears thousand-dollar suits once and then throws them away. His finely tailored Italian suit was complemented by an off-white knit shirt. He wore no tie. His black leather shoes were spit-shined to perfection.

"So much for my private security," I said.

"Actually it's a good system," the old man said to me. "You have to know your way around them."

"I'd love to have your secret."

"I can imagine," he said. "I hope you'll excuse the intrusion."

"That depends on whether you're going to leave me here in one piece or not," I said. "Mo Goldman, I presume?"

"Correct," he said, raising his eyebrows to show he was impressed. "Not to worry, we're not here to cause you harm."

Now I was really confused. "Now that really explains the shootout over at the pet cemetery over there," I said. "You mean your boys here weren't trying to bury me next to Fido?"

He smiled at this, showing straight, white-capped teeth. I wish I had his dentist. "I wouldn't worry about them now. They'll behave."

Otto grinned at me. His expression said he'd kill me if his boss hadn't been sitting three feet away.

"Ever check him for rabies?"

Another smile. "He can be quite scary if he wants."

"That's like saying Mother Theresa can be nice if she wants," I said. "Now what do you want with me?"

"Yes, well, it's a bit complicated." He had a way of talking that was affected, but it sounded funny under the heavy tones of what had surely once been a hefty Brooklyn accent. "I want to first apologize for the incident yesterday. Most unfortunate."

"That's such a nice way of putting it."

"Let me explain."

"Please." I had been sitting on the couch the whole time,

but just then felt at ease enough to lean back.

"Your client, Miss Maxwell and a—how shall I say it?—former employee . . ."

"Karl Blitz."

He seemed impressed again. "You're as good as they say you are," he said. "Yes, Karl. I sent him here to invest some of my client's money, legitimately, of course. There were a couple of projects of particular interest to us, high-budget, high-yield action movies that were cash-poor. Our deal was we supply the green, we share in the back-end profits.

"Karl," he said. "Karl was very good at this. Then he got greedy."

"You mean he decided the Hollywood lifestyle was too hard to resist. I'm shocked."

"Not exactly," he said, turning to baseball cap. "Johnnie, the knapsack, please."

I started to rise in protest, but the muscle did his job. He rummaged through the knapsack, strewing my stuff all over the floor. He found the two computer tapes and handed them to Goldman.

"Those are mine," I said.

"Not to worry," he said, producing a third, identical tape out of his coat pocket. "Bring Ian in."

Once again, Johnnie moved, this time into my bedroom. He came out a moment later with a good-looking kid who bore a faint resemblance to Goldman. He set a large briefcase on the table and opened it, revealing a laptop computer complete with a tape-backup system.

"Ms. Moses," Goldman said. "Meet my grandson, Ian."

I could only nod. I was tired and I was wondering how many other people he had stashed in my house.

"What are you doing?"

Ian started to speak but deferred instead to his grandfather.

"We're merely making a few changes to the information you so kindly retrieved for us."

"I need that."

"We know," he said. "If you'll let me explain."

I slumped back on the couch. I was so tired I wasn't about

to put up a fight. Ian was busy banging on his computer.

"Ian here turned out to be a computer whiz," said Goldman, actually beaming. "Full academic scholarship to Cal. He's not erasing your tapes, he's just extracting a couple of names for us."

"What do you have to do with Guru Tai?" I said, my anger rising. "Did you kill Danny, too?"

"No, no," he said. "We had nothing to do with that unfortunate situation. We needed your cousin."

Now I was confused. "I thought you guys were in the middle of Latisha's case."

"Let's get back to our friend Karl."

"Let's," I said.

"Your cousin's Guru has been an—how shall I say this? An important business associate of ours for years. He . . ." Goldman rubbed his chin as if he was in deep thought. "He . . . cleans things for us."

"You mean launders your dirty money?"

Goldman seemed hurt by my remark. Big deal. I felt like I was in the Twilight Zone. A gangster with feelings.

"You're so hard on me," he said. "At heart, I'm just a businessman."

"And a killer."

"Only when it's necessary." He said it in such a matter-of-fact way that I almost bought into his logic. "But that's not important. Mr. Tai has been helpful in other ways, hiding associates of ours when the need arises, and so forth."

"So? What's that have to do with those tapes?"

"Your cousin Danny discovered the scheme," he said, adding quickly, "but we didn't kill him. There was no need. He wasn't going to expose it. He had other ideas."

"And those were?"

"Mr. Tai is quite a greedy man," he said. "What's on those tapes is very valuable. It's all you need to bring him down, to finish what Danny started."

"How do you know all this?"

"I had a, uhm, similar discussion with your cousin shortly before his untimely demise."

"You mean you shook him down?"

"You watch far too many mobster movies." His eyes were smiling, as if he was enjoying our repartee. "We just wanted to talk to him."

"I'll bite," I said, not sure whether to be angry at Goldman. Part of me was pissed Danny hadn't come to me first, and while I was sure I'd eventually have figured all this out, I had to admit this was a lot easier than doing it the hard way. Let's not overlook the positives of having Goldman as my ally rather than the opposite. I'd already found out how dangerous that could be.

"What did he tell you?"

"Let's just say he had revenge on his mind," he said. "Oh, and about a million dollars."

"A million what???!"

He was grinning as much as I thought a man in his position could, an ear-to-ear smile that showed appreciation for another man's handiwork. I decided right then and there I didn't like this guy and couldn't wait for him to go back to where he'd come from.

"Your cousin was a clever man," he said. "He found out years ago that the Guru was into all sorts of illegal operations. The biggest was his, uhm, appropriation of his followers' identities."

"What's that mean in English?"

"Whenever you join his little group, you're suppose to renounce your given name and all material things. What his followers didn't know was that he was using their names to open up bank accounts, get lines of credit, and to print phony credit cards. It's brilliant, really."

"I'm glad you think so," I said. "But why do you care?"

"We didn't, that is, not until Danny came to us with proof that Tai was using *our* money."

I was beginning to see the picture.

"So you see," he continued, "Danny's death was unfortunate for us as well. He was bringing us the bank information so we could take back what was ours."

"That's what's on those tapes?"

"That and something even more interesting," he said. "You'll figure it out."

"Why are you telling me all this?"

"Because I feel I owe you. And despite what you must think, I believe in things like honor."

And blowing people's heads off, I thought. And sat back on the couch, trying to piece more puzzles together.

"There's one more thing you should know," Goldman interrupted my chain of thought. I was glad. It was making my head hurt.

"What?"

"You might want to know that Danny made off with a million dollars of Tai's stash."

"What? Where is it?"

He shrugged. "We have no idea."

"You're a big help," I said.

"Maybe this will be of interest to you," he continued. "As I was saying earlier, Karl had become a problem. He also got word of Tai's scheme. Instead of telling me, he continued his betrayal by blackmailing the Guru."

"He had him killed?"

"Possibly."

"And why was he following me?"

"Ah. Now that's the sixty-four-thousand-dollar question, isn't it? It seems your friend Ms. Maxwell put him up to that."

"What? Why?"

He shrugged again.

"Let me get this straight. Latisha was having Blitz follow me. Why?"

"You'll have to ask your client that."

"Wait. If it wasn't you guys, it was Karl who broke into my house and stole the Walther," I said.

Light bulbs popped off in my head like firecrackers. Latisha was a lot of things I didn't like—but a murderer? That just didn't fit the profile. But Karl was a pro.

"So he followed me to Mexico, killed Harry, and came back here, where you finally caught up to him."

"Someone beat us to it," he said.

"Who?"

"I don't know," he said. "We thought it was you."

"Me?"

"Yes. Otto followed you to the woman's house that night. He waited until you were gone and that's when he found Karl's body."

I held my hands up. "I didn't kill him."

"I believe you," he said. "It doesn't matter, though. It's a closed chapter as far as we're concerned."

"I still don't understand why you shot at me," I said.

"Mistake." He eyed his muscle, still quietly hanging in the background, taking everything in. "We only wanted the tape. I am sorry if our methods were crude. Ian?"

The mobster kid nodded that he was finished, gave the two tapes back to Goldman, who put them on the side table next to my couch.

"See, all yours," he said. "No damage done."

I hoped not. "I suppose I should thank you for the information, but it still doesn't help much. Your word wouldn't go too far with the cops, would it?"

"Not likely," he said, rising to leave. "But I can give you this."

He handed me a Polaroid. It was the tired, tear-stained face of a young woman, looking confused and hurt. Her hair was unkempt and her familiar eyes were heavy, staring back at me with a depth of pain, hurt, and betrayal I could only begin to imagine.

"It's Sara Maxwell," I said. "Latisha's sister."

Goldman was at my door and had opened it to let himself out.

"Sara Jane *Bodoni* Winchester, to be precise," he said and shut the door behind him, leaving me standing in my living room starting to put the pieces together.

FORTY-TWO

In the time it had taken me to shower and change and make myself some breakfast, I began to hatch a plan to take on Latisha and her lies, but I was going to need help from Brooks to pull it off.

I had gotten several calls from the producer who scheduled guests for "Latisha Live!" and had no intention of returning any of them. But that didn't mean I wasn't going to make an appearance at the studio.

I left word with the woman's assistant that I would be there and to make sure I could get inside. Needless to say, they were surprised and thrilled.

Next I called Brooks, who answered with a boisterous hello.

"You must be a morning person," I told him. "That makes us entirely incompatible."

"I can adjust," he said. "So you keeping your promise?"

"This is ridiculous," I said. "You know I didn't kill him."

"Them," he said. "The Mexico murders? Your gun, too."

"I didn't kill anybody."

"I know." He softened. "Let Watkins have his interview. That's all I ask."

"How about if I give Watkins the real murderer?"

"That would cheer me up but I don't know about him. Remember, Lennon's his boy."

"Figures. Do me a favor then," I said.

"What's that?"

"Make like you got me cold on the murder," I said. "Put an APB out for my arrest and whatever else you do. Say I'm a fugitive. Tell the press."

"Are you on crack?"

"Hardly," I said. "There's one catch, though."

"I'm waiting."

"You can't actually arrest me."

"You *are* high."

"Maybe," I said, explaining to him my plan of action.

"You're gonna have to give me a real good reason to pull off a ruse like that."

"You'll never guess who just left my abode."

"Try me."

"Mo Goldman."

He was silent for so long I thought he'd hung up. "Still there, Jonathan?"

"Yeah," he said. "Maybe I shouldn't be talking to you about this."

"Don't worry," I said. "I already know about the task force and Karl Blitz. The way you guys keep secrets, I'm surprised it took so long. I think I was the last person to know about it."

He grumbled at this. "I won't tell," I said. "You're safe."

"What did Goldman want with you and why are you still breathing?"

"I'd like to say it's my amazing powers of persuasion, but I'd be lying. Truth is he wanted to apologize for shooting at me yesterday."

"That's rich. What next? Did he invite you to his country house for tea?"

"Give it time, we just met," I said. "But seriously, Jonathan. He gave me a photo I think you should see."

"Of what?"

"Let's just say it's a good motive for the Blitz murder."

I told him about the photo, who was in it, and as many details as I could about Latisha and her father and why she hired me.

"You might want to check her bank records," I said. "See if she made a big deposit recently."

"We did. No activity."

"That's not what Goldman told me."

"Since when do you take the word of a mob boss?" he said, plainly irritated. "You know, it might've helped if you'd given me all this information sooner."

"For what? Up until now, I didn't suspect Latisha."

"And you do now?"

"I don't think she actually killed anybody, but it makes sense she was behind it. Goldman says she hired Blitz to follow me."

"She's got a shaky alibi for the night Blitz was murdered."

"What? That she was with her sister in the hospital? Did you guys check it out?"

"Yep," he said. "We found the hospital but nobody will talk to us. I wanted to subpoena the records, but Watkins shot me down. He doesn't see Latisha as a suspect."

"Do you?"

"I don't know," he said.

"But you're not certain she's not involved either," I prodded him.

"What you're asking, it's difficult."

"How hard would it be to convince Watkins?" I said. "He already thinks I'm guilty. If everything blows up, at least you'll know exactly where I am. You can arrest me then if you want. What do you say?"

"I say you're insane," he said. "But I'll see what I can do."

Even if Brooks was able to give me the slack I needed, I'd still be pushing my luck; I was just hoping things would fall into place and I wouldn't end up looking like a fool, or worse.

Latisha would be in her element at the studio, with her show about to go on the air live, and she would have a good reason to make me look even more guilty than I already did.

I had no idea what she would do to protect herself and

her sister, but she'd already proved to me she could fight dirty. I looked at my watch. The show was scheduled to air live at 5 P.M. Pacific Standard time. Prime time on both coasts. Yikes. At least I had a few hours breathing room.

First, I needed to put a call in to my new friend at the IRS, Marcia Atwood.

"Sorry to bother you on New Year's Eve," I said. "But I was wondering if you could help me out with something.

"I can't put off the audit, if that's what you're asking."

"No, no," I said. "I've uncovered some information that might make your career. Interested?"

"Is this a trick question?"

"No, I'm serious."

"Well," she said. "What have you got?"

"Does it interest the IRS that a major religious organization is laundering drug money?" Goldman had told me he'd removed any evidence of his partnership with Tai. The only place the money would point to is Blitz. It would look as if the mob had a maverick.

I hated to see Goldman get off, but it was worth it if it meant nailing the Guru and clearing Danny's name.

"It's worth a look. What do you have?"

"I'm not sure, it's on a computer backup tape."

"Tell you what," she said. "Can you come by my office now?"

"On my way," I said, and for the first time in a while I felt that I really was.

FORTY-THREE

I picked out a pale red silk suit for my visit to
"Latisha Live!" I had no plans of ever going on the air, but
I wanted to make them think I was following through.

So far, Brooks had made good on his promise to stir
things up. The noon news had a report that I was on the lam,
but rumors had it that I was planning on turning myself in
on Latisha's show.

They had even scored a sound bite from Latisha's producer, who lied and said they had not spoken to me, but that
they had heard the same rumors as everyone else. She said
the show had hired extra security, was cooperating with the
police, and would turn me over to them as soon as the show
was over.

I left myself plenty of time to dress and drive to the studio, which was in West Hollywood. It wasn't too far away,
but I was sure I would be fighting the first wave of New
Year's Eve traffic. Besides, I had some loose ends to tie up.

It seemed that over the last year, the IRS had been working with a secret informant from the Guru's inner circle, but
about three weeks ago the lines of communication suddenly
stopped. Now they were back in business.

I left the house thinking about Danny and how perhaps
I'd misjudged him again. He had been working in his own
mysterious ways and now, with his help, I might have found
the reason for his murder.

I dropped off the tapes with Marcia Atwood and stayed
just long enough to see what was on them. The one Danny

had given me contained photocopies of death certificates, including his own.

"Those names look familiar," I said, peering over Marcia's shoulder. She was in much better shape than the last time I'd seen her, though she locked the door to her office after she'd let me in.

I compared the names with those on the list Danny had given me and the ones he had underlined were all there.

"Dead people with bank accounts," I said.

"It's an old trick," she said. "Reusing social security numbers of the deceased."

"If there are records of the death, then how can they get away with it?" I asked.

"My guess is they have someone on the inside at the court of record. Just because someone fills out a death certificate doesn't mean it gets filed forever. And it certainly doesn't always mean the social security department hears about it. I'm going to need more time with this information." She looked up at me. "But it looks solid. Thanks. I see a promotion in my future."

"Is there still an audit in mine?"

I didn't give her a chance to answer.

Santa Monica Hospital was quiet for New Year's Eve, but it was still early. I walked through the white, lonely hallways, the sound of my heels echoing like gun blasts.

Brooks was waiting for me on the third floor outside the room of the man who'd attacked me.

He was the short, stocky one with the mean eyes and the bald head. Only now he had a thick white bandage the size of a grapefruit stuck on his temple and two fading shiners, one under each eye. I noticed the top of his head got slicker in the few seconds after we made eye contact, and as I walked toward him, he looked to Brooks for help.

I grabbed his chart and made like Dr. Kildare.

"Mm," I said. "Bruises, broken nose, abrasions. You're one lucky guy, Mr.—" I looked back at the chart. It said

"Frank Burnhall." "—Burnhall. Mind if I call you Frank?"

"Actually," said Brooks, "his spiritual name is George."

"What the hell is she doing here?" he growled at Brooks. "Don't I have any rights here?"

"You do," Brooks said to no one in particular. "Let me see if I can find out who's in charge here."

To Burnhall's horror, Brooks left the room, whispering to me over his shoulder, "You got exactly two minutes. Don't leave any bruises."

I spent the first thirty seconds of my time alone with Burnhall staring down at him. He wasn't going anywhere, not with one arm handcuffed to the bed and the other strapped to an IV drip. He started to say something, but I put my finger to my mouth and pulled my Walther out from under my jacket.

He followed it wide-eyed as I placed it gently on the table at the end of his bed.

"What do you want?" he said, never once taking his eyes off the Walther.

"What do you think, George?" I said. "Tell me who killed Danny."

"I don't know," he said. "That's the truth."

"You look good for it," I said, picking up the weapon, knowing my time was running out. So was my patience.

"You ain't gonna shoot me," he said. "Not here. Not with the cops outside."

I walked to the door and opened it. The cop on duty was nowhere to be seen.

"You can't do this," he squirmed. "I didn't kill anybody. It's against our beliefs."

"You just kick ass, then?"

"No one understands," he said. "They think we're all quacks, but Guru Tai is like a father to us. He's a kind and peaceful man. We just want to be left alone."

I walked over to him, holding the Walther, and sat down on his bed. He actually cowered. Guess I had that hard-ass look down pretty good. I had practiced watching Bobo.

"Is that so?"

"Yes." He had his spiel down to a science. "We live, work and pray together. We help each other. There's no need for material things or money. Our goal isn't to acquire more material wealth, but to reach a higher spiritual plain. To become perfectly—"

"I know, I know. Perfectly realized beings."

He nodded.

"So Guru Tai is a great and good man who wouldn't hurt a fly. Do I have it right now?"

He nodded again.

"It's him or you," I said, slipping the safety off with my thumb and putting it against the bandage on his temple. He closed his eyes, preparing for the afterlife. If I were him, I wouldn't be so ready to go. "I'm already wanted for three other murders," I said. "What's one more?"

He didn't move at first and I thought he might just call my bluff, but then he started sobbing.

"We didn't mean to kill him," he said. "We just wanted the tape and the money. The whiz kid, Danny. He stole a million dollars from us. He was threatening to go public with these lies. We didn't have a choice."

"And now you have your stinking money."

"No, and we couldn't find the tape either. He'd hid it before we could get to him. That's why we went after you. We thought you had it."

Brooks had come back into the room and when he saw the Walther I smiled sheepishly and stuck it back in its holster under my jacket.

"Why don't you tell your story to Detective Brooks here," I said.

"She threatened me," he said. "You saw it."

"Saw what?" he said.

I got up, giving Brooks a sad smile.

"You off to the studio?" he said.

I nodded.

"Good luck," he said and I crossed to the door, but stopped and turned back to Burnhall.

"Perfectly realized beings?" I repeated and he nodded,

sniffling from his crying bout. "More like perfectly realized assholes."

I could hear Brooks's laugh echo all the way down the hallway.

I took my time driving to Hollywood, trying to get my thoughts in order.

Goldman's visit had cleared up a few things for me, but I wasn't sure just what it all added up to. Sara Jane Bodoni Winchester. I knew there was something about it that had seemed familiar. I'd had to go way back to my first newspaper job as a layout editor for a small weekly in Marin County to recognize the name as a typeface.

Harry had named one daughter after a font, why not another?

Sara's medical problems coincided with the start of those stalker letters, which meant the author must've known something about her past.

I checked with the Beverly Hills Police Department and there had been no police reports filed by Latisha on behalf of her sister, and certainly the hospital, from the records I'd read, had no clue as to what had caused Sara's episodes. As public as Latisha's life had been, she had managed to keep this one family secret under wraps.

If Harry knew anything about his youngest daughter, we'd never know, and with Latisha's mother gone as well, there was only one person who had the answers.

I knew she had left home because of Harry, but what I was wondering now was what horrors had driven a seventeen-year-old away from her home so young, never to return. And what of her mother and younger sister? Why had they stayed, and how much damage had been done?

There was, I knew, only one way of finding out.

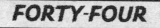

FORTY-FOUR

I made it to the studio a half hour before Latisha's show was scheduled to go on, and was waved in the side entrance.

Like most studios in Los Angeles, it was a nondescript, warehouse-size building whose only identifying mark was a logo that featured a lightning bolt. Several of the daytime shows based out west were taped here.

Two interns were waiting for me when I arrived, both barely college age and extremely perky. They led me into the building, down some musty hallways and into a white-walled room they called the "red room."

I declined the refreshments. I wanted to see the host. But the interns said she was in meetings and wouldn't be available until right before air time, when I would be given my briefing.

I waited until they had left, got up, and went in search of Latisha myself. The security the producer had promised the noon news reporter was nowhere to be found. I pretty much went up and down hallways without being bothered.

I found Latisha's dressing room more by sound than sight. I could hear her anxious voice yelling at someone and I followed the noise until I found the door with her name on it.

I must've been close to the stage because I could hear someone warming up the studio audience with a comedy routine. That's showbiz.

I knocked lightly on the door, and to my surprise Latisha yelled for me to come in. Her mouth dropped when she saw it was me, but it was a momentary lapse. She recovered in milliseconds and was Latisha the talk-show host again.

"Miss Moses," she said, grabbing my shoulders and kissing me on both cheeks. Her producer was standing in the corner and Lawrence Kay was sitting on a couch. He had his stocking feet on a coffee table covered with fruit baskets and flowers, many with good-luck cards.

"I knew you'd come." She stepped back and replaced her smile with a grim look. Her serious mode. "It must be so tough on you. Don't you worry, I'm sure you will find this quite cathartic for you."

"I'm not going on the air with you, Latisha." My words were undercut with the anger I felt at this woman lost in her celluloid world. It changed the mood of the whole room. The producer was smart; she got up and left, murmuring something about having to tend to some last-minute details.

Kay, who was cleaning his fingernails with the blade of a pocket knife, didn't move. Latisha looked at him.

"Get out, Lawrence," she said. Kay just shrugged and left, flashing me a smirk on his way out. I had the urge to trip him.

I was watching the clock. Fifteen minutes to air time. My time was running short. Latisha turned to the mirror, making last touches to her makeup, which was thick and noticeable in regular light, but I knew would look perfectly natural to the folks watching at home.

She was wearing a bright red dress with a gold brooch in the shape of a soaring hawk on her left breast and matching red shoes. Simple, elegant. She was a knockout.

"I don't know what you think you're doing," I told her, "but you're not dragging me into the middle of this."

"It's too late," she said. "You're already in the middle."

"You put me there. You can get me out, too."

"For what?" she said, a rancor in her voice I hadn't noticed before. "I have more to lose than you'll ever have."

It was a nasty, biting, petty comment meant to cut me down to size, but it only made me feel sorry for her and she saw this immediately.

"I don't need your pity," she screamed at me. "I don't

need anybody's fucking pity. You just don't understand."

"Don't go through with this, Latisha," I said. "I know about everything. I know about Jane Bodoni. I know she's your sister."

This stopped her and she stared as much through me as at me, the same hurt and anguish I'd seen in that picture of Sara, somewhere at the back of her eyes. There was a time when I would have reached out to that pain and tried to help ease it, but we were both beyond that now.

"You don't know anything," she said. "You have no idea what's going on."

"I know enough to go to the police," I said, though I had nothing good enough yet to get myself off the hook.

Someone knocked on the door.

"Yes," she snapped.

"Five minutes," the voice said.

Latisha checked herself in the mirror again. "I'm going on." She turned toward me in defiance, the performer returning. "Do what you will, but I'm still going on."

She pushed by me and out the door, leaving me no closer to the truth than before.

FORTY-FIVE

I had no choice but to stick around and see what happened. Live television be damned. It was the truth I was after.

I switched on the monitor in Latisha's dressing room and sat down to watch the show. When she swept out onto the screen, microphone in one slender hand, her head slightly tilted back, a broad smile on her face, she showed not a hint of our confrontation.

She started her show with the ease of someone used to being watched, but then stopped suddenly, as if a thought had just popped into her head. Uh-oh, I thought as I leaned forward in my chair and the camera closed in on Latisha's beaming face.

"We do live television so rarely," she said, "that we wanted to give you something extra special today. Are you ready?"

The audience went wild and as the camera panned, I could see they adored her. Another icon built out of the millions of tiny pixels they call television. No wonder when cultural heroes fall, they fall hard. There is nothing below to catch them. Nothing but air.

"As you know, we have in our studio today a woman who is being sought by authorities in a grisly murder of a man on my own property." The audience gasped. They of course knew all this, but the way Latisha spoke it was impossible not to play along as if you'd never heard it before. "Well, we are going to hear her story *right now*!"

Oh shit, this I hadn't expected. I heard my name being announced and then footsteps in the hallway and the door was flung open. The producer stood there, panting and seemingly near a nervous breakdown. So this was television.

"We were afraid you'd left." She was out of breath. "We're at commercial now. Please come on the air. We'll look like fools if you don't."

I had every intention of walking away, of telling the producer and her whole goddamned show to go to hell, but something made me stay. Latisha had all but offered me a challenge. She wanted to meet me on her turf, and while it was risky for me, it remained my only chance.

I was going to take it.

"Hurry." The producer was looking scared and very young. "We need to get you into makeup."

"Forget the makeup," I said. "Let's go."

She practically dragged me down the hallway and around a bend, pushing me out into the room. I was immediately blinded by the bright lights and made uncomfortable by the wilting heat and the size and fervor of the audience.

The air was filled with hostility and the crowd loudly booed. Zen the outlaw.

Someone yelled, "Stand by!" and the next thing I knew the audience was applauding again and Latisha was back in command.

"So, Miss Moses," she said with an air of superiority calculated, I think, to get a rise out of me. I wasn't biting. "What do you have to say for yourself?"

"Not guilty," I played along and the audience responded with the boos again. I didn't understand their response until I saw a page by one of the stage entrances holding up a sign that said *"Boo. Loud!"*

"Are you ready to face the authorities?" Latisha asked.

"Not until you do," I said. "It is your crimes for which I am being framed, isn't it?"

The audience gasped, then booed again. They didn't need any signs; they were her people.

"That is ridiculous." She laughed. "I'm not on trial here."

"Neither am I," I said.

"You are the accused." She got a few shouts of support from her audience.

"What about your father?" I asked and this stopped Latisha cold.

"He's dead," she said.

"He wasn't dead two days ago," I said. "I saw him."

Another gasp.

"You are mistaken," she said. "My father's been dead twenty years. Whatever he did to me, I'm over it."

"Then why did you hire me to find him?"

Dead silence. I could see the producer waving the "cut" sign, but Latisha waved her off. It was her show and she was not going quietly.

"Did he abuse you, Latisha? Is that why you left?" It was starting to make sense to me now, my mind piecing together the puzzle as I went along. Latisha stood in the middle of her adoring audience, both stunned into silence. Her hand absentmindedly drifted to the gold bird on her chest and I suddenly realized where I'd seen it before. Harry's trailer.

"That's why you left, wasn't it?" I repeated. "But you left Sara with him. You went away and left your sister there."

Tears were beginning to pour down Latisha's face. The producer stood stunned, the cameras still rolling. I wished now they would turn them off.

"She was weak," she sobbed. "She couldn't handle him. Then those horrible letters. I thought he was out of our lives forever. Sara was doing so well, now . . ."

The letters? I realized suddenly with horror that the stalker's letters were from Harry. They were written on the same typewriter as all his letters to the editors. He wasn't stalking them. It was much worse than that.

The audience was in their seats stunned, Latisha's perfect makeup was running down her face. It made me think of my cat's ashes running off the sidewalk. It seemed like years ago.

"It wasn't your fault, Latisha," I said. "You did what you had to do."

She seemed to regain her composure, and I wondered if I'd made a mistake. Then her voice took on that ethereal quality I'd heard from her before. It was as if she was channeling.

"I remember once when I was seven or eight." She was addressing the camera now. It was out of my hands. "He was driving us home from a picnic. We were living in Ohio then. A darling little farm town. How I loved that place. We were driving, me in the back seat, Mother up front. The farms flashing seas of green and golden grains. The sky was so blue. It was a family day and we all felt like one, like a family."

The tears started again and she reached up to wipe some away in a defiant manner that made me wonder how such a strong woman could fall to such depths.

Like the rest of the room, I was focused on her, wondering where she was going—and if she was coming back.

"A boy I'd met at the picnic had come by the house afterward. We were just going to take a walk. My father flew into a rage, nearly beating him to death. He said it was my fault. He said he loved me too much."

She caught herself suddenly in a way that made me almost cry. It was as if she'd been transported back in time, to her childhood, a moment she'd tried her whole life to forget but that had burned such a deep scar in her memory that it would always be an integral part of her psyche. What could have happened to her to cause her so much pain? I almost felt sorry for her.

I started to say something, but she stared me down, her strange power showing even through her tears.

"Our relationship . . . changed after that. *There were no more boyfriends*," she said, accenting the last few words with such viciousness, she practically spit them out. "He loved me all right. I was his little darling. I finally couldn't take it anymore. So I left."

"Without Sara?"

"I couldn't take her with me. She was too young. I had no choice, don't you understand?" She was sobbing now, full-out like a child. "I failed everyone. My father, myself, my . . . my child."

It was the last revelation I hadn't expected, but then the painting on Latisha's bedroom wall should have clued me in. Sara Jane's father was Harry, but her mother was Latisha.

"Sara is your child," I said.

Latisha turned to me, a look of fury and hurt and rage in her eyes, and she shot her hand out at me like a preacher pointing at the sinner.

"He had to be stopped."

"So you hired Karl Blitz to kill him."

"Ha," she said, the defiance back for just a moment. "I killed my father." The audience gasped again, this time there were no cue cards. "You should've seen the look on his face. He was *proud* of me then. I earned his respect by pulling the trigger. Isn't that a laugh?"

She faded off in a pile of sobs and I walked offstage. I'd had enough. Brooks was standing in the doorway and he nodded as I went by.

"Got what you need?" I asked him, not proud of what had just happened. It's one thing to watch someone fall apart, it's quite another to see it along with a million other people.

"You're not sticking around?"

"No," I said. "I can't take it anymore." I walked out, brushed past Kay and the producer and found my way out into the parking lot.

Some cops were mulling about outside, one my old friend Lennon. He saw me, flicked away the cigarette he'd been smoking and stepped in my path. "We were told not to let anybody leave," he challenged me. A tough guy.

With the force of the pain and anguish I'd been carrying around for a week and the rest of the baggage I'd had since the day I was born, I hauled off and punched the young cop in the hard part of his jaw, catching him by surprise.

It should have been the first thing he expected, but it was

the last and he lost his balance and went crashing to the pavement.

I left him there, losing myself in the growing commotion around us and sneaked away into the night.

FORTY-SIX

I'd done all I could do for the day and sat, drained and restless, in my living room, another year ready to pass into obscurity. It'd been two hours since Latisha's on-air revelations and the local news was already on it like vultures to a carcass.

It all happened in time to make the 11 P.M. news back east, which would make the night for news directors all over the country.

Brooks had called to tell me Burnhall had had a change of heart and was ready to give up his leader, though it would be a long time before they sorted everything out. It was doubtful, he said, they would ever tie Guru Tai directly into Danny's murder. One could always hope.

"We got a call from a friend of yours at the IRS," he said. "Looks like the Feds have a pretty solid case of tax fraud, and that's only the beginning. And even if we don't nail him on Danny's murder, we've got eleven other counts pending."

"What?" I said.

"Those 'suicides' twelve years ago?" he said. "Burnhall says the Guru made them jump. Seems Danny was running the scam back then, but he got religion and tried to get out.

"But before he could get to them, he got caught," said Brooks, his tone low and reverent, trying to soften his words for my sake.

"But how did Danny survive? Why did he stay?"

"The peace-loving Guru decided to make an example of Danny, but he needed his expertise. So he had eleven of his followers killed instead. He wanted to make sure the Feds stopped looking, so he made it known that Danny had jumped also.''

''And all this time Danny has been cooperating with the FBI?''

''Not exactly,'' he said. ''He stayed underground for years, building up the proof. The Guru is nothing but distrustful, and of course he had reason not to trust Danny. About three years ago, he went to the FBI. Needless to say, they were shocked and thrilled. He was cautioned to stay dead but it was only a matter of time before the Guru caught up to him. I guess he came looking for you and Sam when he knew he was running out of time.''

It was a difficult thing to hear but it explained a lot. Danny's letter to me dripped with guilt and now I knew why. All these years he wasn't just trying to make it up to me and Sam, but to eleven other families as well.

''You okay?'' he asked.

''Yeah,'' I lied. ''It's all so hard to take, you know?''

''Need company?''

''Thanks,'' I said and meant it. ''But I need some time.''

''I understand,'' he said. ''By the way, you should know one other thing. The money that was in Danny's bank account.''

''The million dollars?''

''Yep.''

''What about it?''

''It's gone. A man fitting his description cleaned it out two weeks ago.''

So a million dollars was out there somewhere. Knowing Danny, it would be a long time before anyone found it.

''If you find it . . .''

''Don't worry,'' I said. ''I'll make sure to leave it on your doorstep.''

''By the way,'' he said. ''I had to talk Lennon out of pressing charges.''

''He's so arrogant, he's dangerous,'' I said. ''But if it helps, I'm sorry I hit him.''

"I'm not," he said. "It made my New Year's Eve."

It hadn't made mine, though.

I had changed back into jeans and a sweatshirt and had an unopened bottle of Anchor Steam on the table, the Sunday *New York Times* Crossword on my lap and Sassy by my side.

My heart wasn't into any of it.

It didn't seem right sitting there by myself. Some other time, I might've taken Nat up on his offer for a few brews to toast the New Year, but tonight I didn't feel up to it.

There was a group of reporters on my front lawn and I had to unhook the phone. Some New Year.

There was somewhere else I knew I should be. I grabbed my jacket and crept out the back and hit the road again.

The rain had returned as disheartened as I felt, coming down lazily and casting a wet glossy sheen on the streets of Santa Monica, catching the glow of every street lamp and every Christmas light.

I was driving south toward the Marina. Traffic was light, and when I stopped at a liquor store, they surprisingly had a few bottles of good champagne left.

"Nobody drinks anymore" was the lament of the guy behind the counter. "It's not politically correct."

Sam's neighborhood was hopping. The sounds of revelers could be heard clearly from the street and I had to circle his block three times before I found a spot to squeeze the Alfa.

The light was on in his living room, but when I rang the doorbell it was a while before he came to the door. He looked as if I'd interrupted a nap, but when I apologized he waved me off.

"I was going to call you," he said. "But I thought you'd be tied up."

"You saw the show?"

He nodded.

"By the way," he said. "I looked up Danny's note. It's from the Deuteronomy."

"The what?"

He pointed to the mezuzah. "It's in there, the scroll. It's the beginning of the blessing inscribed in the mezuzah. The last line is 'And write them on the doorposts of your house and upon your gates.' Wonder what he was trying to tell us?''

I knew then, and smiled at Danny's cleverness. I reached over to pull the ceramic casing off the door; it came off easily. I dug out the scroll inside and underneath was a tiny key, a post-office box number in Santa Monica stamped on the tag.

It was, I was certain, where Danny had stashed his loot. I dropped it in my pocket. Nobody would miss the money tonight.

"Maybe we should've called him Daniel," I said. "He might have become a rabbi.''

"At least in the end he came home to us," said Sam.

He looked tired, but his eyes were bright and his smile told me he was glad to see me. He gave me a hug and I held on until the tears started to flow. It must've just struck nine o'clock—midnight in New York—and we heard a few cheers and the night's first rendition of "Auld Lang Syne" sung loudly off-key somewhere nearby.

Neither one of us moved, there on Sam's landing in the rain, holding to an embrace we were both afraid to break. Three thousand miles away, a new day and a new year had begun. For Sam and me, it was a different kind of beginning, and a different kind of end. We didn't want to let go of either.

ZEN

AND THE CITY OF ANGELS

Earthquakes scare the hell out of me. It's not so much the shaking. Or even the noise, which during significant quakes is like a steam engine bearing through every living room, breaking china, everywhere, all at once.

It's knowing that nothing, not even the ground you're standing on is solid enough to keep from breaking apart at any moment. The revelation there are greater forces at work every second of every day tearing down what you and every person who ever lived spent building up.

The funny thing is I never think about this while my world is shaking to bits, or even after it brings a whole damned city to its knees, making nervous wrecks out of even the most grounded among us. It only comes to me when I'm working a case, mired in the muck of some poor slob's personal trash heap, trying to make sense of why people who live such tenuous existences do such horrible things to each other.

And why knowing this doesn't make them try any harder to keep from falling between the cracks.

Some cases remind me of this more than others. Like this one. Here I was slumped low in the driver's seat of a nondescript rental car on the last legs of a September evening, mainlining Jamaica Mountain from a Thermos and listening to Albert King's blues, trying to remember what had led me here. I was on a stakeout, a stakeout for a fucking dog.

It all started with a favor. Come to think of it, everything bad in my life has started with a favor. Maybe it's the burden of being a private eye or maybe it's just because deep down I'm nothing like I pretend to be, a hard ass with gun.

Truth is when I let my guard down, I'm a sucker of mam moth proportions. It's a quality I hate even more than my eyes, two green-colored traitors, ready to betray my inner-most feelings at the most inappropriate moment. Problem is I have no control over any of it.

I've always had jobs that trade on favors. When I was a sportswriter, it came in the form of swapping information and I find it's been good practice for my present profession. But there are all kinds of favors. Some carry more weight than others and require a greater investment of yourself. The kind you do because at the end of the day, you understand there is no choice. All you can do then is hope you survive it.

Two weeks ago, James Leroy Gray made such a request. The lesser part of me was still pissed I had said yes and I didn't even know why.

The Santa Anas were blowing fierce that dull fall afternoon I drove to Century City to see Jim. It had been a relatively une-ventful season. Summer came and went and except for the usual two weeks in August, it hadn't melted any asphalt. No riots, no big celebrity murder trials, no earthquakes and only a half dozen car chases. A mundane Los Angeles summer.

The Santa Anas don't come every year, but when they do, they churn up the sky like sharks to chum infested waters. It's not the only thing they stir up.

September isn't the month most people would choose to be here. Some call it Indian Summer, those days that hang on in a desperate attempt to fend off fall, only it's like a gene is missing and the result is some mutant form of summer and fall, with a whole new heat of its own.

The Santa Anas have a lot to do with this, dragging thick, hot winds across the Southland with such ferocity, they seem to pick up every free particle that's not nailed down. It makes for some uncomfortable weather, the kind that gets up your nose, into your eyes and underneath your skin. There's a theory, too, that it makes people do crazy things. Like they needed any help.

We were heading for October with no sign of the Santa Anas and everyone was hoping they'd stay away this year. But I could hear the roar of the wind outside my open bedroom window just before sunrise and when I finally crawled out of bed, the back of my throat was raw and hoarse.

It seemed like a bad omen to me. I have this thing about omens and even as I made the short drive to Jim's high-rise office building, I felt a queasiness in the pit of my stomach.

I turned my radio up trying to drown out my inner voice with some Lucinda Williams country kick-ass, but it wasn't working. Even the scars on my chest from where they'd removed my cancerous lung eighteen months ago were starting to itch.

I parked the Alfa in the massive parking garage that covers three or four city blocks under Century City. It was built on what used to be a part of the Twentieth Century Fox lot back when studios owned movie stars and not vice versa. I hoped I'd be able to find it when I got back.

Jim's office was on the upper floors of a forty story building, a monument of glass and steel that reflected the daily Southern California sunshine as if it was trying to send it back to its source.

I strolled into the sterile lobby with the late-morning stragglers and visitors and seeing an open elevator door, quickened to beat it shut. I knew at least one person saw me hurry to make the elevator, because I locked eyes with him as the doors closed, leaving me alone in the massive lobby.

His shrug meant my feelings of dread were founded. Any other day, he would have held the door one more second. But the Santa Anas were back and like the moon and bad seafood, they made people turn on themselves. As if all the silt and debris they blew up were ominous harbingers of things to come, as if the very wind was a carrier of evil.

I was cursing them the whole thirty-nine floor ride up the next elevator to Jim's office suite.

The doors opened into the wood-paneled splendor that is home to J. L. Gray, Attorney-at-law. It's pretty fancy digs for a guy who represents people like me. But that's just one of Jim's many contradictions.

A former cop, Jim drinks with us at Father's Office, as comfortable belly-up to the bar as the neighborhood drunks and yet as a lawyer, he can tear apart a witness with the conscience of an office shredder.

Jim's a deeply private man who looks for answers inside himself and finds strength in the singularity of his own soul and the certainty it will get him through the night. I don't quite understand this in him, but I know I share some of the same qualities and while his mysterious nature irritates me, I still find it admirable.

Born in Minnesota and raised in Santa Monica, Jim is three-fourths Dakota Indian, a bloodline he can trace back to the Battle of Little Bighorn.

We've known each other for years. My friend and some-time partner Bobo introduced us back when we were all still living up in San Francisco. Jim was a cop, working the streets of San Francisco and going to night school.

He migrated south before we did and got a job with the LAPD while he was finishing up Law School at UCLA. He was the one who introduced me to Father's Office, my local pub. But times have changed and outside my occasional visits to his office, we don't see each other much anymore.

He's always been my lawyer but sooner or later many of my clients end up knocking on his door too. Particularly here in LA where despite popular opinion, people would rather the scandal of the moment be someone else's problem.

I walked the fifteen feet from the elevator to the main reception desk across a wood floor so well polished you could probably ice skate on it, staring at my disheveled reflection on the floor. Long, kinky hair, baseball cap, blue jeans, boots and leather jacket—LA practiced casual. A few more years and I'd pass for a native.

I smiled at the receptionist, a woman named Betty who

doesn't like me. I think it has a little to do with my appearance, but mostly she's like a lot of people who find my profession distasteful. Most days I don't disagree.

I walked up to her desk and started to speak, but she cut me off.

"One moment, Ms. Moses," she said, not even bothering to look up at me. I'd been snubbed. "If you'll just have a seat . . ."

"I'd rather stand," I said, immediately feeling like an idiot for being so petty. "I'm sure it won't be a long wait."

"Suit yourself," she said, and returned to her phone, computer, a pile of mail and her cup of coffee. Her own private dominion.

The wait was longer than expected. It was a good twenty minutes before his paralegal, a skinny kid in a blue suit and an earring named Myron, came out to take me back to see Jim.

The hallway opened up to a small divided office with two desks, one for his secretary and one for Myron, who left me at the open doorway to Jim's office.

He was on the phone, but he beckoned me inside. It was a big room, with a bookshelf on each side, a leather couch, a wet bar in the corner and a floor-to-ceiling window that offered a view that on those rare crystal days could reach halfway across the city. This wasn't one of them. The blue sky was more gray than blue, more cloudy than clear. The Santa Anas would change this. Tomorrow I was betting you could see Catalina, maybe even Japan from here.

Next to that window, Jim's desk was the most dominant object in the room. It's massive oak top was carved out of one big tree and was misshapen, almost angular. It was wider by a foot or more on one end, more narrow on the other.

It's not a lawyer's desk but it fits Jim perfectly. He doesn't look like a big-city lawyer, not in his soft denim shirt, bolo tie and smooth khaki slacks that have the sharpest crease I've ever seen. Like he'd used a steamroller for an iron.

His shirt sleeves were rolled up to just below his elbows, showing tanned, muscled arms. He wasn't very tall, six feet with shoes on, but he was solid, carrying his even 200 pounds as if every ounce had a perfect place on his body. His hair was blue black, cropped close to his head and styled with mousse—his only nod to current fashion—so it stood up in places.

"Sorry," he said again, wiping his face with both hands. "Pull up a chair, Zen. We need to talk."

There were two big leather chairs in front of his desk and it was only then I noticed someone was sitting in one of them. It was Bobo.

He nodded at me as I sat down.

Bobo's the kind of person whose presence can dominate a room or disappear into the walls. He was a good four or five inches taller than Jim, built like a mountain but with wide shoulders and legs like redwoods.

He's my mentor, my sometime partner, my savior, my soul-mate, my friend and a hundred other things for which there are no names. Our relationship is complex, still being molded, yet never changing. Its base is as solid as Jim's desk. I like to think we keep honor and loyalty from going the way of the dinosaur.

There is no one, not even my beloved Uncle Sam, who I love more deeply or trust more completely. Most people think Bobo shows very little emotion and the truth is that the burden of having spent his life in often violent worlds has turned him inside himself.

But to say he's unemotional is not to understand him. He speaks a very fluent, rich language that is specific to only him and in our years together, I have learned how to read it.

Of West Indies descent mainly, Bobo La Douceur is a part of more cultures than he'd been able to keep track of, among them French Canadian, Cajun and Italian. He has deep brown skin, a beautiful angular face and two mismatched eyes, one hazel which makes sense with the rest of him. The other was deep-sea blue that would have stood out even if it didn't have the tendency to wander when he was tired.

He was wearing all black. Cargo pants, knitted turtle neck,

black leather jacket and as usual somewhere expertly hidden from the casual observer, he was well armed.

"What the hell are you doing here?"

"Nice to see you, too," he said.

Jim was watching us, a hint of bemusement in his eyes, which I noticed look tired. I looked at my watch. It was barely 10 a.m. Already he looked like he'd put in a 12-hour day.

"You look like hell," I said, ignoring Bobo. "It's not even lunch time."

He laughed, suddenly. A big, booming sound that would have scared the shit out of me if I didn't know better. It was one of Jim's endearing idiosyncrasies, that crazy laugh that bursts out of him at the most inappropriate moments. Like a Texas rancher, leaning against a split rail fence, laughing his ass off at the joke he's told a hundred times to half as many people.

"What's so funny?"

"You," he said. "You never mince words, do you?"

I shook my head. "Nope. So what the hell am I—are we—doing here anyway?"

He laughed again but this time, got control of it faster, rubbed his eyes and reached onto the floor for a pile of folders I hadn't noticed before. He sifted through them, found what he was looking for and tossed a manila envelope across his desk.

The three of us stared at it as if it was a deadly spider. I don't know why, but I didn't want to look inside.

"I need a favor," he said.

"I got a bad feeling about this," I said, feeling stupid for being so edgy. I blamed the Santa Anas. "I don't know why but I do. You sure you can't get someone else?"

"Damn Zen," he said. "I haven't even told you what I need and already you're calling up your demons."

"Tell me I'm being stupid."

"You're being stupid."

He said it. We all heard him say it, but somehow his tone wasn't right. I can't tell you why or how, but deep, down I knew he was keeping something from me.

Jim's got to be pushing fifty, but he looks ten to fifteen years younger than that. Today, he was showing every minute. I could see the lines around his mouth and the shadows under his eyes, deep enough to make me think he'd been spending his nights staring at the ceiling.

"What's going on, Jim? You look like you haven't slept in a week."

"You really know how to make a guy's day," he said and I watched his face, the setting of his jaw, the deliberate breathing and for a moment, I got the feeling he was about to say something important, something he'd never told another soul. And I wanted to get out of there.

For a private detective, I don't handle inner confessions very well. I was the same way as a reporter, cringing even as my interview subjects were revealing things about themselves I wouldn't tell my own mother. It always made me nervous, as if I was giving up secrets, not them.

But then the moment passed. He leaned back in his big chair, took a deep breath and then smiled. It was an instant transformation that grin on his face, as if he had just shed ten years and even more worry. I wouldn't have believed it if I hadn't seen it for myself. Maybe I had made the whole thing up.

"Jesus," he said. "I'm getting melodramatic in my old age. I'm just in the middle of some tough cases and sometimes all this work just gets to me."

He pointed to the folder on his desk. "This client has been one royal pain in the ass and I want to close this out. It shouldn't take more than a couple of days. And don't worry about fees—he can handle it and then some."

"Okay," I said, not convinced. "What's the job?"

"Missing um, persons," he pointed to the envelope.

I picked it up, unlatched the metal clasp and pulled out the most amazing photo of a dog I'd ever seen. It wasn't just any snapshot. This was a perfectly posed, black and white Hollywood still. A traditional head shot, the kind that frame an actor's face in an ethereal glow as if a godly light follows him everywhere he goes.

The dog, some kind of terrier, was staring straight into the camera, its head slightly tilted, eyes glistening, nose moist. I couldn't help but smile.

"Do I look like Ace Ventura to you. I find missing people, not animals. Maybe Doolittle does have calls," I said, turning to Bobo. "You know about this?"

He shrugged, but didn't say anything. Bobo could go days without saying more than three words and depending on the situation, I either loved or hated him for it. Right now, I could use a verb.

"What if I told you that dog is worth more than your house?"

He got me there. "Okay, I'll bite."

He smirked at this. "You're staring at Noodles. Six time undefeated champion show dog," he said. "He belongs to one of my clients and he's been kidnapped."

"I think you mean dog napped."

He ignored me again and I thought I was being wonderfully witty. "The ransom note is inside the envelope."

I looked inside and pulled out a small, white card, the kind that people use for thank you notes.

CHANGE OF PLANS.
DON'T MAKE US KILL THE DOG.

"Change of plans? What the hell does that mean?"

"We think it's the client's wife," he said.

"What? His wife kidnapped their dog?"

"Actually, they're in the middle of a pretty nasty divorce and we suspect she took the dog to up the ante on the settlement."

He was leaving something out. I knew it, he knew it. I was sure Bobo knew it too, but he had decided to sit back and listen. Probably the smartest thing to do.

"There's something else, right?"

Jim got up, walked over to his window to the world and

turned toward the pale blue sky, the glare of the sun sending tendrils of bright light through the dense air and clouds. Like the movie version of God speaking from the heavens. He clasped his hands behind his head and I could see wet spots under his arms.

"What?" I said.

He turned back toward me, a grave look on his face.

"This isn't just any dog," he said.

"Yeah, you told me. It's a damned show dog. So?"

"Let me finish," he said. "This is difficult, a difficult thing for me to say, but the truth is I've got a mess on my hands. And you're the only two people I can trust."

His voice cracked and faded and for the first time since I'd known him his face revealed more about what was going on inside than out.

"This new client of mine has put me in a very, very awkward position," he said. "I never would have taken him on in the first place, but I had no choice. He found out something about my past, something that could destroy my career."

He let that sink in and my mind raced. I looked over at Bobo to see if he had known this was coming, but he had his head back and his eyes closed. His expression gave up nothing.

I looked back at Jim, my jaw down to my shoes. He has plenty of faults, but he's a good, kind, honest guy with the most solid heart I know. He doesn't act rashly and I've never seen him get really angry. My perception of my whole world was being shaken to the core. If Jim had skeletons than nobody was safe.

I started to say something but he held up his hand.

"The details aren't important," he said. "But I think I found a way out. I wish I could tell you more, but the silly thing is I'm bound by my professional ethics. I'm in a bind here and I'm flying by the seat of my pants."

"Technically I'm an employee," I said. "Doesn't that mean you can tell me."

He shook his head.

"You probably could say that's true," he said. "But I'm not gonna tell you anyway. It's bad enough I got this shit on my conscience. No way I'm gonna get you involved too."

"I'm already in it," I said, waving the ransom note.

"And you're gonna be out of it as soon as you find that dog," he said. "I'm not looking for you to be the cavalry here. I can deal with my own problems, my own way. I need you to go along with me on this. The less you know, the better for both of us."

"How can I find this dog if you won't tell me anything about the case?"

"All the details you need are in that envelope," he said. "We've been able to determine the dog is here in Los Angéles, probably in plain view somewhere. We need someone to do the leg work is all."

I sat back in my chair. I didn't like what was happening here. For one, it was crazy, not to mention dangerous, to take on a case without knowing more about its background. You never knew what you were walking into to. And for another, I was concerned about Jim. This wasn't like him and it was scaring me.

"Jim," I said quietly, evenly, making certain he understood the weight of the words. "How long have we been friends, you, me and Bobo? Whatever is going on you can tell me. You know that. I'd go to the wall for you. So would Bobo."

He plopped down in his chair, buried his face in his hands. For a minute, I thought he was going to cry.

"I need you to understand," he said finally. "Some things you have to handle yourself. I made some mistakes in my life and I knew someday I'd have to pay for them. I might go down in flames over this, but I'm not taking my friends with me."

I looked over at Bobo again. "You agree with this crap?"

Bobo nodded and I expected him to continue the silent treatment, but he didn't.

"He sounds like you," he said. "Let's go find the dog."

"I can't believe you two," I said. "Can't you at least tell me who your client is?"

Jim stared at me hard, determined, the look of a man who could survive the worse kind of torture and not give up his secrets.

"Believe me, you don't want to know," he said.